TROUBLE ME

The Madison Ridge Series: Homecoming

ELIZA PEAKE

Caffeinated Words Publishing, LLC

TROUBLE ME

By Eliza Peake

Copyright © 2019 Caffeinated Words Publishing, LLC

All Rights Reserved

ISBN #: 978-0-9912976-3-4

Published by Caffeinated Words Publishing, LLC

Cover design by Julianne Burke at Heart to Cover

❀ Created with Vellum

ONE

Burgers and Bills

EMMA TWISTED her lips into a semblance of a smile as she served Jimmy, her last customer, his usual heaping plate of cholesterol disguised as a double burger and fries. Maggie's Diner served the best burgers in Madison Ridge, or so she'd heard. She'd never been able to bring herself to try one after smelling grease all day long.

Once back behind the counter, Emma breathed deep and pulled the mortgage bill out of her apron pocket. Once upon a time, avoidance came easy. She'd learned to evade any situation that exposed her vulnerability. But avoidance was a safety net she no longer used.

She ripped the envelope open like a bandage off an open wound and forced herself to focus on the bright red all-capped letters that made her stomach churn. The amount in bold was much larger than she anticipated. So much so her vision momentarily blurred.

Emma tapped a finger on the Formica countertop, her mind calculating her bank balance. Even if she could liquidate the last two pieces in her fine art collection tomorrow, she'd never make enough to pay the past due payments and save the family estate. Not by a long shot.

Winning the lottery wouldn't hurt.

Hell, no. Gambling had been her father's main vice and look where it had landed him.

Emma blinked back tears and shoved the letter into her apron, along with the thoughts from her mind, when Jimmy shuffled up front to pay his bill.

She punched the check total into the register and waited while he pulled out his wallet. "It's getting late. Vera's going to wonder where you've been."

Jimmy grunted as he handed over a twenty. "Nah. She's at some artsy wine and painting thing tonight. Probably not thought of me once."

Emma chuckled. "After forty-something years of marriage, I seriously doubt that's true."

With a work-worn hand, he waved away the change she tried to give him. "Nah, you keep it."

Emma's smile was genuine in spite of her fatigue. "Thanks, Jimmy. See you tomorrow."

He waved as he walked out the door, the bell above the front door ringing in his wake. As she set about the mindless task of refilling ketchup bottles for the next day, dread tightened her chest like a vise. She needed to nail her job interview tomorrow. The operations director job at a local winery was the only job in town that paid anywhere in the vicinity of what she needed.

Emma slid her hand into her apron and rubbed the white chip she kept with her. The surrender chip was the hardest to earn and held more significance to her than her bronzed two-year chip. As she did several times a day, Emma recited the Serenity Prayer silently in her mind. The pills and booze had stolen so much from her. Her family's estate would not be one of them.

A winery was not a good place for Emma, but she needed the job. She was out of choices and out of time.

When the diner was empty, she bused Jimmy's table and dared to dream about a hot shower and fresh sheets. Just getting off her feet sounded like a heaping slice of heaven.

The bell announcing another customer rang, sounding like a siren in Emma's ears. Yanked back to reality, she had to bite back a groan. Mentally, she'd already clocked out for the day and was at home, in bed. But she shook out the ache in her feet and plastered on her best fake smile.

Turning to greet the customer, "hello" died on her lips. Even in the dingy surroundings, the man filling the doorway stood out like a beacon in a storm-darkened night. He glanced around the empty diner, his chestnut-colored hair glinting under the harsh lighting.

When her mouth and brain caught up with each other, she managed to say, "Sit anywhere you like."

He stared at her for a few heartbeats before he muttered, "Thanks."

In spite of herself, her sleepy lady parts sat up and noticed him even though a frown marred his full lips. His moves were slow and deliberate, like a panther stalking its prey, settling into a booth at the back of the place.

With a heavy sigh, Emma pressed a hand to her lower back and stretched. Standing on her feet for long periods was difficult after she'd broken her back two years ago. She moved a hand to rub the puckered skin on her upper thigh, one of the more visible scars that reminded her of darker days.

Most of the time, she was laser-focused on the future. But every so often, the past would reach out and bitch-slap her. Right now, her tired ass was just ready to get home and curl up in bed with a pint of chocolate ice cream.

Squaring her shoulders, she walked around the L-shaped counter toward her just-stepped-out-of-a-Ralph-Lauren-catalogue customer. She pulled out her tablet and pen as she approached him. Mystery Man perused the well-worn, plastic-covered menu, snapping it closed when she walked up to the table.

"Hey, I'm Emma. What can I get you?"

When he looked up and met Emma's gaze, her lips parted, her eyes widening of their own volition.

Holy hell.

Long, dark lashes framed intense cerulean-blue eyes that reminded her of the South Pacific Sea. They seemed to bore right into her soul when he looked at her.

Damn. The man had sex appeal in spades.

He blinked at her then glanced down at the menu, rubbing a hand across his strong jaw. "How are the burgers?" His voice held a husky quality that made her tingle in all the right places.

Prying her tongue off the roof of her mouth, she kicked her brain into gear. "They're the best in town. You won't be hungry when you finish."

While he figured out what he wanted, she studied him from under her lashes, pen hovering over the notepad. A lock of dark hair fell over his forehead and the thick, rich mane held a slight wave that all but begged her to muss it up. One side of her mouth quirked up. Women paid good money for the hair color this guy was born with.

"I'll take a cheeseburger with fries and a soda."

She bit her lip in an effort not to smile. The hot mystery man must be an out-of-towner. All the locals simply referred to a soda as "Coke." "What kind of soda?"

"Coca-Cola, please."

Yep, definitely a tourist. She nodded, not bothering to write it down. "Will do."

He put the menu back behind the napkin dispenser, dismissing her. When she returned a few minutes later with his drink, he'd lost the navy blazer. His crisp, white button-down shirt accented his broad shoulders, causing her heart to flutter. She'd always been a sucker for that classic male physique. "Here ya go. Your burger and fries will be up in a few."

He muttered an absent-minded "thank you," his attention focused on the phone in his hand.

Emma frowned and walked away. He may be hot as sin but he had all the social skills of a grizzly bear. Not that it mattered to her as long as he left a tip.

While she worked to ready the diner for closing, she kept an eye on the level of his drink, but otherwise left him alone. When Bud, the night cook, popped the bell and called out, "Order Up!" she grabbed the plated food and headed toward her definite last customer of the day.

She was locking the damn door this time.

"Here ya go."

Her customer moved back so she could put down his plate, his focus still on his phone. Irritation flared and weaved its way into her voice. "Need anything else?"

"No." His tone was brusque, putting her teeth on edge. She spun on her heel, but only made it a couple of steps before he called her back.

"Yes?" She tried to hide the aggravation in her voice. She wasn't expecting him to fall all over her or anything. He was way out of her newfound league. His clothes and demeanor screamed money and power. These days, hers screamed desperation. But was it too much to ask for a little courtesy? Eye contact, or a "thank you" she didn't have to strain to hear?

She walked back and leaned a hip against the edge of the table. Her body hadn't been her own for the last two years, and the longer she stood on her feet, the more it revolted. All she wanted to do was get this guy out of here and go home.

He looked up with the intense blue eyes that she tried to ignore. "Can I add a slice of pie to my order?" he asked.

"We have apple, peach, and cherry."

"Hmmm." He tapped his finger on the rim of the turquoise-tinted coke glass. "Peach, please."

"Okay. Be back in a few."

"Thanks." One corner of his mouth lifted in a half smile that was obnoxiously heart-stopping. She could only imagine what his full-on smile would be like. Angels probably broke into song. A ping from his phone diverted his attention and she was subtly dismissed.

Her teeth clenched until her jaw ached, and she barely resisted the urge to stomp back into the kitchen. With jerky movements, she sliced a piece of pie and slid it onto a plate.

Emma closed her eyes and pinched the bridge of her nose. She needed to get a grip. She was overly tired and didn't need a man she would most likely never see again to get under her skin. Blowing out a deep breath, she pasted a smile on her face and sailed out of the kitchen to his table.

"Here's your peach—"

As she moved to set down the plate in front of him, he lifted his glass up to his mouth. Plate and glass collided, sending a shower of Coke all over his very white, very expensive shirt.

Her gasp and his string of curses filled the air.

Shit, shit, shit. They were both still for a moment, with her holding the plate and him holding the glass in mid-air.

Heat spread up her neck until her ears burned. Mortified didn't begin to cover the emotions that ran through her veins. "Oh, my God, I am so sorry. Here." She set the plate on the table before pulling a handful of napkins from the dispenser and patting his shirt dry. "Let me clean you up."

"It's fine," he said, his tone sharp. He put down his glass with a thump and stilled her hand by covering it with his own.

Their faces were close enough for her to see the bright blue irises darken. Her heart raced and warmth spread through her body. Mixed with the smell of soda and peach pie, hints of pine mingled with laundry detergent teased her. Despite her embarrassment, she wanted to bury her nose in his chest and take a deep breath.

He cleared his throat and leaned back, dropping his hand and putting distance between them. "It's fine. I have other shirts. Just bring the check."

Determined to save face, Emma pulled herself to her full height, ignoring the hearty protests from her back. "Give me a minute," she said, matching his cold, clipped tone.

After she brought his ticket, it wasn't long before her last customer of the night walked out the door without so much as a thank you, then climbed into an SUV parked at the curb.

"Good riddance," she muttered to herself, heading to the now-empty table, bus tub in hand. She didn't care how hot he was, or how well he'd filled out his dark jeans.

Her movements were slow, weighed down by exhaustion in her bones. She cleared the dishes and scooped up the ticket, only to send the cash fluttering to the worn-out concrete floor. Groaning, she bent over and snatched the bills up.

Wait a minute. She shifted the bills in her hand and counted. Holy shit.

Mr. Surly had left her a one-hundred-dollar tip.

TWO

So We Meet Again

INSOMNIA WAS an old friend of Shane Kavanaugh's. The type of unwanted friend that came begging for money they swore they'd pay back and never did. Yet, you still gave in to their pleas.

Mr. Sandman didn't have the address of the fancy cabin his assistant had rented for him, which was how he found himself in his office, clicking through pictures of some property his father wanted him to scope out in the area.

The thrill of wheeling and dealing thrummed through his veins. He'd missed that rush, the eagerness to work. After Marlene's death two years ago, there hadn't been much he'd wanted to get out of bed for in the mornings. He closed his eyes and pinched the bridge of his nose. The heaviness he'd felt in his chest for so long after she'd died had abated. Even after all the shit he'd gone through with Marlene, he missed her. Well, he missed the woman he'd thought she was, not who she'd turned out to be.

Now that Dad was sick, he needed to get his shit together. The business needed him to step up and be the heir he was supposed to be, to be a leader. KVN Incorporated had been around for over a century and helmed by a Kavanaugh the entire time. The company was not going to die out on Shane's watch.

Of their own volition, his thoughts turned to a curvy little waitress with big, amber-colored eyes. His body tightened at the thought of her dangerous curves even the threadbare, pale peach uniform couldn't hide.

He rubbed a hand over his jaw and sighed. Shit, she was hot, but the last thing he needed was to add a woman to the mix.

On second thought, maybe he should release some stress before he went into full-on workaholic mode. He could head down to Maggie's Diner for some breakfast, see if Emma the waitress would be interested in a drink—preferably one she didn't spill on him—or something. Emphasis on "or something." All he needed was one night.

Shane jumped when his cell danced a jig on the desk. "Shit."

He narrowed his eyes when the name *Jenn* flashed across the screen. "It's a quarter to five in the morning your time," he said by way of greeting. "Shouldn't you be sleeping?"

His assistant's tone was testy. "Shane, I know what time it is. Even in utero, babies are on their own schedules. Mine's an early riser, apparently. Besides, you never let me know if you received the résumés I sent you for the ops director position."

"You really should try to rest. I can hear you pacing."

She huffed and Shane imagined her rolling her eyes at the phone. "Did you get my emails or not?"

"Yeah, I got them." He scrolled through his emails until he found the one in question. A couple of clicks and the résumés for each candidate appeared on the screen.

"Perfect. I scheduled them pretty much back-to-back because your afternoon is booked. Your first interview is an Emmaline Reynolds, at nine."

"Got it." He read over Emmaline's résumé, raising a brow at her vast experience. "Who's next?"

"Ryan Carlisle is at ten and Andrea Smith is at ten forty-five. By the way, I've arranged for your temp to show up at eight. Her name is Lindsey. Be nice."

"I'm always nice." When she scoffed, he grinned. "I'll be sweet." He glanced at his watch, noting he only had about ten minutes before the temp showed up, if she was prompt. He hoped like hell she was.

Shane directed his attention back to the document he was reading. Ryan and Andrea's credentials didn't wow him like the first one had, but they were respectable. "Do you have any other candidates?"

"I have another three if those don't work out."

"What would I do without you?"

"You'd lose your mind."

Shane chuckled. "Other than it keeping you up at all hours, how's that baby doing?"

She groaned. "I've got six more weeks of this misery. Sorry I was irritable at first."

"Don't worry about it. I'm used to your mood swings by now." Her silence told him he wasn't a funny guy but he grinned anyway. "You know I don't expect you to keep the hours I do on the East Coast. Your husband will kick my ass if something happens to you."

"I'll be fine. How's it going in the mountains?"

Shane swiveled his chair toward the wall of windows behind him and stood. Laid out before him, bathed in the golden light of the rising sun, stood rows and rows of grapevines. There was a lightness in his heart looking at those vines. He used to run through the vineyards as a kid with his brother, Colin, and work side-by-side with his grandfather. He frowned, pissed and saddened at the same time, noting the condition of the vines. "Well, I've managed to find my cabin and eat in a greasy spoon."

"A greasy spoon? You mean like a real diner?" Jenn's voice ticked up a notch.

"Yeah." Shane paced in front of the large windows, the image of the waitress floating through his mind. Why the hell did he keep thinking of her? "Why do you sound so shocked?"

"Because, you're Mr. Organic. Well, at least you have been since you've been back from your leave of absence."

"Yeah, I know. But having landed here well after nine, I didn't exactly have a lot of choices. Madison Ridge isn't exactly a hotbed of activity on a weeknight."

"You have a fridge full of food in that cabin you rented. I know, because I arranged to have it all stocked."

"For which I am forever grateful."

"Well, you hit the ground running today. You have the three interviews and a large block of time carved out for Noah Reynolds at three-thirty this afternoon." She paused. "I wonder if he's related to your nine o'clock appointment."

He sighed, taking in the state of the outside buildings and recalling the state of the place from when he'd come in. "I have no idea. But that's going to take a while with Noah."

"Oh, and don't forget about the conference call with that bottle distributor today. It's on your calendar. That'll be at seven o'clock your time, by the way."

"Shit, I forgot. Where's Colin right now?"

"En route to Italy. He's going to look at a new system they implemented. Do you need me to contact him?"

Of course, Colin was headed to Europe. It was too early in the implementation phase to check the system, but Colin did what Colin wanted. "No, I'll call him later. He's probably not even up yet. I wanted to see if he could sit in on that meeting, but it's fine. I'll get a status update on the bottling issues. But can you find out when he returns from Europe and set up a meeting for me, please?"

There was clicking in the background on her end. "Done."

"You're a rock star."

"Then give me a rock star bonus. I'm going to have another mouth to feed this year."

"Don't worry, I'll take care of you." He paused. "Has my dad been to the office since I left?"

"Yeah." Jenn's voice was tight. "Alan doesn't look good. I've gotta warn you Shane, I've never seen him this way. His face is drawn and he looks so…small." She sniffled.

Shit. Shane's fingers tightened around the phone. He couldn't allow himself to worry about dad at that moment. Alan would be fine. Plus, Shane had no desire to make a pregnant woman cry. Jenn was an honorary member of the Kavanaugh family. She'd worked for KVN in one capacity or another for over a decade.

He ran a hand through his hair. "Fucking cancer." Composing himself, he continued. "Listen, I'll be back tomorrow for his birthday, but I'll only be there for a day. There's a lot of work that needs to be

10

done here and I really need to hire the operations director as soon as possible." He stopped pacing, rubbing a hand over his chest where it felt tight. "While I'm here though, I need you to be my eyes and ears with Alan. I don't expect to hear much from Colin. I never do."

"Okay, I'll keep you updated."

"Appreciate it. You know Alan. He'll just pretend all is well. For now, get off the phone with me. Be with your husband. Keep me out of trouble."

"Shane?" The serious tone in her voice alarmed him. Jenn was unflappable most of the time.

"Yeah?"

"I'm so glad you're back at KVN. Colin...well, he has a lot to learn. The company needs a leader. The year you were gone was rough on everyone."

Shane swallowed, a storm of emotions running through him. Gratitude and regret led the charge.

"Me, too. Thanks."

"Talk to you later, boss."

He ended the call and put the phone down on the desk. Scrubbing his face with one hand, he plopped back down in his chair. Before he could think much more about his father, Lindsey showed up, right on time. By eight-thirty, she was settled in at her desk outside his office and reading over HR paperwork.

"I have an appointment coming in at nine, Lindsey. Buzz me when she gets here."

"Yes, sir, Mr. Kavanaugh," she said eagerly, bobbing her head. When the wire-rimmed glasses she wore slipped, she shoved them back in place.

Jesus, she looked like a private school student in her cardigan, tweed skirt, and sensible shoes. She made him feel every second of his thirty-six years. "Please, call me Shane. Mr. Kavanaugh is my father."

She wrung her hands in her lap and smiled shyly. "Yes, Mr.—I mean, Shane."

He nodded his head once. "Could you make some coffee?"

"Would you like a cup, sir?"

Guess it was going to take some time for her to call him by his name. "That would be great. Black, please."

"I'll do it."

Shane started to step away but then came back. "Oh, is there a good dry cleaner around here?"

Lindsey pushed her glasses up her nose as she nodded. "Yes, sir. The best one is right off the square, in town. Mrs. Richards has owned it forever. There's not a stain on the planet that can get past her." She paused and swallowed hard before speaking again. "If there's something you need me to take, I'd be happy to do it for you."

He shook his head. "No, I can handle it."

"I really don't mind, sir." Shane appreciated Lindsey's eager to please attitude, but for God's sake he wished she'd stop calling him "sir."

"No, thanks. I'll take care of it."

"Let me know if you change your mind." Head bobbed, glasses slid as she stood slowly. "I'll get your coffee now."

He couldn't help but grin at her. "Thanks."

"You're welcome."

Minutes later, he was sipping a perfectly made cup of coffee and analyzing a contract for a new distribution center lease.

His desk phone buzzed. "Emmaline Reynolds is here."

"Thanks. Give me five minutes, and you can send her in."

"Yes, sir."

Five minutes later on the nose, Lindsey opened the door to his office. Shane stood and came around the desk. "I'm sorry to keep you wait—."

He froze midstep. His gut clenched and his blood ran hot.

The woman in the doorway stopped in her tracks. Those amber-colored eyes he'd thought of more than once since last night widened in surprise. Standing before him, impeccably dressed in a sharp suit, was none other than Emma the waitress.

THREE

Interview with a Kavanaugh

IT WAS ALL she could do to keep her jaw from hitting the floor. The ridiculously hot, but unfortunately rude, great-tipping stranger from the night before was Shane Kavanaugh?

Seriously, the universe was enjoying this joke right about now.

They stared at each other for a few beats as the air crackled around them, his intense ocean-blue eyes holding her captive across the office. Desire darkened his eyes to a nearly navy blue that made her skin flush underneath her suit.

Finally, he moved forward with his hand outstretched. "I'm Shane Kavanaugh."

His large palms were warm and a shade rough. They were more working man's hands than those of a man who sat around pushing papers all day. She swallowed hard. It was an intriguing layer to the man whose vibe screamed money and power yet seemed to know the value of hard labor. Emma's interest kicked up a notch.

No. She mentally shook herself. She could not find this man intriguing. *Focus on why you're here, Emma. Work, make money, save the house.*

"Emmaline Reynolds. But please, call me Emma."

He held her gaze—and her hand—for a few seconds longer than

was probably appropriate, but when he released it, she instantly missed his warmth.

"Nice to meet you again, Emma." He smiled and gestured for her to sit down as he settled in behind his desk.

Crossing her legs, she sat on the edge of the seat, her back ramrod straight. In his slacks and button-down shirt, Shane exuded an air of prestige that fell in line with the company he represented. It wasn't as though Shane was the first handsome, powerful man she'd dealt with in a professional setting. She could handle this, even if he was the first man in the workplace that made her breath catch every time she saw him.

Focus on the job, Emma.

He leaned back in his chair, the wine-colored shirt stretching across a chest she figured wasn't a stranger to the gym. She caught herself and met his eyes. "Why don't you tell me about yourself?"

She blew out a breath and straightened her shoulders. Her work experience was one thing she could talk about with confidence. "Right. I grew up here in Madison Ridge, but left for college after I graduated." Her eyes darted away and she swallowed, pushing back the growing ball of sorrow in her throat. She returned her gaze to his again and lifted her chin slightly. "I started out as a marketing associate for a bank in Atlanta while I worked on my MBA."

"You were there for a few years with several positions," Shane glanced up from reading her résumé, one brow raised. "Deciding what you wanted to do?"

"I call it learning the ropes, Mr. Kavanaugh. Later in my experience, it came in handy." Her tone was sharper than intended. She resisted the urge to wince, but just barely.

He held her stare for a beat. "Fair enough." His gaze shifted back to the paper in his hand. "How did you end up working for one of the world's largest beverage companies?"

"By that time, I was a marketing manager and ready for a change. A recruiter called me at an opportune time and I made the leap." Banking had been a boring, uptight atmosphere for her younger, party-hungry self. Her counterparts at the time all seemed to work fabulous jobs with all kinds of fun perks. The call from her recruiter friend had been both a blessing and a curse.

Shane nodded. "And you worked your way up into a C-level position before leaving and starting your own firm." He laid the paper down on the desk in front of him, tapping a finger against full lips that made her lower belly burn. His gaze remained fixed on hers. "Tell me about your company."

She inhaled a small breath. At least this was part of her accomplishments and not her royal screwups. "I owned a marketing firm that employed around one hundred employees all over North America."

His brows shot north when she told him her firm's two most lucrative deals for some of the largest companies in the world. She bit her lip to keep from breaking out into an unprofessional grin. She'd been damn proud of her crew when they'd landed deals that put her firm on the cover of the Atlanta Business Chronicle a few years ago.

On the heels of her swelling pride, her heart landed with a thud in her chest. Giving it all up nearly broke her spirit.

He was quiet for a moment. "Why did you sell your company? With deals like that, it would be an understatement to say you were doing well."

She bit back a sigh. There's no progress without struggle, right? Talking about her past was inevitable. Who sold a highly lucrative company at the pinnacle of their career, only to interview for a middle management position two years later?

Recovering alcoholics with a shitload of debt, that's who.

She cleared her throat and looked down at the desk calendar before bringing her gaze back to his. "My family went through some rough times. They needed me to be here with them. While it may have been a career-changing decision, it isn't one I regret making."

No, she didn't regret coming home to be with her parents for what turned out to be their last years. But she did regret the circumstances under which she'd had to sell the career equivalent of her heart and soul. She'd used a substantial chunk of her proceeds to dig her parents out of the debt they'd been in, but her own medical bills and the rehab facility she'd spent six months in to get clean had put a sizable dent in her earnings as well. It made Emma's gut twist with disgust at herself.

But telling a prospective employer you'd sold your company in part because of alcohol addiction? Especially an employer that made its earnings on alcoholic beverages?

Her stomach twisted again. Maybe this hadn't been a great idea. But a girl had to do what a girl had to do.

How else are you going to save the house? Think about the house.

Shane nodded once before leaning forward. "What do you know about our company?"

The knot in Emma's stomach loosened slightly when he didn't press her for more details. "I know KVN is a family company, and the largest distributor of wine in the world. It's been in your family since the 1800s, and thus far, the company has always been run by a member of the Kavanaugh family. Headquarters are in Napa, California, but there are offices in London, Sydney, Rome, and Auckland. KVN is also the second largest producer in North America of non-alcoholic sparkling grape juice." She took a breath and continued when he stayed silent. "You have several hundred thousand acres of vineyards around the world, and the brand continues to grow with the addition of tasting rooms and lodges at various locations in California and Europe."

He smiled and the large leather chair creaked as he rocked back. "You did your homework."

"I like to be prepared."

"I can see that." Shane averted his gaze to her résumé, frowning. Damn. Frowning was not a good sign.

"There's no doubt in my mind you're qualified for the job. Your references are stellar." He tapped his fingers on the desk before looking back at her. Emma stayed silent, unsure if she should add anything that would help her case. Unfortunately, Shane had a poker face.

"With your background, you could hit the ground running." He rapped his knuckles on the wood of the desk, his stare riveted to her résumé. After a pause, his eyes met hers. They really were a mesmerizing blue.

For all that is holy, Emma, focus!

"I need an ops manager in here quickly. I have two other interviews coming in today, but I will be making my final decision within the next day or two." Standing, he held out his hand. "Thank you for coming in, Emma. I'll be in touch."

Emma surged to her feet. While working for a winery wasn't ideal for obvious reasons, the truth of the matter was, she was beyond desperate. In a town like Madison Ridge, jobs that paid like this one didn't come along very often. She'd never find another one like this in time to save her family's land.

"I don't know why you don't want to hire me—"

He dropped his hand and his eyes narrowed. "I never said that."

She rolled her eyes. "You didn't have to. I've used that exact same line on candidates before. I know what it means. 'We will keep your résumé on file and never call you again. Next.'" She mimed a big check mark in the air. "You said yourself I'm qualified. And I know for a fact you'll be hard-pressed to find anyone in this town to fill the position as well as I can."

His lips tightened in a thin line and he crossed his arms over his broad chest. It was a feat to keep her eyes from lingering on the play of muscles in his arms when he moved. The business casual slacks-and-shirt ensemble only served to heighten his raw masculine power.

"You think Madison Ridge is my only resource for candidates?" His smile was wolfish. "You underestimate me."

She shrugged a shoulder, feigning nonchalance. "Maybe. But if you want anyone from Atlanta or the northern suburbs, you're going to have to pay a lot more for them, to make it worth their time to sit in the traffic that will no doubt plague them."

"I can afford to do that."

"But why, when you don't have to?"

"I don't owe you an explanation, Ms. Reynolds," he replied, his tone cold. He paused and looked away, a small pulse under his cheek. He turned back to her, his eyes serious. "But I'll be honest. You're overqualified. You have a résumé that reads like a Who's Who of *Fortune 500* employers and clients. And yet, here you are interviewing for a position that, while vitally important to *my* business, is something you surpassed a few years back." He jammed his hands on his hips and stared her down. "I don't know what your situation is, but I don't want my business to be a stopgap for you when one of your recruiters lures you back to the city."

Emma couldn't fault him for his reasoning, even if she knew a block of ice had better odds in hell than her recruiters calling to lure her away. She was *persona non grata* in that circle, which suited her fine. That life had nearly killed her.

If she were smart, she'd leave it alone and be on her way. But desperation and all. Her gut had never let her down before, at least when she was sober and listening to it.

She raised her chin. "You're right, you don't. But before you kick me out, hear me out." Her stomach was a ball of knots but she forged ahead. "I need this. Besides being the best person for the job, I'm a local. I know people in this town who could help you. It would give you an edge over the other wineries in the area."

A thoughtful look crossed his face, and before he could say anything, she pushed on. "My family is one of the founding families of Madison Ridge. The local university was named after my aunt Stella's family. I may have left to pursue dreams in the big city, but I love it here. My roots run deep. There's nothing more I'd love to see than this community thrive and your company can do that by offering jobs during the remodel and into the future once the winery opens." She smiled when he narrowed his eyes as though processing implications. "I have a vested interest here, Mr. Kavanaugh. More than any of the candidates you'd get from Atlanta."

He studied her for several moments with another frown, his fingers tapping against his hips.

"I'll take that into consideration, Ms. Reynolds." One side of his mouth curved into a half smile. Emma decided at that moment if she ever did see a full-on smile from him, she would probably faint. "You're persuasive. I'm beginning to see why you landed so many deals." The low, deep timbre of his voice vibrated across her skin. "I'll be in touch tomorrow."

It wasn't a yes, but it wasn't a hell no either. She'd have to take it for now.

When he held out his hand again, she slid hers into it.

"I look forward to hearing from you. Thank you, Mr. Kavanaugh."

He kept her hand clasped in his but leaned in ever so slightly, the smell of pine and man surrounding her. It made her knees weak. "I admire your guts, Emmaline. I'm going to need that here. And please. Call me Shane."

She looked up into his face. "Thank you, Shane." Her voice was breathy and these were not at all the signals she needed to give off.

His Hollywood-esque smile made her lightheaded. The brooding, grumpy man from the diner made her want to lighten him up by any means possible. But this guy, with the sexy smile?

Yeah, he was definitely going to be trouble.

The fact he could be her future boss put things in a different light. There were no exceptions to her business-and-pleasure rule. Even with her careless ways during her active addiction, it was one rule she had never, ever broken.

That wasn't going to change now.

He released her and stepped back. His eyes were unreadable as he rounded the desk and crossed the room to open the door. He stood beside it and gave her an expectant look. "Thank you for coming in."

Mr. Kavanaugh was effective with his dismissals.

Of course, she had no reason to stay. The interview was over. She'd pled her case, and while she may be on the verge of losing one more piece of herself, she had to have some shred of dignity. *Fake it 'til you make it, baby.*

She nodded and without another word, turned on her heel and left his office with her head held high. It wasn't until she made it back to her car that she let the starch out of her spine, leaning her head on her hands curled around the steering wheel. She inhaled and exhaled deep breaths until her heart finally beat normally.

If she went to work for him, she was going to have to reinforce her business-and-pleasure rule with a brick wall.

Something told her he would be more dangerous to her well-being than the wine.

FOUR

The Cancer Within

THE FLAT EXPANSE of the Napa Valley passed in a blur outside the Town Car windows. Shane's thoughts were three thousand miles away, centered on Emmaline Reynolds. Not for the first time, she intrigued Shane. And that troubled him.

When he'd seen her in the diner, it seemed like she didn't belong there. Emma had an air of class about her one was born with and rarely taught. Born into a family whose money was centuries old, Shane recognized wealth when he saw it.

The woman he'd met in his office was Emmaline. Classy, polished, and sophisticated. Ice princess beauty, with her hair pulled back away from her face and the expensive, sharp navy-blue suit tailored to her body.

She was just as beautiful, but less approachable than the smiling waitress who had served up one of the best burgers he'd ever eaten. The one constant was she'd smelled the same, of clean vanilla with a hint of citrus.

Who was the real Emma? Small-town waitress or high-powered executive?

Shane was certain of one thing. The woman who waited tables in a greasy spoon and wore a suit worth a couple thousand dollars was a puzzle. But Shane no longer did puzzles when it came to women, especially after Marlene.

He also knew after interviewing the other two candidates, it was obvious Emma was head and shoulders above the rest. Shane worried about Ryan's ability to stay on task and be a leader and Andrea's ability to take charge. Shane wouldn't be there daily to oversee his leaders and he needed people he could trust.

Shane grinned to himself. Damned if Emma wasn't right about the pool of talent in the area.

"We're here, Mr. Kavanaugh," the driver announced.

"Thank you, Arnold."

Shane alighted from the car and stopped to take in the grounds of the expansive estate that was his childhood home. The dark beige and natural-colored stone façade of the Tuscan-style home sprawled out in front of him, with the lush greenery, punctuated with dark pink bougainvillea, flanking the double doors beneath the arched entryway. The fountain in the center of the stone-paved, circular driveway bubbled a soft welcoming tune.

It seemed like a larger-than-life home, one that didn't appear to be a place for children to grow up. But Shane had never known anything else and wouldn't want to. There were memories, good and bad, wrapped up in this place. He always enjoyed coming here, even when what had waited behind the doors had brought him more sorrow than joy.

He jogged up the stone steps, and the front door opened ahead of him. His father's butler, Abe, stood off to the side of the door, dressed impeccably in his black suit.

"Good afternoon, Abe."

"Good afternoon, sir." He nodded once and shut the door behind Shane. "Your father is in his study."

"Thanks, Abe. How's the family?"

"Very well, sir. Thank you for asking." Even after forty years in the states, Abe still held on to his British accent.

Shane ducked his head to hide a smile as he followed behind the older man leading him to his father's study. He'd always found the formality of coming to his father's house amusing. It was as though he hadn't grown up here and run the halls like a banshee with his younger brother.

Before Abe opened the heavy wooden door, he hesitated, then turned to Shane. "I'm not sure how much you've been told about the change in your father's condition over the last few days," he began.

Shane's sigh was heavy. "Only what Jenn told me on the phone the other day, which wasn't much. Last time I talked to him, he sounded worn out." He rubbed a hand along his chin, his mouth dry. "It's worrisome." Shane wasn't prepared to think about any alternative.

Abe nodded and averted his worried gaze. "Yes, it is. I just wanted to make sure, sir. To give you warning before you see him."

After opening the door, Abe stepped aside for Shane to walk through. A knot formed in Shane's stomach that made him ill. At first glance, the room looked the same, with its dark, wood-paneled walls and built-in, book-lined shelving. The sturdy mahogany desk and the oversized, worn black leather chair that sat behind it were familiar. But the room that had once smelled of leather and his father's cologne now smelled like antiseptic. It was an odor that took Shane back to a hospital room when he was twelve and visiting his sick mother.

In addition to all the things that made the office the quintessential gentleman's cave, it now included a large recliner for his father's chemo treatments, IV stands, and various other medical equipment. He paid his doctors and nurses well to take care of him in his own home.

Heavy curtains stood open halfway, revealing the fields surrounding the estate and allowing sunlight to filter into the room. His father reclined in the tan chair, staring out the window while receiving a treatment and sucking on a grape Popsicle.

Something twisted in Shane's chest at seeing his father looking small and frail in spite of his height. For all of Shane's life, his father had been an imposing figure. Tall, broad, and with a booming voice that carried through the vineyards, Alan Kavanaugh was larger than life. He was a decent, honorable man who lived for his family, the two sons he'd raised on his own, and the business his family had spent a century making. He was someone Shane had no trouble wanting to emulate, in life and in business.

Too bad he'd failed to follow through so far.

Alan's gaze slid over to Shane and his eyes lit up. "Shane, my boy. What brings you here?" He motioned to the uncomfortable wingback chair next to his recliner, smiling. "Come, sit."

"Hey, Dad." Shane sat down next to his father and leaned his elbows on his thighs. "How are you feeling?"

Alan shrugged. "Okay, at the moment. I have my Popsicles and a view I never seem to grow tired of."

Shane studied the older man, worry a hard knot in his stomach. Jenn hadn't exaggerated. His father had seemed to age in just a few days. "What's going on, Dad?" Shane asked softly.

Alan sighed the sigh of a man who was resigned to something but hated the fact of it. "The chemo is finally kicking my ass. The doctors thought I could sit out a round, but they want me to do more. And I ended up with an infection." He frowned. "This stuff just seems to snowball. I'm trying not to let the fucking cancer kill me, but in order to get rid of it, I have to do things that make my system vulnerable." He clenched a fist on the armrest and leaned his head back, his eyes closing.

His father sounded like he was giving up. Fear snaked through Shane and made his blood run cold. The last time fear gripped him that way he was a kid lost in one of the vineyards, thinking he'd never make it home. "You have to keep fighting this, Dad. You can beat it."

Alan rolled his head to face Shane. "Don't count me out yet, son. Now," he sat up straighter in the chair. "Give me a status update on Gold Mountain." He sucked on the purple icy treat and looked at Shane expectantly.

At that moment, Shane laughed. It was hard to reconcile the sharp president of a worldwide corporation with the man gnawing on something children ate on a hot summer day, purple mouth and all.

Alan's brows came together in a look that brought Shane's laughter to a halt, but a smile still on his lips. "Yes, sir. Gold Mountain..." For the next hour, they talked about the area, marketing, budgets, and rehabbing the facility.

"Did you move forward with hiring the director of operations?" Alan asked, shifting positions in his chair.

"I met with three talented candidates and I've made my choice." Shane stood and came to his father's side. He studied the machine dispensing the lifesaving poison. "Are you okay? Do you need anything? And how the hell long does this treatment take?"

Alan waved away his questions. "I'm fine, and too long. Continue, please."

Shane sat down on the chair he'd vacated and leaned back, kicking his legs out in front of him. "Okay," he replied, thinking about Emma, "Like I said, I've made my choice. A woman named Emmaline Reynolds. When I get back, I'm extending the offer to her."

Alan nodded. "Good. We need someone in there to look at the numbers and make sure we stay on track. Especially if we decide to buy some property. It may need some work, and our budgets will need to be in order. I have news on that. But first," he paused long enough to bite into the Popsicle and swallow. "Tell me about Emmaline."

This time, it was Shane who shifted in his chair. Where did he start? With the whiskey-colored eyes? Or dark hair shot through with fiery red strands? Or the curves Emma tried to hide under her clothes? He rubbed the back of his neck.

"She's a local. Grew up in Madison Ridge and owned a marketing firm in Atlanta for several years before selling it two years ago. Prior to that, she worked in several industries, including the food and beverage industry. Passed the background check. Went to a local prestigious business school and has several other letters behind her name that say she's certified to handle numbers, finance, and all things marketing. She's sharp, and exactly what we need."

Before he'd decided to make her the director of operations and extend the job offer to her, he'd thought she was exactly what he needed to end his sex drought. But now he'd gone and made her a KVN employee, Emma was no longer in the running for *that* particular job. He shoved away the thoughts that would get him in nothing but trouble.

Alan narrowed his eyes. "What's she been doing for the last two years?"

"When I asked her, she said she moved back to Madison Ridge because of family issues." Shane didn't mention she waited tables in the town's diner that probably didn't pay her much more than minimum wage.

Alan pursed his lips. "What about her references?"

"She had a list of references and clients as long as my arm. Jenn checked them. They all love her. Couldn't say enough about her work ethic."

Alan nodded. "Good. We'll see how she does." His eyes lit up and a smile touched his lips. "So, you went by and saw the property. Loved it, huh?"

Shane nodded and moved to the edge of his chair. Adrenaline rushed through his veins, and he was relieved to move on from the topic of Emma Reynolds. "Man, Dad. It was just as you said. Rolling hills, wide expanses of grass, a pond. Perfect for the horseback riding we talked about offering," he said. "Well, at least what I could see of it. I didn't exactly go walking the property. I was trespassing as it was." Shane rubbed his hands together and grinned. "You said you had news."

"Yeah. James, our broker, said the house is six thousand square feet and was once a bed and breakfast before the owner nearly lost it to gambling."

Shane's eyes widened. "No shit. So, it's already set up for guests." His pulse quickened. "It doesn't get much more perfect."

"It appears there are some unpaid mortgage payments and it will be going up for auction." Alan grinned. "It sounds like we can get it for a phenomenal deal. We need to cash in on it."

Shane's muscles tensed and he frowned. Properties with ties to foreclosure could be a huge pain in the ass. "Tell me the price is right. Land like that can be wrapped up for a while trying to clear it all up. How much are we looking at?"

Alan winced. "I know. I remember what happened with the property in Sonoma." He shifted in his chair. "James and his team need to get some more details. This is just prelim intel he picked up. But the fair market value isn't outrageous." Alan rattled off a number and Shane's brows lifted.

"That's reasonable. We may be able to come in a good bit lower. I'm sure it's going to need work if it's been sitting awhile."

Alan frowned. "There's a catch. Word on the street is the owner isn't interested in selling. The house is actually owned by a trust now since the owner passed away a year or so ago. So, we will have to sweeten the deal."

"Meaning we will need to come in a bit higher. Hmm..." Shane pulled at his bottom lip. "I'll call James and get the ball rolling this week."

"Sooner than later, Shane."

Shane nodded, but a small trickle of fear ran down his spine. Was there something his dad wasn't telling him about his condition? "I'll call him today."

"There's one more thing," Alan began.

Shit, here it was. The tension in his shoulders tightened further.

Alan closed his eyes and turned his head toward the window. The way the sunlight hit his face showcased the wrinkles that seemed to have appeared overnight. His eyelids were almost transparent and his face was more drawn than normal. Shane's heart broke at the sight, and he looked away. He wasn't sure he would ever get used to a fragile Alan Kavanaugh.

Shane feigned nonchalance and leaned back in the chair, crossing an ankle to his knee. "Okay, what's up?"

Alan opened his eyes and turned his head to face Shane. His stare was sharper than Shane had seen it in quite some time. "I received a call from the board of directors. It appears your ability to take over as CEO when the time comes is being questioned."

Shane raised a brow and his fingers gripped the arms of the chair. "Really? Who has a problem with me?"

"Colin."

Shane froze and his mind blanked. "Colin, as in my brother, Colin?"

Alan swallowed hard and nodded. Shane shoved up from his chair and paced the room. "What the fuck, Dad? What the hell is he doing?"

"Vying for the job it would seem." Alan sighed and it was the sigh of a man resigned to his fate. "Shane, we have to play this close to the vest. Colin doesn't realize how much I know about what he wants to do."

Shane stopped in front of Alan, hands on his hips. "What do you mean?"

"A source tells me that Colin is looking to take over as CEO and then sell off the company, piece by piece."

"What the hell for? This is our legacy here." He paused, staring at his father. "And why aren't you more upset about this? You've worked your ass off your whole life for the company. To give us what we need."

"I've calmed down a bit since I first found out."

"How long have you known? Have you talked to him? What did he say?" Shane swallowed hard. "And how the hell does he think anything he's done is any better for the company's interest?"

Alan held up a hand. "One thing at a time, son." He settled back against his chair, looking more like the man in command that Shane was accustomed to seeing.

"The board called me two days ago. I'm calmer now, but..." He waved a hand away. "Anyway, I talked to him and he said he was worried you were still reeling from Marlene's death and it would be in the best interest of the company for the board to look at him since he's the next in line as heir." He paused. "And no, he didn't mention anything about why. A trusted member of my team told me about it. They're looking into finding out why he wants to sell. Other than money. He has plenty. It has to be something else." Alan sighed. "As far as what he's done being any better? He was questioned on that and explained his way out of it claiming paparazzi and things not being as they seemed."

Shane began pacing again and ran a hand through his hair. Fucking Colin. Shane loved his brother but over the last year or two, Colin was not the same. Not that Shane paid a lot of attention since Marlene died. But in the periphery of his mind, he'd seen changes in Colin. He drank too much and partied too hard. Colin even managed to land in some gossip rags over the last year or two.

"Shane, sit down. I need for you to hear what I'm about to say."

He paused before sitting back in the chair he'd vacated. "I'm listening."

"You can't let Colin take over. Even if he weren't planning to sell, he's not ready for the responsibility. But the fact that he plans to sell the family business..." Alan's face reddened and his nostrils flared. He blew out a hard breath before continuing. "Anyway, buying that land and house is imperative. It's the way you're going to prove to the board you're back in the game."

"Dad, you know I'm back. I've already—"

"I know. Trust me, I understand losing a spouse. Especially the way Marlene went. But the fact of the matter is I can't do my job anymore. At least not right now while I do these treatments." His voice was strong in spite of the frail appearance. "I believe you're ready because I know who you are, son. But there's just enough newer board members to make this hard for you now that Colin's made them doubt."

Shane dropped his head into his hands. His mind was a swirl of emotions that all seemed to land back at the doorstep of "What the fuck?"

He lifted his head and looked into his father's eyes. There were lines in his face that weren't there the last time he saw them. After the news he'd been dealt it was no wonder his father looked older in a matter of days. It wasn't just the illness.

But Alan had to kick some cancer ass. Gold Mountain was Shane's responsibility, and one he planned to take care of. It was his first solo project since he'd returned from his year-long hiatus, and he didn't plan to fuck it up. He couldn't fuck it up. Thanks to his brother, his back was against the wall. A place Shane didn't care to be.

"I'll take care of this, Dad. I'm not going to let you down." He reached over and patted his father's hand. "Enough talk of business today. You relax until the chemo finishes, okay? I'll be back shortly."

Alan didn't open his eyes, just nodded his head. "After a treatment, I'm not much of a good time for a while. I don't know that I'm going to be up for having a birthday dinner. Why don't you head back to Madison Ridge?"

Shane pursed his lips. "Are you sure?"

Alan nodded. "I'm positive, Shane. The next time you're in town, we can celebrate. I'll feel better then." He patted Shane's shoulder. "Now go. Make me proud, son."

He planned to do just that. Shane gripped his dad's hand in his and squeezed. The return squeeze was weak, but there. Shane smiled. The old man did have some fight left in him.

"Anything I can get you before I go?"

"Tell Abe to come see me."

"I'll do it." Shane released his hand and stood. He studied his dad for a moment longer before turning to leave. At the door, Shane turned back. "Love you, old man."

Alan turned his head and smiled at his oldest son. "Love you too, rugrat."

It had been their exchange for as long as Shane could remember. His throat was thick with emotion, and, unable to speak, he left the room.

When he found Abe, he relayed his father's message and left the sprawling mansion, lost in thought. Now that he'd seen his father's condition for himself, the urgency to get back to the small town and start work ramped up.

He wasn't running. His father was right. There was nothing more Shane could do for him in Napa. He needed to get back to Georgia and get that winery up and running. It was imperative to Shane that his father see he hadn't chosen badly when he'd picked Shane to be the next in line for CEO.

Arnold opened the door to the car when Shane strode out the front door. "Where to, Mr. Kavanaugh?"

"Back to the airport. Call ahead and make sure the plane is ready to go." His voice was brusque.

"Yes, sir."

Shane slid in and leaned his head back against the headrest, blowing out a ragged breath. As they started to pull away, Shane glanced at the house, not knowing the next time he'd see it. He prayed when he did, his father's voice would be booming through it again.

He sat up, squaring his shoulders, and pulled out his phone. Daylight was burning and he had things to do. He sent an email to Jenn checking on some loose ends he had at another vineyard. Next, he emailed Lindsey with a list of things to get for Emma's office, including a new laptop.

He tossed the phone on the seat beside him and leaned his head back, closing his eyes. The image of Emma sitting across from him at the interview slid through his consciousness. His body responded by tightening in several places, one of them an inappropriate place.

"Fuck," he muttered, running a hand through his hair. He set his lips in a hard line. There was too much at stake for his cock to start thinking now. "She works for you, you bastard. There's no fraternizing with those who work for you. So, just sit your ass back down."

Perfect. Now he was talking to his crotch.

He clenched his fists and took a few deep breaths. It was crucial he get his feelings of lust under control when it came to Emma. He was going to need her more than he'd planned. She was going to be an integral part of the winery. She was the best he'd seen on paper in quite some time, and regardless of what he'd told her, he couldn't afford to waste time trying to find a different candidate.

There was no way he was getting involved with her personally. While he was going to have to spend a considerable amount of time with her, Shane was just going to have to keep her at arm's length and his hormones would just have to cool it.

The clock was ticking, and Shane didn't plan to fail his father—or his family—again.

FIVE

Sweet Beginnings

"GOOD MORNING, SUNSHINE," Emma called out. Her cousin, Amelia, stood in the kitchen of The Sweet Spot bakery dumping brown sugar into a commercial-sized mixing bowl.

"Morning." Amelia glanced up at Emma, her brow furrowed. "Did I lose track of time? I thought you were coming in later."

"I was." She shrugged. "But I was up, so here I am. Ready to help." Emma leaned on the island with one hip and peered into the bowl. "Chocolate chip cookies?"

"Yep." Amelia dumped in the white sugar. "Having trouble sleeping again?"

"Sometimes." Amelia scoffed and lifted a brow. Emma rolled her eyes. "Okay, yes. Insomnia and I have become well acquainted."

"How did your interview go?"

Emma sighed, her heart skipping a beat as she thought about Shane. "It went great."

Amelia cracked two eggs into the bowl. "You don't sound very excited about it. What kind of job is it? You never said."

Emma was dying to lick the mixing bowl. "I'll tell you in exchange for some cookie dough."

Amelia's answer was to turn on the mixer. "I can't hear you," she shouted over the whirling noise, a smirk on her lips.

"Are you going to withhold cookie dough until I tell you? That's just mean. Even for you."

Amelia chuckled and measured out vanilla. "Tell me about the job."

Emma frowned and pulled out the stool before perching herself on it. "Fine, evil queen of cookies. The job is for the director of operations. There will be a lot of moving parts to the job, which I like." She paused.

"And? Is that it?" Amelia asked, her lips pursed. "Who is it with?"

Emma rubbed her brow and sighed. Her cousin drove her crazy with an incessant need to know things. But it was that persistence that made Amelia's bakery one of the most talked about up-and-coming bakeries in North Georgia. It was a trait Emma recognized in herself. Or at least, once upon a time she did.

"KVN Incorporated." When Amelia didn't respond, Emma slid off the stool and began to pace the room. "Yes, it's at the Gold Mountain winery, before you ask what you already know. But it's not like I'll be around alcohol all the time. And they sell more than just wine. They make grape juice as well."

Amelia stayed silent but kept her eyes on Emma as the mixing bowl circled between them. "That's the Kavanaugh family, isn't it?"

Emma nodded, thinking about Shane, and tried not to remember his intense blue stare.

"Ah, yes." Amelia stopped what she was doing and stared into space, a faraway look in her eyes. "I met Shane a couple of months ago when he and his brother, Colin, were here for a Chamber of Commerce meeting." She fanned herself. "Whew, those Kavanaugh men are hot. Shane is a dead ringer for that British model, what's his name? David something."

"David Gandy?"

Amelia snapped her fingers and pointed at her. "Yes, David Gandy. And his brother, Colin?" She rolled her eyes in a mock swoon. "Man, they grow them well out there in California. I'm serious—when they smiled at me, I nearly had an orgasm right there in the middle of the meeting."

Emma rolled her eyes and tried not to laugh. "Oh my God, stop it."

"I had to stick my head in the freezer when I got home."

Emma couldn't hold back her laughter any longer.

Amelia scooped some dough onto a cookie sheet. "I wonder if they're single." She bobbed her eyebrows at Emma.

Emma shrugged and ignored her quickened pulse. "I have no idea. Anyway," she continued, "I should find out today if I got the job, but he made it clear at first he didn't want to hire me. Gave me the old 'don't call us, we'll call you' line." She waved a hand. "I've heard it before. Hell, I've *said* it before."

Amelia wrinkled her nose. "Did he say why he didn't want to hire you?"

"Because I'm overqualified." She leaned back against the counter. "I pled my case. Told him that to hire anyone from Atlanta would cost him a lot more. *If* he could get anybody to drive this far to do it. More than likely he'd have to move them here."

"Yeah, even someone from the northern suburbs would have at least an hour commute." Amelia's lips pursed. "I really wish I could hire you full-time, Em. But I'm just not there quite yet."

Emma smiled at Amelia. "I know. Everything you have is tied up in this place, as it should be. I wouldn't take your money, anyway." She held her smile even though her stomach nosedived when she said, "I don't know how much room you have in the loft upstairs, but keep the couch open for me just in case. Okay?"

Amelia nodded. "Deal." She paused, narrowing her eyes. "I'm guessing you didn't mention your issue to the handsome Mr. Kavanaugh." Emma shook her head. "I figured," Amelia continued. "Don't you think he might find out? A lot of people in this town know about your fall from grace."

After living in the city for so many years, Emma didn't miss the small-town grapevine. In spite of the growth and the influx of tourists, there were still locals who made it their business to know everything that went on in town. Being part of the Reynolds family tree didn't let one stay off the radar for long.

Emma averted her gaze from Amelia's forceful stare. "I know I probably should tell him, but not right now. I'll lose the job before I even start if I mention it now. I need to prove I'm the right person for it. Besides, he won't be here all the time once the winery opens."

From her back pocket, Emma's phone rang. An Atlanta number she didn't recognize flashed across the screen. "Hold on, let me take this call."

Emma walked into the small office and shut the door behind her. "Hello?"

"Good morning, is Emma Reynolds available?"

"This is she." Emma's stomach clenched, praying this wasn't someone else from the mortgage company.

"My name is Tim Ford. I'm a real estate broker from Hattersley Brothers, in Atlanta. How are you today?"

"I'm fine," she replied, her tone clipped. Her brows drew down. "What can I help you with?"

"I'm glad to finally get you on the phone. I've left you a couple of messages recently."

Emma sighed. What the hell did this guy want? She hoped by ignoring the messages, he'd get the point she didn't need his services. Were agents that hard up these days? "I received them. I'm not interested in selling, but thanks for the call."

"Even if—"

Annoyance simmered under her skin. "I'm not interested in selling my home right now or anytime in the future. Now, please stop calling me." She hung up and slid the phone back into her pocket with a growl.

"What was that?" Amelia asked when Emma stomped back in the kitchen.

Emma waved a hand. "Just an annoying sales call. Anyway, I need this job to save the house." Especially since it appeared the vultures were circling thinking she was going to sell.

Amelia picked up the cookie sheet and turned to the oven behind her, shoving the pan inside. She brushed her hands on her apron. "Do you think that's the best way to go about it?"

Emma lifted her chin and gave her cousin a cold stare. "It's the only way to go about it right now. I don't have another option."

Amelia rolled her eyes and shook her head. "I don't understand why you feel the need to keep that monstrosity of a house and all that land. It's just you. It's not like it's going to bring your parents back."

As soon as the words were in the air, her mouth formed an O and her eyes went wide. "Emma, I'm so sorry. I didn't mean it like that."

Emma straightened her spine and pushed away from the counter. "It's fine. Don't worry about it." She jerked an apron off the hook near the door and started to put it on, her hands shaking with a combination of anger and anguish. Loss and regret ruled her life for too many years.

Her cousin walked over and covered Emma's hands in an attempt to keep her still. "Look at me."

She blinked back tears that burned her eyes before looking into the face of one of the people she trusted most. She found pain swirling in Amelia's eyes and sighed, then drew her into a hug.

"I love you. I know you didn't mean it that way." She pulled back and looked down at the floor between her red Chucks. The ache in her chest was almost overwhelming, and she blew out a breath, meeting Amelia's denim-blue eyes.

"I made a promise to my parents, Amelia. I told my dad I'd take care of my mom. And I told her I'd keep the house in the family. One day, maybe I'll open it as a B&B again."

The shimmer of hope in her heart was chased away by the reminder of the bank breathing down her neck. "I've gotta do what I need to do in order to keep my word." She swallowed back the tears that threatened to fall. "I have to make amends. It's the only way I can move forward."

"Oh, Em. I'm sorry." Amelia's eyes filled with tears. "Damn it, now I feel like a real shit for what I just said to you. Me and my damn mouth."

Emma grinned. "You always did get us in trouble with your mouth. I don't know how Stella doesn't have a headful of gray hair."

Amelia smiled and wiped the tears from her eyes. "I know. I can only hope I look like her in my sixties. We kids caused her so much angst."

Emma's gaze took in the rich chocolate-brown hair and deep blue eyes of her cousin. Of all her cousins, Amelia looked the most like

Stella. "I'd say you have plenty of your mama." The hollowness in her chest grew thinking about her own mother, who had been as blonde as Emma was dark.

She moved away toward the island and picked up a cookie scoop, dropping dough onto the waiting pans. The repetitive exercise soothed her nerves. "It won't bring my parents back, I know. But it's the least I can do to make her proud, defend the family name, and prove I'm not a screw-up anymore."

Amelia frowned, her eyes still damp although the tears were gone. "You're not a screw-up. You were a freaking CEO of an international company, a company you built. I'm sure you made a ton of money in addition to all your success of climbing the ladder."

"Yeah, but I wasn't happy." Disgust churned in her stomach. "I fell down a slippery slope and used anything I could to explain away my actions and bad judgment. It took losing it all, including my parents, before I figured out what the hell I needed to do."

Coming back home had been the first step toward finding the peace she craved. The peace she needed to stay on recovery road.

Amelia picked up the pan Emma filled with the sweet dough and put it in the oven before turning back to her. "Well, you're making good now. Give yourself some credit."

Emma nodded and looked at her watch. Thank God, it was time to open. She backed toward the doorway that led out of the kitchen. "How about for this morning, you man the kitchen and I'll go open up. Trays of pastries already out here?"

"Yeah, I took them out just before you got here." Amelia cocked her head to one side. "You don't usually like manning the counter first thing."

Emma pursed her lips. "Yeah, well, I'm doing a lot of things out of my comfort zone lately." Before Amelia could respond, she turned on her heel, shoes squeaking on the floor, and moved out into the dining area.

She hustled, starting the multiple commercial coffee pots brewing and sliding the trays of fresh-baked goodness into the glass cases. Less than five minutes after she opened, Shane Kavanaugh walked through the door, looking better than he had a right to in a flannel shirt and faded jeans.

Stopping his forward motion, his eyes widened in surprise, then a half smile curved one side of his full lips. "Emma. I wasn't expecting to see you here."

She swallowed hard and stood tall, ignoring the butterflies in her belly. Her mouth finally cooperated and kicked into a smile. "Hi, Shane. How are you?"

"I'm good." He walked farther in, the door closing behind him, and glanced around the bakery. "Hmmm...it smells good in here." His gaze came to hers. "You're all over the place in this town, aren't you?"

She chuckled at his slightly bewildered look. "My cousin owns the place. I help her out sometimes when she needs it."

He nodded, shoving his hands in the front pockets of his jeans. Walking over to the glass cases, he studied the wares. "Are all these pastries baked in-house?"

"Every morning."

"Good to know." Shane stepped up to the counter, his eyes roaming her face. "It's nice to see you again." His voice was low, the deep timbre of it dancing along her skin like a live wire. She was spellbound for a moment before her brain fired again.

"Yeah, you too." Emma blew out a breath, trying to bring herself back to rights. "What can I get you this morning?"

He pulled his stare from hers and looked up at the chalk-drawn menus behind her. "What's your favorite of all those?" He waved toward the boards.

"You can't go wrong with a medium roast."

He nodded. "Medium roast it is."

"What size?"

"Large, please."

Emma pulled a large cardboard cup out and began to fill it with the steaming liquid. "Cream or anything else?"

"Black, please."

The butterflies continued to swirl in her belly. Her kind of guy. No, wait. What was she saying?

After securing the lid, Emma slid the cup across the counter with a smile. When Shane pulled out his wallet, she held up a hand. "First one's on the house. Enjoy."

"Thanks." Shane dropped a five-dollar bill into the tip jar. Emma raised a brow. The tip was more than the coffee cost.

A tendril of steam rose from the cup as he sipped. "Ah…You're right. That's good." He focused in on her for a moment before a smile touched his lips. "It appears I saved myself a phone call. Can we talk?"

Emma grinned and tilted her head. "I thought we were talking."

Shane returned her grin and shook his head. "I mean alone."

Emma swallowed hard at the way his "alone" came out in a low gravelly tone that sent chills down her spine. "Um, sure. Let me get Amelia. One sec."

He nodded. "Sure, no problem."

Emma hightailed it to the kitchen, where she ran smack into Amelia as she entered the doorway.

"What the hell are you doing?" Emma hissed. "Eavesdropping again?"

Amelia leaned around Emma, craning her neck to get a better look at Shane. "Damn, Em. He's as gorgeous as I remember."

Emma growled at her cousin. She was going to step on the top of her foot—Amelia's weak spot—the next time they were alone. She grabbed Amelia's wrist. "You need to go out there. He asked to talk to me," Emma whispered frantically.

"I know. I was listening."

Emma closed her eyes and prayed for patience. Yep, she was going to stomp hard. She shoved at Amelia. "So, go, I need to…look presentable, or something."

"Alright, alright." Amelia sailed through the door. "Hi, Shane. I don't know if you remember me—" Before Amelia could finish, the bell on the front door chimed. "Well, good morning, ladies."

The elderly, feminine voices of what was known as the "Poker Posse" wafted to her. She stifled a giggle thinking of how the four Southern-to-the core, eighty-something-year-old women that made up the posse would react when they saw Shane. The twins were shame-less flirts.

But first, she needed to get her head on straight before she talked to said man. He had a way of scrambling her brain.

She kicked her Chucks into gear and whipped off her apron, making tracks to the small restroom in the back. Facing her reflection, her cheeks were pink and her eyes bright. She finger-combed her hair with trembling hands, almost pulling out a couple of strands when she hit a knot. "Ow, damn it. Of all the places to get coffee in this town, he had to walk into The Sweet Spot," she muttered, rubbing flour off her check.

A light bulb came on in her head. "Lip gloss!" She rushed out of the bathroom and over to where her purse hung with her coat. After a hurried search and some cursing, she managed to unearth said lip gloss. She finished her primping in the small closet of a bathroom in under sixty seconds.

The fact that her heart slammed against her chest had nothing to do with the man himself. It was just because she needed the job to save her family home. And by extension, her sobriety.

Keep telling yourself that, sweets, her libido taunted.

Shut up, her brain shot back.

Emma turned her head from side to side, analyzing her handiwork. "That's as good as it gets." She brushed off her shirt one last time, making sure there was no more flour making an appearance.

When she walked back out into the dining area, shrugging into her coat, she was greeted by the sight of Shane, standing head and shoulders taller than the four women that surrounded him.

Rooted to the spot, Emma crossed her arms over her chest, intrigued by the sight in front of her. He gave each of them a genuine smile as they chatted like magpies around him, oohing and aahing over him.

They were a colorful sight, all dressed in track suits of different colors with matching fanny packs, each carrying a pale pink box in one hand and coffee in the other.

It was their daily attire and routine. They all took turns leading the local, daily *Silver Sneakers* class, right before they came into The Sweet Spot for their coffee and baked goods, leaving a cloud of Aqua Net in their wake.

"AnnaMae, look at all that hair. It looks like how your Harold's looked. May he rest in peace." This from EllaMae Goodwin, Anna-Mae's twin sister.

The ladies crossed themselves, murmuring "rest in peace."

AnnaMae laid a liver-spotted hand over her heart. "Same color and everything." She sighed. "I miss my Harold."

"You're really tall. How tall are you?" Clarice Martin, queen of all things yellow—including her track suit—eyed Shane up and down like one of her prized horses from back in the day.

Before he could answer, Faye Casteel, the ringleader, piped in. "Cheese and rice, girls. Leave the boy alone." She frowned at her friends before turning back to Shane, who graced her with his magazine cover worthy smile.

"My stars, you have one of the prettiest smiles I've ever seen on a man," Faye said to Shane.

Emma's eyes widened. Was he blushing? "Thank you, ma'am."

The older lady giggled like a schoolgirl. "Goodness, you're handsome." She sighed. "We have to go. Poker game to get to. Hope to see you again, blue eyes." She turned to the girls. "Let's go, ladies. Y'all got some money to lose."

Shane opened the door for them, and they waved, calling out goodbyes and protests over who had the better poker face.

He shut the door behind them and turned, stopping when he found she and Amelia were watching him. "What?" he asked, rubbing the back of his neck. "They remind me of my grandmother and her friends."

Emma bit her lip to keep from laughing and decided to show him a little mercy. "You wanted to talk?"

His smile was slow to form, but when it did, she felt the power of it low in her belly.

"Yeah, care for a quick walk?"

"Sure." She glanced over at Amelia, who was sporting a Cheshire grin. "Behave," she muttered low enough for only her cousin to hear.

When they stepped on the sidewalk, the cold February morning air hit her face, making her eyes water. She shoved her hands into the coat pockets and huddled down inside it as they walked side by side.

"I see you met the Poker Posse," she said with a grin.

"Yeah. They're...something," Shane said, sipping his coffee.

Emma laughed. "They've been a staple in this town for seventy years or so. They're all widows now, but they've always been friends. Well, AnnaMae and EllaMae are twins who married twins. So, they still have the same last name."

"No way." Shane shook his head with a chuckle. "Didn't know that kind of thing happened in real life."

"You wouldn't believe some of the things that have gone on in this town."

Shane looked out toward the town. "Maybe you can tell me about it sometime." Before she could formulate a response through the shock in her brain, he cleared his throat and continued. "This coffee really is amazing," he murmured. "What kind is it?"

Emma shook her head. "Can't give away trade secrets."

"Damn," Shane responded, playing along. "Can't blame a guy for trying."

She laughed while Shane took another long pull on the cup, his gaze lingering over the town before glancing down at her with a smile. "Madison Ridge is as charming as I remember from the first time I was here. It's got a historic, artsy feel, mixed with the fun of a college town."

His smile made her belly quiver every time. She cleared her throat and swiped at an errant lock of hair that blew across her face. "Well, it has a storied history, art, and Hardiman University on the other side of the square. All in all, it has character. So, did you come by to get a rundown of the town?"

"No."

He stopped and faced her, causing her feet to halt forward motion. His face turned serious, looking away before bringing his gaze back to hers. "I want you for my director of operations. You're exactly what I need for the winery." A wry smile played on his lips. "Like you said, there's no one around here with your experience, expertise, or vested interest in the community. There's no one I want to captain this ship more than you."

He named her annual salary and bonus potential, then paused. "Do you accept?"

Slowly, Emma nodded, her eyes on his, vaguely aware of people walking around them on the sidewalk. Her body vibrated with excitement, but she needed to play it cool. "I accept."

A huge grin spread across his lips, revealing straight white teeth. It was like looking into a bright light that held her spellbound.

"Great. When I get to the office, I'll draft the offer letter and email it to you. HR will be in contact for any other paperwork they need." He extended his hand. "Welcome aboard, Emma."

God, his eyes were impossibly bright blue against his blue-checked flannel shirt. She returned his smile and extended her hand, her coat swishing with the movement, and placed it in his. His palm was warm against hers, and tingling shot up her arm, landing squarely in her chest. When appropriate, she pulled her hand back and stuffed it in her pocket. "Thank you, Shane. I look forward to getting started."

"Me too." He gestured toward the bakery. "I'm sure you have to get back, and I don't want to keep you any longer."

She nodded and started back the way they came. "Yeah, Amelia's probably wondering where I am."

When they came to the door of the bakery, Emma turned and looked up at Shane. The man was so tall next to her. "Thank you so much for the opportunity. I'm excited to get started."

"Can you start Monday?"

A grin curved her mouth. "Absolutely. I'll see you then."

Shane saluted her with his coffee cup. "See you then." That devastating smile appeared again. "Take care, Emmaline." His eyes held hers for a beat longer before he turned and walked away. A feeling akin to a caress danced along her skin when he used her full name.

"Oh," Shane turned back to her. "I was serious about you giving me a tour of the town sometime."

"A tour?" Emma tried to play it cool despite her heart pounding. What was it about him?

He grinned, and Emma nearly fanned herself. "Well, you did say knowing the town worked in your favor. And I'd like to get to know it better. Goodwill and all."

42

"Right." Emma looked away, letting her gaze linger over her hometown while she caught her breath. Cars cruised through the roundabout circling the old historic courthouse in the center of town as people milled about on the sidewalks, moving in and out of the boutique shops, the general store, the bank. The town bustled in the way of small southern towns.

Watching the activity helped bring her body temperature back to normal. She turned back to him and smiled. "Of course. I'd be happy to show you around sometime."

He nodded, a cocky grin in place as he turned to leave. "See you Monday."

She let out a deep breath. It was wrong on so many levels, she was sure of it. But she couldn't help but admire how his ass looked in those well-worn jeans. Emma liked the casual Shane as much as she liked the powerful businessman attire.

No, no, no. Accepting his job offer slammed the door on any other kind of relationship. That beautiful man was now her boss.

And totally off-limits.

SIX

Tangled Vines

THE FOLLOWING MONDAY, Shane's gut was a ball of nerves at the prospect of seeing Emma again and in a professional capacity. He occupied himself by reading over a report from his agent regarding the local real estate market. The property values of the area were on the rise and he wanted that nearby property before prices became prohibitive. James's firm had yet to get in touch with the trustee to see if any sort of offer could be made.

He stood and began to pace. How could they sweeten the deal? All Shane knew was he needed the property, even if that meant spending more to secure it. That six-bedroom estate was part of the plan to make Gold Mountain a viable location and now, to keep Colin from destroying their legacy.

His thoughts were interrupted by a knock at the door. "Come in." Testiness worked its way into his tone.

Lindsey opened the door. "Emma's here to see you."

His thoughts of real estate took a back seat when he saw Emma standing just behind Lindsey at the door, but he kept his face impassive.

"Send her in."

Lindsey stepped aside and Emma walked in. Shane swore the temperature of the room inched up a few degrees.

Sliding his hands into his front pockets, he studied Emma from under hooded eyes. She'd come prepared with a notebook hugged to her chest and a cup of coffee. When the stirring started deep in his gut, he tore his eyes away from her form and looked at her face. To his dismay, her face didn't dampen the desire that heated his blood.

Expensive clothes were not foreign to Shane. His late wife had worn them all the time. The black dress Emma wore was tailored to fit her soft, curved frame. The jacket didn't cover much, rather it enhanced the curving neckline that dipped down to the tops of her breasts. His eyes drifted down to the swell of skin that played peek-a-boo with him as she moved.

"Come in and take a seat." He gestured to the small conference table in his office and sat across from her. "Lindsey, can you bring Emma some fresh coffee?"

"Yes, sir. Would you like anything?"

"I'm good, thanks."

Lindsey closed the door behind her silently.

Emma sat across from him and crossed her legs. The whisper of her pantyhose in addition to the flash of leg before she pulled closer to the table made Shane bite back a groan.

She seemed to have no idea of the effect she had on him and he thanked God for it. Not that he would act on the attraction, anyway. She was an employee and he couldn't afford any distractions. Or legal issues for that matter. Experience had taught him temptation could be messy and deadly.

He just needed to get the rest of his body on board with his brain.

"Did you get settled in okay?" he asked.

"I did. Lindsey showed me around, got me everything I needed."

Shane nodded. "Good. If you need anything at all, just let her know. She'll take care of it for you."

"Thank you."

"You're welcome."

There was a light rap at the door before Lindsey walked through, a steaming cup of coffee in one hand. She set it next to Emma and dropped a couple of sugar packets and creamer next to it. "I wasn't sure how you took your coffee, so I brought you a little bit of everything."

"Thank you, Lindsey." Emma looked up at the younger woman and sent her a genuine smile that made Shane want to do whatever he needed to do to keep the smile on her face all the time. The smiles she'd given him so far were guarded, and her eyes held shadows.

They were similar to shadows he'd seen in the mirror every day for the last eighteen months.

"Shall we get started?" He slid a packet of papers across the table to her. "This is the current year budget for the winery and vineyard. Let's start there."

She picked up the papers and clicked her pen. "You're the boss."

He expected to see the nerves in her eyes that had shone through at times during her interview. But this time, her eyes were clear, bright, and held a determination he admired. His gaze traveled down to her lips, where she tapped her pen as she read over the numbers. Shane tore his gaze away, his jaw tightening until it ached.

Blowing out a breath, he focused on the numbers. "Let's start at the top. Revenue…"

For the next hour and a half, they went over every line of the budget, adjusting numbers here and there until Shane wanted to jab a pen in his eye. Emma, on the other hand, had a calculator for a brain. A confidence exuded from her that he found sexy as hell. He really wanted to know what made her tick. How many facets were there to the lovely Emmaline and which one was the real her?

"I think if we can cut some of the office expenses, there will be more room in the budget for marketing. That brings in business directly affecting revenue." When he didn't respond, she looked up and frowned. "Do you not agree?"

Shane leaned back in his chair. "Yeah, I do. Let's throw more dollars at marketing. We're going to need as much advertising as we can get when we open the place."

"Okay." She scribbled something in her notebook. "I'll start looking for a marketing manager. The sooner we get someone in, the sooner we can start on an advertising strategy."

He smiled while he rocked in his chair. Oh yeah, she was good. "That's why I hired you. I need someone to jump in and take this on. I'm here now, but once this place opens, it'll be all yours."

She bit her lip as some sort of shadow crossed her face and then disappeared. Nodding, she sat up straighter. "Right. Okay, I'll dig into seeing what we can do with cutting costs." She scribbled some notes in her notebook, her handwriting a collection of looping, feminine curves.

He glanced out the window while she took more notes. Shane was twitchy, and he found the way to tame the restlessness was to walk the land. He figured it was as good a time as any to show her the vines, and he could walk off the agitation that seemed to consume him.

"Come with me." He pushed his chair back and stood, his hand clenched in a fist to keep from holding it out to her. When she raised her eyes to his, he said, "I want to show you the vines. It's important for employees to know how the business works, starting with the land."

"Okay." Emma stood, and the scent of vanilla surrounded him as she moved closer to follow. The smell was warm, fragrant, and tugged at something deep in his gut.

He led Emma downstairs and through the open space once used as a combined lobby and sitting area. When Emma's steps slowed, Shane glanced behind him to find her gazing at her surroundings. "This is a really beautiful space. Large and open. It feels like you're in the home of a friend."

She walked farther into the space and turned in a slow circle, nodding her head. "I can see where this has the potential to be a world-class wine facility, with a restaurant, and various tasting rooms. All you're missing for the ultimate wine connoisseur experience is lodging. And, to my knowledge, there isn't a winery around here offering that."

"At least, not yet," Shane stated. When she glanced over her shoulder with a raised brow, he continued. "We have a total of six rooms upstairs on the back side of the house we plan to renovate into guest rooms. But we want more. A main house, so to speak. There's a lead on some property in the area we may be able to buy for that purpose."

He followed her into the room, mesmerized by the way she moved as though flowing through it, owning it. She crossed to the wall of windows, her hand running across the long, wide window sill. The clicking of her heels echoed off the walls, made louder by the emptiness of the room.

"When do the renovations start?"

"Next week, if the weather holds. Rumor has it there could be a weather system coming in."

She nodded. "Yeah, I heard we may get some snow."

"Does that happen often?"

She shrugged a slim shoulder. "Winters in Georgia can be tricky. It feels like spring one day, the dead of winter the next. But we haven't seen snow the last couple of years up here in the Ridge. Being in the mountains usually ensures we'll get something. It's the ice that kills us here."

When she stopped at the wall of windows, he joined her. "Does KVN have their own building contractors they use in the wineries?" she asked.

"No. We always use local contractors if they meet our standards of craftsmanship. If not, we look outside the immediate vicinity."

She turned her head and leveled a gaze at him. "Who's your contractor?"

"Reynolds Construction and Restoration."

"Really?" Her head jerked back. "I didn't realize you'd hired them."

"Any relation?" Shane asked, not that it mattered. He didn't have time to find a new contractor if this one was no good, but he would if necessary.

"As a matter of fact, yes." A smile played on her lips. "Noah's my cousin."

"So, you can vouch for him, right?" Shane teased with a grin, crossing his arms and leaning against the wall.

"Noah's a great guy. He's more like an older brother than a cousin. I practically lived with his family as a kid."

It was an interesting tidbit of information that made him want to know more about her. He pushed away the thought and focused on the topic at hand.

"The company has a stellar reputation."

Emma nodded. "My uncle started the company with the intention of having his sons go into business with him. But Del went to California, and Aidan went into the military. Noah is the only one who stuck around the Ridge, so he owns it now." She turned to Shane. "I'm sorry. I derailed us. Lead me to the vines."

He wanted to learn more but nodded and gestured for her to walk ahead of him. "Ladies first."

"So how many of your cousins disappointed your uncle?" he asked as he steered her through the large room and down the hall past the kitchen.

Emma stopped and turned back to him. "What makes you think my uncle was disappointed?"

Shane smiled and held open a door leading outside. "I know all about the dynamics of a family business, remember?"

"Right. Anyway, it was two sons."

"Let me guess. Noah's the oldest?" He smiled when she nodded. "No wonder he and I get along so well."

She raised a brow in question and he shrugged. "We walk around with the weight of the world on our shoulders."

"Yeah, that would be Noah," she commented while they walked toward a small brick storage building that sat on the edge of the vineyard.

"What's this?" she asked, following Shane toward the structure. It resembled a barn, but on a smaller scale.

"This is where we house the hand tools used to work on the vines." He pulled a set of keys from his pocket and unlocked the padlock on the barn door. It swung open, revealing a wide, open space with a wood plank floor, the smell of earth rising up to him. The sun filtered in through two large windows on either side of the barn, casting shadows through the cool room.

She walked in ahead of him, looking around at the variety of commercial-grade garden tools. She turned back to him, her brow furrowed. "These are the tools you use?"

Shane laughed. "No. We'd never get a bottle of wine produced if we used hand tools on a vineyard this size. We keep these on hand for smaller, more delicate projects if they're needed. There's another storage facility on the other side of the vines that houses all the heavy equipment. But here,"—he motioned her to follow him to a bench against the far wall—

"is where we get our boots to walk the field."

She wrinkled her nose as she studied the shin-high rubber boots lined against the wall. They were caked with the red clay associated with the area's earth, but the soles were still solid. In the silence, Shane's arms crossed his chest and he leaned against the wall as if he had all the time in the world. He bit his lip in order not to laugh at the look of disdain on her face.

Damn, she was cute.

He eyed her shoes. "I don't know a lot about women's designer shoes, but I know for a fact you spent a pretty penny on those shiny, red-soled heels."

Emma looked over at him, a sheepish look on her face. "They're my weakness." She glanced down at her shoes, something akin to adoration in her voice. "They don't make these in this color anymore." She paused, meeting his eyes again. "Anyway, I'm not afraid to get dirty, but I draw the line at mud on my shoes and dress clothes."

Shane chuckled softly. "Well, your best bet, then, is to wear the boots. The ground is pretty dry right now."

Emma walked over and plopped down on the bench along the back wall. "Fine. I'll wear them." She gave the rubber boots the side eye. "I guess it would be too much to ask if you had a size seven."

Shane laughed and passed her a pair before picking up one for himself. "One size fits all."

She pursed her lips, but gamely slipped off her expensive shoes. With both hands, she pulled on the dirty, black rubber boots. Shane studied her as she went through the motions of putting on the boots gingerly. He supposed it was so she didn't tear those silky, translucent hose that ran up those long legs.

He leaned against the wall and changed into a pair of boots, then pushed off, walking to the large area where the doors stood open. If he could just not look at her, he could talk to her like she was anyone else. She was beautiful sure, but she was also smart as hell and it was a powerful combo. A combo he had no choice but to fight.

"What do you think?" Emma asked walking in front of him with her arms outstretched.

He couldn't help the smile that curved his lips. "They suit you."

The ugly black boots should have detracted from the way she looked in her dress. Instead, she simply looked like a little girl wearing her father's too-big shoes. It was adorable.

Fucking hell. He couldn't think of her that way.

Shane cleared his throat to cover a groan. "Let's go." His voice came out harsher than he'd intended, if her raised brows were any indication. Emma stepped aside in a silent gesture for him to go ahead of her. As he passed her, she stiffened and looked away.

He struck out toward the far end of the top level of acreage, where one section of the vines started. The more he walked, the more the coils of tension settling on his shoulders eased. As they walked in silence, Shane looked over at Emma with a sidelong glance. Although he had about six inches on her, she had no trouble keeping up with him. She never said a word, just followed wherever it was he walked. Shit, he'd been an asshole. Time to start over.

"I wanted to show you where the magic starts. The vines." Shane waved a hand to the rows along the left side. "These produce a deep burgundy. Mostly merlot and cabernets." As they walked, he pointed along the rows on the other side of them. "These are also red grapes but they will produce a slightly sweeter wine. Not as dry."

Shane led them down a row with towering vines, with various stages of grape growth. Some were plump, dark red grapes, other were tiny, baby globes of a lighter red. Emma looked around, then at the ground around the vines. "What do you do when it rains or snows and there's excess water? It seems to me it would run downhill and drown them."

For someone who was new to a vineyard, her mind was sharp as a tack.

He pointed to a bunch of grapes growing along fruiting wire attached between two wooden posts. "We're using the mountain slope to our advantage. We put in a new drainage system to divert the excess water from the vines."

Emma leaned forward, fingering one of the flowing towers in front of her. "How do they know to grow like this?"

"We employ what's called vine training. The vineyard master trains the vine with the vine trellis so it can grow upward using these wires" —Shane pointed to the top three pair of wires, near her hand—"called the catch wires."

She was close enough that if the wind blew slightly, her thick, cherry cola-colored hair would sweep over his face. He inhaled quietly, and the scent of vanilla and citrus filled his nostrils. His heart beat in his ears, and every muscle in his body tightened to the point of pain.

Clearing his throat, he took a step back from her. Bringing her out to the vines was supposed to help her learn the ropes, instead all he'd done was fight off urges he had no business having. She was an employee. It would be nothing but trouble. After Marlene's death, Shane tried to stay away from trouble. He had to get away from being so close to her. "Listen, I hate to cut our tour short, but I need to head back to the office."

Emma nodded, her gaze averted from his. "Sure, no problem."

Damn it, he was an asshole. Again, his tone was sharper than he intended. But the claws of desperation were in his throat and he had to get away from her before he did something he regretted. Like kiss those full lips until they both couldn't breathe. He had to stop looking at her like a woman he wanted and see her only as an employee. Shane needed her fascinating brain and nothing more.

Still, it didn't mean he had to act like a dick.

They started the hike back to the storage shed to change shoes. With each step, the apology worked its way up his chest. He stopped and turned to face her, finding her trailing behind. "Look, I'm...are you okay?"

A grimace marred her face and she gripped her left thigh as they hit the steeper area of the terrain.

"I'm fine." Her response was curt—a mirror to his own—and she passed him without sparing a glance in his direction.

His hand shot out and curled around her bicep. "Emma, stop."

She looked up at him, fire in those amber-colored eyes making them look as if they glowed.

"Shane, I'm fine. I swear."

"You didn't look fine when pain marched across your face. Are you going to tell me what caused it?"

"No, I'm not. It's none of your business, frankly." She sighed and looked away, her cheeks coloring a slight pink. "Please let go of my arm."

He released her immediately, but she didn't move away from him. The heat from her body warmed him like a blazing bonfire. When she turned her head to look up at him, their faces were close enough her breath whispered across his cheek.

The amber brown of her eyes darkened as her eyes searched his face. All he would need to do is lean in slightly and press his lips to her pink ones. Would they be as warm and soft as her hand?

She swayed slightly toward him, her eyes intent on his before her gaze averted away. A moment later she looked back at him, and the desire had all but melted away from her eyes. "I'm sorry for snapping at you that way. It was very unprofessional." All-business Emma returned. She stood straighter, her shoulders back. "It won't happen again."

Before Shane could respond, Emma walked past him, and he closed his eyes for a moment before following her. He thanked God that she came to her senses and moved away from him.

He caught up to her and, in silent unison, they continued the walk back to the storage shed and the main house, although they both moved a bit slower and farther apart than they had before. His head was muddled with the closeness of her. He needed to get back into professional territory.

When she stopped to change into her heels, he paused briefly. "I'll be tied up in meetings for the rest of the day. Take your time, get settled in. We'll talk more tomorrow. If there's anything you need, let Lindsey know or shoot me an email." He booked it back into his office, ditching the work boots at the back door.

It should have been a relief that they were on the same page in that their relationship was strictly business. Instead, it left him cold and empty.

SEVEN

Last Man Standing

THE PIERCING RING of her cell phone startled Emma out of her work flow. "Damn it," she muttered.

She scrambled to pick up the phone to stop the incessant trill but a quick glance at the screen flashed Shane's name. There was no stopping the small thrill in her belly seeing his name, even though she'd hardly seen him. He'd been in California for nearly a week.

"Hello?"

"You're still at the office, aren't you? Don't even answer that. I know you are. Isn't it like seven or something?" Shane's deep voice greeted her. Emma ignored the tingling that danced under her skin at the sound of his voice.

She looked up and found that it was pitch black outside the windows of her office. The clock on the bottom of the screen told her she'd missed dinner by a couple of hours. "I'm doing fine, thank you." Emma smiled and shook her head.

"Sorry. Let me start again."

"Should I hang up and let you call me back?"

Shane chuckled. "Ha ha. You're cute. Wait, I didn't mean it that way..."

Warmth that had no business spreading through her body did just that. She could make out a couple of curse words under his breath, causing her to grin. "It's fine. Don't worry about it."

He blew out a breath. "Okay, starting over." He paused. "Hi, Emma. What's up?"

She leaned back in her chair. "Work. What's up with you?"

"Same. But it's four here, not seven. You should head home."

"I was just about to shut down for the day. I had to finish the inventory download. Tomorrow starts the cross-checking with the accounting system."

Shane made a snorting sound. "Inventory. Accounting. Can you hear me snoring over here? By the way, if the guy you work for makes you stay so late, he might be a demanding prick. Do I need to kick his ass?"

Emma raised a brow and snickered. "So, Mr. Kavanaugh does have a funny side. Learn something new every day."

"Hey, I can be a funny guy." Mock hurt came through the line before he paused. "Um, I probably shouldn't have said 'prick' or 'ass' to you. I apologize."

"That's not necessary—I'm not offended."

"Maybe not, but HR would have my ass...butt if they knew."

Emma smiled. "It's all good. Thanks for the offer to kick his ass. But I can handle him."

"I have no doubt that's true." His voice was low and rough. She closed her eyes against the storm of pure hormones racing in her blood. He sighed. "Okay, so what were you working on before I called and made an ass out of myself?"

She silently thanked him for bringing the subject back to the equivalent of a cold shower. "Inventory, accounting, you snoring."

"Right. How does everything look?"

Emma paused before answering. "Fine. But..."

"But what?"

"The accounting software is outdated. It's an old version and doesn't run like it should."

"What's your recommendation? I know you have one."

She tapped a finger on the desk. "Okay, but remember you asked for it." With a deep breath, she dove in. "You need a complete system overhaul. And not just the accounting software."

He groaned. "I was afraid you were going to say that. What else? Lay it all on me."

"The computers here are slow and outside of their useful lives. You need cyber security for the local network here and a server upgrade." He grunted on the other end of the line, but she kept going. "With more server space, we can get rid of all the paper around here and digitize—"

"Stop. My brain can't take it right now. La la la." She giggled at the image of him plugging his ears.

"Did you just giggle?" he asked.

Emma tried to stop but it just made her giggle more. "I am a girl after all and sometimes we giggle."

"Hmmm...I like it."

Her smile faded and she swallowed hard against the dry desert that set up camp in her throat. "Yeah, so if you want to go over this when you get back, let me know. I'll have all my recommendations written up with quotes for new software and hardware."

Shane cleared his throat. "Yeah, that'll work. I'll be back the day after tomorrow." He paused. "Emma, you've done an amazing job already. I haven't exactly been the best manager to you. You've been there more than a week and we've hardly spent a moment together. Shit, that didn't come out right." He sighed. "And I probably shouldn't have said 'shit' just now. Ahhh...I'll just shut up now."

Emma laughed and shook her head. "Cut yourself some slack, Shane. Shit, fuck, damn, ass. Feel better? Now HR can write us both up."

Shane joined her laughter and then sighed. "Thanks. I needed that."

"I aim to please," she replied and rubbed a brow. She tried not to be too friendly with him but Shane was easy to talk with. Note to self: tread lightly with the casual conversations.

"Hey, this is random. But you said the other day one of your cousins moved to California. Which one?"

Emma tilted her head. "Delaney. He moved out there a decade or so ago to work in television. Why?"

"I knew it. Your cousin is the host of *Property Ace*."

She smirked. "I didn't picture you as one who sat around watching home improvement shows."

"I don't, but Del is pretty popular in any circle. He was here last weekend. We've played golf a few times."

Her eyes widened. "Golf? Del played golf?" She laughed until her side ached. "Oh boy, I can't wait to talk to him again. He used to make fun of the guys who would come around here and golf. I may call him when I get home just to mess with him." She hummed. "Did you tell him I worked with you?"

"No, I didn't make the connection until later."

"Ha! Perfect, he'll wonder how I know what he's been up to and it will drive him crazy. Del's hard to get one over on. Yes!" She fist pumped the air. "Thank you, Shane."

He chuckled. "Anything to help in the war of sibling rivalry. Or cousin rivalry in your case." A pause. "I should let you go. Plot world domination and all. I assume you're alone."

His low, throaty voice shot a zing through her body. She bit her bottom lip. Of course, she was in a two-year-long sex drought and she was beginning to crack. Anything the man said to her lately made her think of sex.

"Last man standing."

"I figured. Be careful on your way out."

"Care about my well-being, Shane?" She intended it to be a joke, but as soon as his name left her mouth, she closed her eyes and wanted to kick herself. What the hell was she saying? It was like poking the proverbial bear.

"Of course, Emma," he said, his tone soft. He cleared his throat as the tense silence drew out. "I care what happens to all my employees." His voice had lost that throaty, intimate quality.

Right. Employee. Her lips twisted into a grimace and she fought back the emotions that crawled up and landed in her chest. "You're a good man, Shane. Well, I'm going to head out. I'm starving. Talk tomorrow?"

"Yeah, sure."

All teasing was gone and it was back to business as usual. "Bye, Shane."

"Bye, Emma."

This phone conversation confused Emma. Shane ran hot and cold with her, as though he'd forget their circumstances and then catch himself. She should be grateful that he'd backed off. The way he made her blood run so hot, she wasn't sure she could do the same if he didn't stop.

She sank back into her office chair with a deep sigh. It was time to head to a meeting, pronto. She hadn't been to one in weeks and needed to find a way to take the edge off. Her old go-to habits were no longer an option.

Liquor was obviously out of the question, as was picking up a stranger in a bar—something she'd quit doing even before she became sober—and, thanks to the pin in her femur, running was out as well.

No time like the present. A glance at her phone told her that a meeting would be starting soon, but she could still make it if she hauled ass.

Thirty minutes later, Emma sat in a folding chair in the musty basement of a Methodist church, stirring powdered creamer into a Styrofoam cup of coffee that resembled motor oil. She glanced around at the few people milling around the room, relieved to find strangers.

Madison Ridge had their own meetings three times a week in a church basement as well, but while most people knew about her demise, it didn't mean she wanted to know about anyone else's issues or fuel the town gossip further. There was a reason why the program was "anonymous".

"Hey, girl."

Emma turned her head to the soft voice behind her. Shifting her body in the seat, she smiled at Kristen, a young woman she'd spoken to a few times before the meetings started. "Hey, how are you?"

Kristen shrugged, but it was more like a jerky twitch. Her leg bounced as though it were on a spring. "Today's been a rough day." She took a sip of her coffee, tendrils of steam swirling around her dark messy bun. "My court hearing didn't go so great."

"Oh no, I'm so sorry. I didn't realize it was today." Emma reached out over the back of her chair and held out her hand. Kristen dropped her head and grabbed Emma's hand like it was a lifeline. Maybe it was. She had no other words to offer, so she just let the girl cry in silence.

Her heart broke for Kristen. The state recently took her two young kids into custody after she was caught driving under the influence with her children in the car. Kristen faced a load of charges and spent some time in jail before being sent to rehab for the third time. After that stint, Kristen's family had written her off and she had no support system. Emma hoped Kristen could follow the program and string some sober time together for her kids.

But the trembling hand, the bouncing knee, and the clamminess of her skin twisted Emma's gut. If she had to guess, she'd say that Kristen's last drink—or fix, or maybe both—was probably only a day or two ago.

Kristen raised her head, tears coursing down her cheeks. She released Emma's hand and brushed at her face with her sleeve. Emma wanted to hug her and tell her it would all be okay. But the truth was she didn't even know that for herself, much less a young mother who by all accounts hadn't found her rock bottom just yet. Emma could only hope Kristen's rock bottom wouldn't land her in the morgue.

"Okay, everyone, let's get started."

Emma tilted her head to catch Kristen's eye. "Want to talk after the meeting?" she whispered.

Kristen wouldn't meet her gaze. She wiped the last of the tears from her face and leaned back in her chair. "No, thanks. I'm good. I got some help."

"Okay. I'm here if you need me." Emma frowned when Kristen ignored her and brought her arm back over the chair, facing forward. She couldn't make the girl talk to her. Emma could only hope her "help" wasn't in the form of a pint of vodka or a bottle of pills.

Emma sipped her coffee and focused on reciting the twelve steps and traditions. Her heart went out to Kristen, but for now she'd concentrate on her own shit she had to work out. Namely the fact that she had the hots for her sexy boss and that was the road less traveled for a damn good reason.

She blew out a quiet breath as members stood and told their stories. Thumbing the anchor pendant, she dreamed of hope and redemption. Emma needed hope to make it through the day and to save her home. It would be her redemption.

Her curiosity for the boss would have to sit this one out.

EIGHT

So You Like Torture

EMMA ADJUSTED the glasses she'd reluctantly broken down and bought, and clicked through a website, researching new accounting software. She dropped her chin to her hand. As hard as the software company tried with its bright colors, exclamation points, and we're-all-in-this-together pictures, she just couldn't get excited about accounts payable and receivable collections.

"It appears you work as hard as I do when you're intent on something."

Startled, Emma jumped and smacked her knee on the unforgiving wood of her desk. *Ouch! Son of a bitch.* Rubbing the sore spot, she grit her teeth against releasing a string of obscenities. "Hey, there."

"Are you okay?" Shane leaned against the doorframe to her office in all his T-shirt and faded denim glory.

Unlike the pressed pair he'd worn the first time she met him, these were the well-worn-in kind that said they'd been around a while. His black T-shirt stretched across those shoulders that carried the weight of the world according to him. A dark jacket draped across his shoulder and work boots completed his ensemble. He looked more like he belonged on a job site with a hard hat than in an office wheeling deals.

The man could pull off any look and in spite of the more blue-collar look, Shane still exuded an air of prestige.

Against her better judgment, she had to admit he was hot as hell in jeans that accented his slim hips and long legs.

And good Lord, he was a tall drink of water.

She swallowed, catching her breath, and quickly took the glasses off her face. "Yeah. I'm fine. I didn't hear you come in."

He smiled and pushed off the doorjamb and walked into her office, stopping in front of her desk. "You're always so intent on what you're doing, you never notice me."

Yeah, right. Noticing him was never an issue. It was noticing him too much that had her in more knots than a pretzel.

He peered over her monitor. "What's so interesting?"

"Accounting programs." She smirked. "Let the snoring commence."

Shane smiled but it didn't quite meet his eyes. "Don't tempt me." He didn't elaborate but, with a heavy sigh, sat in the chair across from her. He laid the jacket across his lap and kicked his legs out in front of him, his focus on the floor.

Emma looked closer, past the mesmerizing good looks, to the actual man. There were hints of circles under his eyes, and his jaw was darkened with more than a day's worth of stubble.

"How was your trip?" she asked.

Shane rubbed a hand over a cheek. "It was productive. We signed some contracts, closed some deals. Looked over some land in Virginia we're interested in."

Emma narrowed her eyes. "Then why don't you look happy about it?"

Shane's gaze met hers. He looked as though he were weighing his next words. Looking away from her, he pulled his legs in, his elbows on his knees, hands dangling between them. "I spent a couple of days with my dad in Napa, as well."

She stayed silent when he paused, feeling he wasn't done talking, but her stomach dropped. The look of sadness on his face didn't give her a warm and fuzzy feeling.

"My father has stage three colon cancer."

Shit, it was worse than she thought. Her fingers tightened around her glasses that sat in her palm. Her throat ached and her heart twisted. She wanted so badly to reach out to him, soothe the hurt that comes with knowing a parent is sick. "Oh, Shane. I'm so sorry. What's his prognosis?"

"He's on his second round of chemo right now and it's really taking a toll. If it works, his prognosis is decent. But at this stage?" he trailed off, shrugging. One of his hands clenched into a fist. "I hate seeing him this way."

Emma's heart went out to Shane, and she tried to comfort him the only way she could without crossing the line. "I understand. It's incredibly hard to watch someone who you consider an anchor in your life be so frail." Her mind wandered back to the times when first her father, then her mother, lay dying in a hospital bed. "It's a helpless feeling."

"Exactly." When he spoke, she looked up at him to find him watching her. A sort of understanding passed between them. It was a feeling like they were in the same club, but it was one nobody wanted to join.

She swallowed and cast her gaze down to the calendar on her desk. "You never mentioned your mother. How is she doing with all of this?"

Sadness tinged his voice once again. "My mother died when I was twelve."

She closed her eyes briefly as her heart clenched again and she wanted to kick her own ass for asking. "I'm sorry. I shouldn't have—"

Shane stood and put on his jacket before sliding his hands into his front pockets. A sad smile tilted his lips. "Don't be sorry, Emma. You didn't know. It's not like I walk around talking about it."

"Still, I'm an idiot."

"I don't hire idiots." He shot her a grin, making her smile. "Speaking of hiring. How's the staffing going?"

Emma had never been so grateful for a subject change. "I narrowed down a few candidates for the restaurant manager and hospitality director. I've sent you the résumés, if you want to go over them."

Shane shook his head. "No, I trust you know how to hire great talent. I've got the new vintner coming out next week. I hired him away from one of our European locations. He and I will work on staffing for the vineyard."

Trust. Her chest swelled with the knowledge that he trusted her. Something she felt she needed to earn again with her own family. Still, to have Shane's trust made her sit a little taller.

"Other than that, I've been working on the inventory list, and I reconciled it to the audit reports."

"Good. I should have had that done sooner but never got around to it." He smiled. "Great job, Emma. Why don't you head on home? It's late and you're the last one here. Again."

"Yeah, I'm exhausted actually." She stood and raised her arms over her head, working out the kinks in her neck and back. He cleared his throat and walked to the door of her office. "I'll walk you to your car." His voice came out low and gravelly.

"It's okay, I'll be fine. I've walked myself out for the last few nights."

Shane walked back toward her with her scarf and jacket in his hands. "The woman doth protest too much."

Emma tilted her head. "Did you just use Shakespeare on me?"

He held out the scarf to her. "I did. Why?"

She shrugged, taking the colorful fabric from him and wrapping it around her neck. "I just didn't picture you as the Shakespeare type."

He stared at her, his gaze darkened slightly. "There's a lot you don't know about me." He held out her coat to her and when she took it, their hands brushed. Their stare held for a beat while her heart threatened to race out of her chest. She swallowed the lump in her throat.

"So it would seem," she said, forcing her tone to be easy as she shrugged into her coat.

His hands found the front pockets of his jeans again. "Besides, anyone who's ever sat through a high school literature class is the Shakespeare type at some point."

She chuckled and pulled her hair out of her coat collar. "That's true. In my case, I did it again in college."

"Because one session of it just wasn't enough?"

"I took it as an elective," she said, digging for her keys.

He rubbed a hand over his five o'clock shadow. "Huh uh. So what you're saying is you like torture. Good to know."

Emma rolled her eyes but couldn't hide her smile while she dug for her keys. "Get your mind out of the gutter, Kavanaugh."

He held up his hands as though in surrender. "You said it, I didn't."

She sent him a wry smile, before turning her attention back to the task at hand. Where the hell had she put her keys? "Damn it," she muttered before upending the large tote she used as a purse onto her desk.

Shane leaned forward with caution, like a man wanting to see a rattlesnake up close but staying out of striking distance. He averted his gaze. "I'm sure there are things in that pile I don't need or want to see. But what are you looking for?"

"Looking for my keys." Emma shifted through receipts, a small notebook, her wallet, a hairbrush, and various other items before hitting the jackpot. "Ah ha!"

She spied the telltale silver loop of her keys peeking out from under a grocery receipt and pulled them free. She also spied a small white chip under a tampon. *Shit!*

While the tampon would be embarrassing if Shane scoped it out, it would be detrimental to her job if he saw the AA chip she carried with her at all times. Cupping her hand, she slid all the contents on her desk back into her bag. When she glanced up at him, his brows were drawn down. Her stomach bottomed out and bile rose in her throat.

"Carry your whole life in that bag?"

Emma smiled and relief flooded her body. "Just about." She hitched it up onto her shoulder. "I'm ready."

Shane stepped back and held an arm out. "Ladies first."

They walked out into the cold night and darkened parking lot. The only light came from inside the building and a single streetlamp from the far side of the lot.

He looked over at her when she shivered. "Come on, let's get you to your car."

She clicked her key fob, unlocking the doors before they reached her SUV. "Listen, Shane," she began and turned to him, her back against the side of the vehicle. "I've lost both of my parents, and I know how difficult it can be, especially since you aren't with them every day. And even though I try to keep business and my personal life separate, if you ever need someone to talk to, feel free to knock on my door and scare me." When she smiled, he rewarded her with the full force of his smile.

Yeah, she heard angels sing.

"I appreciate that, Emma. Truly." Even in the dark, his eyes were like a blue flame, hot and intent on hers.

"Thanks for walking me to my car," she managed to say, even though her tongue seemed to have lost its ability to function when he looked at her like that. The heat in his eyes warmed her from the inside out. Even in the freezing weather, her skin heated beneath her scarf. The cold air against her skin was a welcome sensation.

"Well, you parked a long way out here and it's dark. I don't want anything to happen to you." He leaned forward, and when she inhaled sharply, his masculine scent invaded her senses. Her eyes slid closed, relishing the heat of his body so close to hers. "You'll be warmer if you get in."

Her eyes popped open and she found he had opened the door for her. "Oh. Right. Good night," she mumbled, nearly diving into the driver's seat and slamming the door behind her. Shane stood outside her door and once she started the reluctant truck, the fan blasting cold air in her face, he motioned for her to roll down the window. She did so grudgingly, because really, she just wanted to get home and wallow in her mortification.

"Yes?" she asked tersely, leaning her face toward the opening.

Before she could react, Shane leaned in and placed his lips over hers. It was just a whisper of a kiss, a brush of lips against hers. But the zing went all the way to her toes. She could only imagine what a full-on kiss would be like with this man.

Pulling back, a grin split his too-handsome face. "Drive safely, Emma."

He turned and walked away.

NINE

Rescue Me

SON OF A BITCH. What the hell was he doing? First, he'd skirted the line of flirting with her at every turn. And now he kissed her? He ran a hand through his hair and sighed. Fuck, he was asking for trouble. He'd crossed a line.

The kiss was really nothing more than a brush of lips together. But now that he'd had that small sample? Shane wanted to taste all of her. Before, his desire for her was based on his imagination. She couldn't possibly taste as sweet as she looked, but damned if she wasn't sweeter.

It was something he couldn't let happen again. Getting involved with Emma could crush his career and land him in hot water legally. Now that he was getting his footing back after Marlene's untimely and avoidable death, he would be seriously fucked if he didn't handle this right. He may as well hand the company over to Colin on a silver platter.

The taillights of Emma's SUV faded out of sight as she turned the slight curve onto the main road, her tires crunching over the gravel on the road. Through the trees, it was hard to make out the vehicle, so he turned to head to his Range Rover. He debated getting some work done when he got home, but jet lag started to settle into his bones.

Once the truck was warmed up and ready to go, Shane headed down the long, winding drive that led to the main road. As he rounded the last curve, his stomach rolled when he saw the night was lit up by the flashing lights of Emma's vehicle.

With his heart pounding, he parked behind her and jumped out, walking up to the driver's side window. She rolled it down, her pink lips drawn into a deep frown and irritation lighting up her eyes. Muscles he didn't realized were tensed up, released.

"You okay?"

"Yeah." A frown line appeared between her brows. "I don't know what happened. It just stalled and wouldn't start again."

"What does it do when you try to start it?" She turned the key and the truck made a hideous groaning sound but never turned over. "Could be the starter," he said. "Need a ride home?"

"I already called Aidan to take me home."

He raised a brow. "Who's Aidan?" And why did he care? Jealousy wasn't a remote possibility.

Somewhere in the back of his head, a little voice whispered, "Liar."

"My cousin."

"I could take you home. No need to get him out."

"He's a cop and working tonight anyway."

Shane chose to ignore the relief that flooded his body. "Well, come sit in my truck. It's cold out here." She rolled up the window and cut the lights.

He opened the passenger door of his vehicle for her and when they were both settled into the warm interior, he turned to her. "Is there anyone you don't know in this town?"

She laughed. The laughter died when she pulled her cell phone out of her purse and looked at the screen. The blue light of the interior cast her face in partial shadow, but a frown marred her lips and caused that V between her brows to make another appearance. "Everything okay?" he asked.

"Yeah," she said on a sigh. "Just some persistent people trying to make a deal where there isn't one." She swiped at the screen and tapped a couple of times before looking back at him, picking up the thread of conversation. "I do know a lot of people, but no. I don't know everyone."

"From where I'm sitting, it seems as if you're related to everyone in town."

She smiled at him and burrowed down in the heated seat. "Aidan will be here in a couple of minutes to get my keys and will take care of getting a tow arranged."

"Pays to know people in high places."

She smiled softly. "Aidan is the baby boy of the family. But since he came back from the military and now runs the police department here, he's pretty much taken on the role of family protector."

Headlights cut through the night at the end of the road and made a slow but steady progression toward them. As the large white truck drew closer, it pulled over in front of her vehicle.

"That was quick," Shane murmured.

"He said he was headed in this direction, anyway." She pushed open the door, the frigid air filling the cabin, when a tall, broad-shoul-dered man stepped out of the truck across from them.

"Hey, Aidan." The three of them stood in the light beams from Shane's truck.

"Hey. What are you doing out here so late by yourself?" Aidan's voice was deep and laced with concern.

"I was working, but I wasn't alone. Shane was with me." She shifted and turned to him. "Shane, Aidan Reynolds. Aidan, Shane Kavanaugh."

The two men shook hands as Aidan sized him up. He had the build of a linebacker and stood an inch or two taller than Shane's own six foot three. Aidan's jacket was dark with large yellow letters reading "police" on the back, and he had a gun strapped to his jean-clad hip.

Aidan assessed him and appeared to be satisfied. "Nice to meet you, Shane," he said. "Thanks for staying with her."

Emma huffed and rolled her eyes. "I'm not some simpering female." She smacked his chest with the back of her hand. "Are you going to help me or not?"

The radio on Aidan's hip went off and he pulled it out of the holster and spoke into it, while at the same time nodding at Emma.

"Reynolds. The tow needs to be sent to..." he trailed off and Shane rattled off the address. "425 Brandywine Drive. The vehicle is about a hundred yards up the road on Brandywine. Over."

Something was said that Shane couldn't decipher, but Aidan seemed to speak static. "Shit," he muttered under his breath. "Is Deputy Wilson available?" He listened again to more static then said, "10-4, thanks, Cara." He slipped the radio back into the holster and, with his hands on his hips, turned back to Emma. "I have another call I have to get to. There's no one else available. I'm sorry, Em." He glanced over to Shane. "You'll make sure she gets home safely?"

"Absolutely."

Aidan nodded once. "You going to be okay in that big house by yourself?"

Emma nodded. "I live there, of course I'll be fine." She pushed up on her toes, laying a hand on his shoulder and pecked his cheek. "Thanks for taking care of this," she said when she pulled away. The cousins seemed to share some sort of telepathic message before Aidan looked back at Shane. "I'm counting on you to get her home in one piece."

"Consider it done."

"Em, I'll have it towed to Henderson's shop."

"Thanks, again. Tell your mom hi for me."

Aidan nodded and touched the edge of his baseball cap before heading back to the warmth of his running police truck. A few minutes later, Emma directed Shane to her house. "I'm not too far from here. About five minutes or so."

His eyes stayed on the road in front of them, hands clenching and unclenching the wheel while his brain worked overtime. The directions she gave made Shane's stomach roll. They sounded suspiciously familiar to ones he'd followed when he'd visited the property KVN wanted to buy. And that the owner didn't want to sell. He swallowed hard and beat back the heaviness in his chest.

"You're close to the winery."

She nodded, looking out the side window. "It's a dream commute compared to what I used to have to deal with."

"I've heard about traffic in Atlanta. Sounds like it can rival some of the jams on the Eastshore Freeway in San Francisco."

Emma sighed. "It can be pretty nasty. Especially if the interstate collapses or something equally ridiculous. I was fortunate enough that after a while I had a car service, but sitting in the car for an hour to go seven miles is no fun, driving or not. The only upshot was that I was productive." She leaned forward peering into the night. "It's right here."

Shane turned and drove down a long road. It looked like he was driving into a black hole, and it was nearly impossible for him to make out anything that would help him figure out his surroundings.

As the headlights of the truck cut through the darkness, lighting up the front of an enormous farmhouse in the near distance, Shane closed his eyes briefly. "Son of a bitch," he muttered under his breath.

"I'm sorry, what?" Emma asked.

He glanced over out of the corner of his eye. "Uh, it's a huge house. I'm surprised you live here all alone."

Emma leaned forward, peering through the windshield. "It is a big house. Much too large for one person. But it's been in my family for generations." The lights of the dashboard only illuminated half of her face, but the wistfulness that crossed her features was clear.

Shit, that was not the reaction he expected.

The driveway forked, one wide path leading to the right side of the house toward a detached garage building in the back. The other circling in front of the house. Shane pulled into the curved part of the drive, slowing to a stop at the bottom of the front steps.

Landscape spotlights lit up the front of the house, which was made of white clapboard siding with black shutters. The large wraparound porch invited visitors to come up and take a load off. The multi-angled roofs and windows dominated the front of the home, giving it a stately, yet elegant feel. It was beautiful and even with its large size, it looked like the perfect family home.

Shock, dread, and a bit of "I can't believe my dumb fucking luck" twisted in his gut. He rubbed his chin. How the hell was he going to get out of this one?

Emma was quiet for a moment. "Are you hungry? I have a huge Crock-Pot of chili."

Shane glanced over to her. The adorable shrug and wry smile hit him in the gut, which meant he needed to put some distance between them. "I need to go. I've got a pile of work waiting for me at home. Thanks for the offer though."

"It's too much food for one person, but a man's gotta eat, right? Or at least take some home with you. Payback for bringing me home." She paused, her amber eyes on his. They held a mix of emotions that he couldn't completely decipher.

Shane stared at her, then looked back out into the night. "I don't need you to pay me back for giving you a ride." It was just a meal. He was a grown-ass man and could control his hormones. No matter what other parts of his body thought. And if it got to be too much being close to her, he could leave. Nothing said he had to stay.

He shut off the car. "Lead the way."

TEN

Not Today, Hormones

THE WARMTH of the house hit Emma in the face and wrapped around her like an electric blanket. Closing out the cold air, Shane shut the door, and after hanging their coats, she motioned for him to follow her. "I'm going to make some coffee. Want any?"

She turned to find Shane looking around the two-story living area, a hand rubbing over the front of his shirt. "You have a beautiful home."

She smiled and walked up beside him, trying to see the massive room from his point of view. "Yeah, this was my childhood home. Well, sort of. My parents ran it as a bed and breakfast for most of my life."

"Well, I can see where it would be perfect for something like that," Shane said, pacing the room and running a hand through his hair.

Her smile faltered. "Are you okay? You seem agitated."

Shane stopped his forward motion and looked across the room at her. His gaze was inscrutable. "I'm sorry. I'm fine. I just need to make a phone call."

"Oh, of course. I'll go make coffee." She walked off toward the back of the house and through the kitchen that smelled of spicy meat and tomatoes. As if on cue, her stomach growled, her lunch long forgotten.

74

She scooped some coffee grounds into the machine and pressed a button. After a few gurgles, coffee poured into the glass carafe below. She laid her palms flat on the counter and took several deep breaths in an attempt to control the butterflies in her belly. She needed a minute to think without him around her. He kissed her. It was merely a brush of the lips, but she had felt it all the way down to her core. What the hell did it mean? *You can handle this, Emma. He's your boss, pretend you're at work. And forget about the damn kiss.*

Now he was in her house—by her invitation sure, but still—with his smiles that made her heart race and her thighs clench.

The skin on her face warmed and she cast her eyes up to Shane standing in the opening from the dining area. A small smile played on his lips as though he knew what she was thinking. Damn it all to hell— the man could fluster her like no other had before. She fumbled with the coffeepot and managed to pour the hot liquid into the mugs without making a mess. "You take your coffee black, right?"

Shane smiled. "Right."

She waved a thumb over her shoulder, toward the Crock-Pot sitting on the far counter behind her. "I think the chili's ready. I was going to put some bread in the oven. If you give me a few minutes, I can put some together for you to take home."

Shane slid his hands into his pockets while his gaze wandered around the room before stopping on her. With his jaw set, he nodded. "If it's okay with you, I'll just eat here before I head out." He rubbed a hand over his stomach with a half smile. "It smells great and I'm starving. The last time I ate was before I left Napa this morning."

Her head bobbed in affirmation and she gestured to the breakfast table that sat in front of the windows. "Make yourself at home. I'll have everything out in a few."

He smiled and reached for the coffee on the counter. "Works for me."

She busied herself with buttering several slices of thick-cut sourdough bread, but his presence made the room feel a size too small.

"So, you grew up in this house?" Shane asked. She glanced over her shoulder to find him looking around the sitting area that led off to the opposite side of the kitchen.

"Um, yeah. Well mostly," she said, pushing the pan of bread into the oven and shutting the door. Emma leaned her elbows on the island and looked around, thinking about her strange childhood. "My parents and I lived in the small detached house out back when we had guests. It was small and pretty cramped. But I was able to play with the kids who stayed here." She twisted her lips and shrugged. "That didn't happen often though."

He looked over at her. "I can understand. My childhood home wasn't open to guests, but the vineyards were. When I was little, I couldn't always understand why strangers walked all over what I considered my playground."

"It's hard to understand, isn't it?" She shrugged. "I think that's why I spent so much time at my Aunt Stella and Uncle Paul's place. It was a real home, like I'd seen on television. The only people who lived there were mom and dad with their kids. I mean, my parents were great." She paused and swallowed, emotions she didn't want him to see starting to surface. "But it was an unconventional upbringing, and they worked a lot."

Especially during the times when her father's gambling addiction had nearly cost them their home and livelihood. To this day, she wasn't sure how her mother had managed to keep it all together. Emma's heart twisted, knowing she'd disappointed her mother with her addiction. Regret filled her soul knowing her mother would never see her make amends.

Shane nodded. "After my mother died, my childhood became a bit unconventional, as well." His blue eyes were intense on hers. "It seems we have a few things in common, Ms. Reynolds."

There went the damn butterflies again. "It appears we do, Mr. Kavanaugh." Emma looked away before she found herself entangled in his stare. Relief flooded her veins when the timer dinged. "Bread's ready."

Minutes later, they sat at the table, blowing on hot spoonfuls of chili. Emma handed him a couple of slices of the fragrant bread. He accepted them gratefully, and promptly dumped one in his chili.

"I think this is the best chili I've ever had," he said around a mouthful. He closed his mouth and swallowed. He paused for a moment before scooping up more of the meaty mixture.

"Thank you. It's an old family recipe." She took a bite of chili and chewed thoughtfully. "So, what's your family like?"

Shane stopped, spoon mid-air. "I would say it was like your aunt and uncle's until my mom died. After that, it was more like yours. It was only me and my brother, but we lived on a family compound of sorts."

She raised a brow. "A family compound?"

He laughed. "Makes it sound like a cult, doesn't it?" He shook his head. "We all lived on the same piece of land, but it was made up of hundreds of acres. So, we had to work at seeing each other. My grandparents, my family, they all have their own houses on the land." He grinned at her. "I have a lot of cousins as well, who are more like siblings. Being in the family business meant there was always family to rely on." A shadow crossed his face. "It came in handy when my mom died."

Before she could think about it, she reached out and laid a hand on his forearm. "I'm so sorry. And you were only twelve?"

"Yeah."

"That's a rough age for kids. I was devastated when I lost my mom, and I was thirty-two. I can't imagine being a child."

He shrugged. "It was a long time ago. But it was great having family nearby, especially during that time. Even when we had our fair share of family squabbles, much like a family your size probably did."

She stared down into her chili as she stirred it. "No, we didn't have squabbles." When he raised a brow, she continued, even though her stomach rolled. "Don't get me wrong. My parents were good parents. They loved me and took care of me. But there were…issues. And it caused problems with the rest of my family at times."

Emma blew out a hard breath to beat back the nausea and sat back in her chair, wiping her palms on her pants. She looked up and into his stare. "My father was a gambler, a bad one. When they first started the B&B, they had a stable of horses as part of the amenities they offered." She looked out the window, her reflection casting back to her in the darkness beyond the glass. Memories of helping her father brush the horses when she was a kid came back to her. Not sure why it popped into her mind since she hadn't thought of it in years.

"Year after year, the stable got smaller. He had to sell the horses to pay back his debts, until finally, there were no more to sell." She thought of the horses—she'd loved and named them all—being trotted into trailers, never to be seen again. Even now, the loss she'd felt back then was keen. "Then, he began to sell off or borrow against anything and everything he could. And yet he kept gambling." Emma couldn't say she didn't understand, because she understood that demon known as addiction all too well.

Several moments ticked by and Shane didn't say anything, just looked at her with an emotion in his eyes she couldn't read. Her stomach quivered and the smile she gave him was shaky. "And that's my tragic little story. Want more chili?"

"No," he said on a groan, laying his hand across his stomach. "I'm full. Thanks for feeding me."

Emma's shoulders slumped in relief when he didn't press for more details on her story. "No problem. I have plenty of food." She rose and started to pick up his bowl.

He stood and picked it up out of her reach. "I got it. Let me help you clean up."

"There isn't really much to do." She waved him away.

He grabbed her hand in his larger one and stared down at her. "Emma. I want to help you. Let me."

The warmth of his hand around hers made her tingle in places that had no business tingling. His hand dwarfed hers, and the slight roughness of his palm against hers gave her goosebumps. His eyes implored hers to let him help her.

She wanted to fight against it, but found she couldn't. He was wearing her down, her resistance to him becoming weaker each time she was around him.

"Okay," she said softly.

"Thank you." He released her hand, but didn't break eye contact or move away from her.

After several seconds ticked by, he turned away and crossed to the large farmhouse sink. She stood a moment longer, her feet like bricks, unwilling to move anywhere. When she finally had her wits about her, she moved to help clean up.

They worked together well, almost like a dance. They anticipated each other's moves and joked around while they did it. The heaviness of the conversation at the table lifted, leaving only good-natured bantering.

As Emma dried the last dish, Shane tried to cover a yawn. "You look beat," she said.

He rubbed the back of his neck. "Jet lag is kicking my ass." He glanced at the clock on the stove. "I should get going. Get out of your hair."

She waved him away. "You're not bothering me." Crossing her arms, she leaned against the counter and eyed him. The shadows under his eyes were prominent and he swayed slightly, making her worry he was going to face-plant on her kitchen floor. "You okay to drive home? You look like you could fall asleep where you stand."

He nodded. "I'll be fine."

"Want some coffee for the road?"

He smiled. "Sure, thanks."

"No problem." Short of driving him home herself—which would be hard with no car—Emma had to trust he would be okay and the coffee would keep him awake.

A few minutes later, Shane was armed with a stainless steel travel mug and had shrugged into his coat in the foyer. At the door, he turned and looked down at her. "Thanks for dinner. It was delicious. I needed a good home-cooked meal."

She smiled, knowing he had to leave, but reluctant to watch him walk out the door. And knowing it was all wrong to feel that way. "You're welcome."

He ran a hand through his hair. "Listen. I want to apologize for earlier tonight. When I kissed you."

"I'm not going to report you for harassment if that's what you're worried about." She averted her eyes for a moment before looking back at him. "I liked it. I wish it had lasted longer."

He moved his shoulders, sending the muscles under his shirt into motion. "Still, I should've never done that. You work for my company. It's inexcusable."

She crossed her arms over her chest. "It was barely more than a brush of lips, Shane."

He rubbed a hand on the back of his neck and looked at her from under his lashes. Her breath caught just looking at him. If a man could be beautiful, Shane Kavanaugh was the poster boy for it. "I know, but I want to do it again. And it can't happen again, Emma. No matter how much we both want it."

Everything he said made complete sense. It was her own rule. Never mix business with pleasure. And Shane would bring about abundant pleasure, that much she knew for sure. The fact she was a recovering alcoholic working in a winery didn't bring about the temptations she expected. The biggest temptation at work was Shane, and he was certainly unexpected. She couldn't let hormones or the fact that she hadn't gotten laid in two years get in the way of her goal—to save her family home. She nodded and straightened her spine. "You're right. Absolutely. If you try to kiss me again, I'll knee you in the balls. Work for you?"

His hand dropped and he shook his head laughing. "You are a spit-fire, Emma. You know that?"

"So I've been told." She hugged herself to soothe the riotous emotions that played under her skin.

The smile fell away from his face as he stared at her. It was just for a few moments, but every time Shane looked at her was intense, over-whelming and spellbinding. His hand lifted and brushed a wisp of hair behind her ear. Her breath caught in her lungs, and for a moment she felt as though she were drowning.

He shook his head hard and stepped back to open the door, causing frigid air to rush in around them. "Thanks for the coffee. See you at the office. Lock the door behind me."

She nodded, one side of her mouth curving up. "I will. Good night, Shane."

"Good night, Emma." He looked at her for a heartbeat longer, and then stepped over the threshold, closing the door softly behind him.

Emma locked up and dropped her forehead against the cool,

smooth wood. A few moments later, the engine of his truck started and eventually faded away. She leaned her head back and stared at the tall ceiling, willing away the aching emptiness in her gut. It felt suspiciously like missing someone. And that was not going to work.

"What the hell am I going to do now?"

ELEVEN

Just a Friendly Gesture

AFTER A STRING of nights ruined by fitful sleep and full of sexy dreams where her boss played a starring role, Emma's mood was bleak. She half expected to see a storm cloud following her around like in a cartoon. She had no patience for issues, which meant anything that could go wrong did. Including her fancy-pants laptop, which had decided it was time to update the operating system. There'd been nothing but a spinning rainbow beach ball in the middle of a black screen for the last ten minutes.

The only silver lining was that it was Friday and she could hide at home for the weekend. Do some baking, binge some Netflix, and hopefully get some sleep. She had to stay focused on that. She was *not* going out, no matter how much Amelia begged, which she was prone to do at times.

It was days like today that tested her sobriety and her judgment on taking the job. But she couldn't run from her problems anymore. That's how she'd ended up in a rehab facility and with a white chip in her purse.

When she'd arrived that morning, Lindsey informed her that Shane was working at his home office, would be in conference calls all day, and if Emma needed him, she should send an email. It didn't help her mood that she suspected Shane was avoiding her. What pissed her off was she couldn't understand why. Hadn't they cleared the air the other night? Sure, it was an air fraught with tension, but they both knew the rules, and Emma needed this job too badly to screw it up with a one-night stand.

"Bastard," she muttered under her breath and banged on the keyboard. It occurred to her she wasn't sure if she meant her uncooperative computer or her temperamental boss.

"Should I come back?" A male voice asked from across the room.

Emma glanced up to see Noah's broad shoulders filling the doorway, tablet in hand and a wary look on his face.

"No." She waved him in. "Sorry, I'm just…this computer is driving me insane and…" She leaned back in her chair and blew out a breath. "It's just been a rough day and I've barely cleared lunch."

"I'll do my best not to add to your misery."

She shot him a wry grin. "Thanks, I appreciate it." After he sat down, she asked. "To what do I owe the pleasure of your visit?"

"Weekly status meeting with Shane." He frowned and ran a hand over his close-cropped dark blonde hair. "Did he not tell you?"

"No…" She mentally counted to ten to keep her blood pressure down and tried to keep her voice neutral. Noah was sharp and would detect any bitterness in her tone if she weren't careful. "Well, let's get started."

It was her job to oversee what happened in the winery in Shane's absence. Emma may as well get used to it, because once the job was over, Madison Ridge would just be a spot in Shane's rearview mirror. Yet another reason to stay uninvolved with Mr. Kavanaugh.

"Okay." Noah tapped a couple of times on his tablet and then launched into his notes about budgets and timelines.

"Hold on. My computer is still being a pain in the ass. Let me write this down." How the hell long did an update take, for God's sake? The rainbow ball was working her last nerve.

"If we work an extra Saturday or two and don't have any more bad weather, we can finish within about two days of the proposed completion date." Staring down at the device in his lap, he rubbed a hand along his jaw. A frown line appeared between his denim-blue eyes, and his lips were situated in a hard, flat line. "That's within the margin of error, but it pisses me off."

Emma fought the urge to roll her eyes. Noah was a perfectionist of epic proportions. "I know there was an issue with the stone for the restaurant fireplace. Did that get straightened out with the vendor?" she asked.

"Yeah, thank God." Noah shook his head. "It's going to be a beautiful focal point, but damn, this vendor has been a pain in the ass. Unfortunately, they were the only ones that had the stone we needed."

Emma smiled absently at her cousin. "I wasn't worried about it. I knew you'd get it taken care of. You always do. But I knew it was an issue and something Shane will probably ask about," she said, making a notation.

When she finished writing, she leaned forward on her desk and dropped her chin to her palm, studying him. After years of being in her own boozy haze, she hadn't taken the time to really see the people she loved the most. Noah Reynolds was a great man, but he carried everyone's burden with him. He always had, even before his father's unexpected death at the age of forty-eight. Being the firstborn, Noah had taken the role of provider to the next level after his father died.

"Noah, why are you here?"

His head popped up, and confusion crossed his strong, masculine features. "What are you talking about? I told you why I was here. The weekly status meeting."

She tossed her pen down on the blotter covering her desk. "First of all, you could've sent an email to cover what we just talked about. Second of all, my guess is you knew Shane wasn't going to be here. He isn't the type of guy to flip the script without telling you." *At least not professionally* ran through her mind, and she shoved the thought away.

Noah had the grace to wince slightly and avert his gaze. Busted.

She pointed at him. "You could have rescheduled with Shane if you needed a face-to-face. So, what's the real reason?"

Noah half sighed, half groaned, and laid the tablet on the edge of the desk. "Okay. When I heard that you were working here, I wanted to make sure you were okay." When she opened her mouth, he raised a brow and a hand, silencing her. "You're doing so well, Emma. But I know you're under a lot of stress right now financially, and taking on this new job is a big deal. Your position in the company is high profile, I can tell. Plus, you're in the business of producing something that is a deadly weakness for you."

"That's why I say the Serenity Prayer every morning, Noah. Every day is a fight with the demon, but for the last two years, he hasn't won. Today is one of those days that I would have gone home and drank a bottle or two of wine. Or made a pitcher of margaritas by myself. Hell, near the end, I wouldn't have waited until I got home to drink my stress away."

Emma looked down at her hands as she twisted her fingers together. "It's the hardest thing I've ever done, not picking up the bottle when things get tough, when I feel like everything will be right if I have just one drink. But then I remember everything wasn't alright when I drank." She shook her head and blinked tears away before looking up at Noah. "I lost years of my life. Years with my parents and your family, the friends I no longer have, my business I'll never get back. I may not have much anymore, but what I do have left, I need to salvage."

Emma leaned back in her chair and swung it toward the window that overlooked the vineyards. "And to get my life back and do something I love requires me to test myself every day. It sucks, but I'm making my peace with it." She paused and was grateful when her cousin stayed silent. "You know, when I look out over the land here, I concentrate on the beauty of it. The whole picture. The mountains in the background and the sky that kind of completes the package. It's... peaceful actually."

It hit her at that moment that what she said was true, and that she wasn't placating Noah. Pride swelled in her chest as she felt more of the burden lift from her shoulders. "The more I look at it that way, the less I look at these vines and think about how they can produce my weakness." She turned the chair back to face Noah. "And that's how I get through the day."

His gaze was steady on her. "I promised my mother I would keep an eye on you. So, here I am."

Emma was touched he was still looking out for her. Even if it was a bit heavy-handed. "Using your mother now, Noah? That's just sad," she teased.

"Maybe. But it's also true. We look out for our own, Emmaline. You know that. And you're a Reynolds. You're one of us."

She raised a brow when he used her whole name, something he rarely did. Out of respect for the family and Noah, she nodded once. "I know. But please understand that I have to save myself. No one can do it for me. I can't be locked away or shielded from being around alcohol by anyone else to keep me from relapsing. That's something I have to do for myself. You know that, right?"

Noah sighed heavily before he stood. Emma figured he knew she was right, but not happy about it. Couldn't blame the guy, really. He was in the business of fixing things. "Yeah, I know that. But it's hard, Em."

She stood and came around the desk. He wrapped her in a bear hug that soothed her and went a long way to making her day better. "Yes, it is. But you can report back to Stella that things are going well."

There was a knock on her door, followed by Lindsey sticking her head in. "Emma, there's something here you need to sign for."

"Okay, thanks." Her brow furrowed as she pulled away from Noah. "Were we expecting any materials today?" she asked him. He shook his head and followed Emma out to the front of the building.

Her eyes widened and her jaw dropped. Sitting in the front driveway was her old SUV. Except it didn't look old anymore. It shone, looking like it had just rolled off the showroom floor.

"Ms. Reynolds?"

Stunned, she turned to the young man standing in front of her. "Yes?"

"I need you to sign here." He held out a clipboard, a large X on the bottom of the yellow paper clipped to it.

"Sure." She scribbled her name and he handed over her keys with an envelope.

The delivery guy touched the brim of his baseball cap. "Have a good weekend."

"Thanks," she murmured walking toward her car. Noah walked with her and inspected the vehicle while Emma tore open the envelope and pulled out a piece of thick paper with the KVN logo at the top.

I figured your ride could use some TLC. The attached invoice should tell you everything the mechanic did. He assured me there was a lifetime warranty. Take the repairs as a friendly gesture, Emma.

Or think of it as one less thing your boss will worry about when you work late.

Drive safe.

-Shane

Emma shuffled the papers and looked over the invoice that covered all the services Henderson had performed. Her eyes bulged at the list. A tune-up, new starter, new tires, an oil change, new wipers, and a whole list of inspections the truck needed. Not to mention the pewter-colored paint shone like a new quarter.

"How the hell did they get this done so quickly?" she asked under her breath. Henderson must have had all of his men working on her truck at once.

Noah read the invoice over her shoulder and whistled. "That's a lot of work. Probably more than what the thing's worth. Who pa—"

Noah's phone rang, and he signed to her that he was leaving. "Yeah. Hang on a sec." He put the phone on his shoulder and gave her a hard stare. "Emma, whatever that is, just be careful."

Not having to ask what he meant, she nodded as he walked away, still dazed. By the time she returned to her office, frustration ran through her body. Didn't he understand that he was making things more complicated? Fixing her car was a ridiculously nice gesture, but now she was indebted to him no matter how she looked at it. And that was the last thing she wanted to be to her employer. She knew in her gut he was avoiding her and now she knew why.

She called Shane on her cell phone, only to have it roll over to voicemail. Growling, she grabbed her purse and keys and strode out of her office. The situation needed to be rectified now or it would eat at her the rest of the day. "Lindsey," she called out, "I need to run some errands, so I'll be out for a little while. Call my cell if you have any emergencies. If I don't make it back before you leave, have a nice weekend."

"Will do." Lindsey continued typing without looking up.

When Emma slid into her practically new SUV, her frustration level ticked up again. "I have my pride, damn it," she muttered, typing in the address to his cabin into her GPS program.

Her hands tightened on the steering wheel, her body tensing from head to toe. They were colleagues. Nothing more.

It was time to remind him.

TWELVE

Sanity Snapped

SHANE RUBBED HIS ACHING EYES. It was after lunchtime but he had been up and working in his home office since before daybreak. He could count on one hand how many hours of sleep he'd managed to get thanks to a bewitching, forbidden brunette. When was the last time a woman had dominated his thoughts so thoroughly and quickly? Never. Not even with his late wife.

During the night, he lay thinking, his cock so hard he ached, that he wasn't sure how working with her was going to play out. She was one of the smartest women he'd worked with, and was more than an asset to the company. Emma could be the new face of KVN. Smart, sexy, and elegant, with a touch of mystery that made him want to pull the layers away.

He was going to have to double down his efforts to find a way to get this desire that was beginning to rule him out of his system. Shane had a contact list in his phone with several willing and able women who could help him satisfy his needs.

The thought of any of those women, women he'd slept with before, left him cold. He had no desire to contact any of them. There was only one woman who would truly work the need out of his system. But Shane couldn't have her.

To make matters worse, his suspicions were confirmed. Emma's house was indeed the property the brokers had found for KVN to buy. He had no idea how in the hell he was going to handle this when they moved forward with the acquisition. For now, he figured it best to not tell her any more than she needed to know. Emma would find out soon enough.

But it was risky. His heart had sunk when she'd told him of her plans for the place. How fucking ironic was it that the job he'd hired her for had put into motion a set of complications he hadn't seen coming?

He ran a hand through his hair and leaned back in the chair, staring at the laptop screen in front of him as if it held all the answers. Lost in thought about a potentially dicey situation, the words on the screen blurred. Hell, now he was hearing alarms in his head.

It took a minute for it to penetrate his thoughts that the dinging sound he heard was the doorbell. And whoever was on the other side of it was insistent, judging by the continuous noise.

"I'm coming, I'm coming" he called out, winding his way through the living area and into the foyer.

Shane swung open the door to find the object of his desire standing on his front porch. And from the glare she was giving him, she was not happy.

Jesus, she was beautiful. He cleared his throat before he could speak. While the sparks in her eyes were awesome to watch, Shane also knew that he was probably the reason for said sparks. And not in a good way. How had he managed to get himself in trouble? He'd worked from home to stay *out* of trouble.

"Emma. I didn't expect to see you here." He stepped back and opened the door further. "Please come in."

She didn't cross the threshold, just waved a piece of paper in his face. "What is this?"

He caught the paper from her hand before he ended up with a paper cut on the end of his nose. It was an invoice from Henderson's Automotive. Impressive. They'd done a fair amount of work in a tight timeframe. He would have to keep that in mind.

Shane nodded and handed back the paper to Emma. "Looks to be an invoice of the work the repair shop did on your SUV."

"An invoice with no pricing on it I might add," Emma said tightly. She jutted out her chin. "I'm paying you back. How much was it?"

"Why? It needed work, Emma. It is a better vehicle for the area, but only if it's reliable."

"Shane—"

"Emma, I'm not going to talk about this with the door wide open. It's cold. Come inside." He realized his tone was a bit demanding, and tempered it with, "Please."

She lifted her chin and straightened her spine. The movement pressed her breasts against the dark green fabric of the sweater she wore. When she walked past him, vanilla and citrus wafted to him. At that moment, Shane was grateful he'd left his shirt untucked earlier. His crotch was beginning to feel a bit tight.

When he turned to her after shutting the door, Emma walked farther into the house, her heels clicking on the hardwood floor, toward the open living area that included the dining area and kitchen. Shoving his hands in his pockets, Shane did his best to keep his eyes from watching her ass in the black form-fitting slacks. Combined with the heels, her legs looked a million miles long.

Son of a bitch. Being in close quarters with her was not a good idea. Time to find out what she needed and get her moving along.

"Nice place," she murmured, running a hand over the granite countertop of the kitchen island. Turning to face him, she pinned him with a stare. "Shane, you really shouldn't have done that with my car."

He sighed, his patience fraying. "Look, Emma. Your car needed to be fixed, and I could help. KVN is a family and we like to help our employees. It really was just a friendly gesture. I expect nothing in return for it."

"I could have handled it myself. I didn't need you to pay for it." Her mouth was set in a hard line. "I'm not helpless. I know how to make my own way."

She wasn't happy. Well, neither was he, truth be told. Frustration began to build in his blood. Frustration that he couldn't have her. Frustration that while he wanted to run from her, he also wanted to be near her. His sanity held on by a thin thread.

Shane shoved both hands through his hair, growling. "I know that! Jesus, Emma. I was trying to be nice." He held out his arms at his sides. "What's the big fucking deal?"

"The big fucking deal is that I don't need to be rescued. Now, how much do I owe you?" Emma crossed her arms over her chest, her voice low, each syllable moderated.

He dropped his arms, hands slapping his thighs. "I have no idea how much it cost. But don't worry. I promise I won't do anything nice for you again." Shane couldn't help it. His eyes went to her breasts that moved up and down with her slow measured breaths. Damn it all to hell, the woman was distracting.

Emma lifted her chin. "What is your problem with me?" she asked.

His brow furrowed. Where was she going with this? "What are you talking about? I don't have a problem with you."

"Bullshit." She slammed the invoice down on the counter and advanced on him, her eyes nearly glowing with anger. "I can't tell from one time to the next how to act around you. One minute, we talk like normal people, you make jokes. The next, you shut down and dismiss me."

"I—"

She poked him hard in the center of the chest. "If you didn't want to hire me, you could have said no. But since you did hire me, the least you could do is act normal. You want to be a cold bastard? Be one. But stop running hot and cold with me. Because I'm done trying to figure out whether or not you want me around."

Her chest heaved with exertion. He gritted his teeth and advanced on her until her back hit the counter of the island behind her. "Don't you get it? I want nothing more than to be around you. But when I am, I can't think straight. You trouble me to no end. It's all I can do to keep my hands off you."

Her whiskey colored eyes widened slightly and she licked her lips.

She was killing him. Slowly, but surely. His cock was hard enough to drive nails into a wall without breaking a sweat. The last line of his sanity snapped. "Fuck it."

Before he could think of the consequences, his hands cupped her face and his mouth crashed to hers. She fisted his shirt in her hands, pulling him closer. When his tongue lined the slit of her lips, she opened for him and he plundered her mouth, his tongue sliding against hers. It was hot and demanding as she met his lust head-on. He turned her head to get better leverage, taking the kiss deeper. The moans coming from her set the blood boiling in his veins. She angled her hips, grinding against him, and stars exploded behind his eyelids. She could, no doubt, feel the evidence of his need against her thigh.

He'd known desire before, but this kiss, just this kiss alone showed him that anything before Emma had been nowhere near passion.

His hands moved up under her thick sweater, the backs of his fingers grazing the soft skin of her stomach and making her inhale sharply against his mouth. He continued his way up to cup her firm breasts, rolling her nipples between two fingers. She cried out and let her head fall back, her dark hair a waterfall behind her. The position gave him full access to devour the long, creamy column of her throat.

"Shane..." she gasped, her hands finding their way into his hair, grabbing tightly. Stepping back, he pulled her sweater over her head and tossed it behind him. The lacy bra that covered her breasts was sexy and elegant all at the same time, but now that he had his hands on her, he needed to feel her skin. He freed those lovely tits of their confines and tossed the bra to join her sweater on the floor.

"Ah, Emma. Look at you." She took his breath away, her breasts bare and on display for him. He wrapped an arm around her waist, pulling her to him and cupped her with his other hand. "So beautiful," he murmured, just before his lips closed over a nipple.

She moaned and gasped his name, her hands buried in his hair again. It was as though she anchored herself to him. His tongue swirled around the areola, before sucking on the hardened peak, first one side then the other. God, she was sweet, just like the peaches and cream of her skin.

He lifted his head and met her eyes, cloudy with desire that sharpened when he slid a hand down her body and unbuttoned her slacks. He pushed the pants and panties down in one motion and she kicked them away when they hit her ankles. Her head fell back on a groan when his fingers found her slick and ready for him. Flames of desire danced along his skin, and as much as he wanted to drag this out, he couldn't hold back much longer.

Her eyes held his while she tugged at the buttons of his shirt. Desperate to be skin-on-skin with her, he lifted a hand and reached behind his neck, pulling the shirt over his head in a single motion. Her hands worked the button and fly of his jeans. Having gone commando, when her hand slid inside his jeans, it closed around his hot erection, causing his vision to blur. "Fuck," he muttered as she stroked his hard length. He had enough wits about him to remember the condom in his wallet.

"Let me," she whispered, taking the foil packet from his hand. With her teeth, she ripped open the package. With deft fingers, she rolled it over his aching cock, making him recite baseball stats just so he wouldn't explode in her hand. In his next breath, he lifted her up on the counter and stepped between her thighs, his focus solely on getting inside her.

She wrapped her long legs around his waist, pulling him close. He gripped her hips and she stared into his eyes as he guided his length into her heat. Twin moans filled the room when he filled her completely, and her eyelids fluttered briefly before opening again. His vision went hazy, but he didn't move, letting her body accommodate his size. Shane bared his teeth in an effort to hold back the ending before they really got started. She was soft and hot and better than any fantasy his brain could conjure up.

Emma twined her arms around his neck and tunneled her hands into his hair. She brought his head down and their lips met in a searing, hot kiss. He pulled his hips back slowly before sliding back home, his fingers digging into her hips, her legs tightening around his middle. With every stroke, they found a pace and rhythm, moving together as though they'd done this hundreds of times before. Her skin burned beneath his hands, and her breasts brushed against his chest with every thrust.

The tingling started at the base of his spine when the muscles of her core tightened around him. They raced toward the edge of the cliff together, and seconds later she convulsed around his cock, his name a half cry, half moan from her lips. The feel of her heat wrapped around him in a death grip nailed him right in the gut, tearing its way through his resolve. With one last snap of his hips, he soared over the edge and into his own nirvana.

When they came back down to earth and their breathing returned to normal, Shane brushed his lips against her forehead and moved away to dispose of the condom. In the small half bathroom, he caught sight of himself in the mirror. He couldn't help but grin at the way his hair stuck up in places all over his head. Warmth spread through his body thinking about Emma's grip on his hair. Desire coiled in his lower belly again.

"Down, boy," he murmured to his reflection before leaving the room.

When he walked back into the kitchen, she slid down from the counter and bent down to pick up her clothes. The sight of her only served to make him want a repeat of the mind-blowing sex they'd just finished. His cock was all for another round.

She straightened, holding her slacks and underwear against her chest. They partially covered her nakedness and it was a damn shame for her to be covered up. He'd have to fix that.

Shane walked over to her and pushed his hands into her soft, thick mane of dark hair. He'd never really thought much about a woman's hair before, but Emma's was as enchanting as the rest of her. She leaned her head back and he kissed her mouth softly. When Shane lifted his head and looked down at her face, he was struck breathless by her beauty. Her eyes opened slowly and still held a sex-dazed sheen to them. "Hello, Emma," he said with a smile.

"Hello, Shane." The smile she returned was that of a thoroughly satisfied woman. Shane wasn't ashamed to admit he felt ten feet tall and bulletproof knowing he'd put that look there.

He ran a fingertip under her eye. "You look like you got about as much sleep as I did last night. I say we take a nap."

Her lips curved into a smirk. "A nap, huh? I know what that's code for."

His hands traveled down her back, caressing the soft skin as he went. Her skin was like satin and he couldn't stop touching her. "Well, we might sleep. We might do some other things," he murmured, rubbing his nose against her cheek. "Wanna go find out?"

Emma averted her gaze to the clothes she held trapped between their bodies. "I should probably be going."

Shane's stomach lurched. She was right. He'd chosen to ignore the voice in his head that told him they'd crossed a line that couldn't be uncrossed. Hell, they'd sprinted across the damn thing. But if Emma was going to put distance between them now, he needed to follow suit.

No matter how much it pissed him off.

He nodded and dropped his hands, taking a small step back from her and the heat of her body. "Probably."

She didn't move, just stood there with her eyes on his. Those enticing amber eyes darkened to a caramel color and her breathing changed, ever so slightly, but it was there. A dark glee formed in his chest to know she wasn't any more immune to him as he was to her.

He raised a brow when she continued to stand there. "So, you're going?"

Emma nodded, but a sexy smile curved her lips. She dropped the clothes she held and walked past him, all of that glorious skin on display for him. At the bottom of the stairs, she stopped and looked over her shoulder, smile still in place. Damn, she was a little minx, and he was hard as stone. Again.

"Which one did you say was your bedroom?" she asked, her voice low and sultry, the hints of her southern accent weaving through it. It was as smooth and potent as a shot of single-malt scotch.

A lightness filled his chest and adrenaline pumped through his veins as he stalked over to her. It was a combination that made him feel on top of the world. "I didn't. But I'd be happy to show you."

When Shane reached her, he plucked her off her feet, and her yelp was mixed with a giggle. The sound of it landed in his chest, making him feel light and carefree. He grinned and carried her up the stairs to his room.

THIRTEEN

I Like the Way You're Made

EMMA STIRRED into consciousness with an arm hooked around her waist and a muscular leg entwined with hers. She leaned back into Shane's hard, warm chest and sighed. It had been a long time since she'd laid in bed with a man and felt safe, content.

A long time? Try never. She'd never been with a man who made her feel safe and content. Satisfied, maybe. She'd had a couple of relationships that had been exclusive, but they'd never crossed into the serious zone.

Whatever this thing was with Shane wouldn't cross that zone either. The fact was, when the sun rose the next morning and they left the cocoon they were surrounded by, reality would set in and they would be coworkers only. That's what they needed to do. Before long, there would be more employees at the winery, the renovations would be complete, and Shane would move on, leaving Emma to run the place alone.

A pang hit hard in her heart and she closed her eyes, steeling herself against it.

"What's wrong, beautiful?" His deep voice rumbled against her neck.

She opened her eyes and mentally shook off the melancholy feeling. *Get out of your head, Emma.* Getting lost in her head was one of her worst habits, one that led her down some nasty paths. She'd missed a lot of life that way. Part of her sober plan was to stay present. And now, what she needed to do was what she should have done earlier. Go home. She'd leave in five minutes. Yep, just five more minutes was all she needed.

She shifted her hips back, feeling his hard length against her ass, and smiled. "What could possibly be wrong with me?"

Shane growled as he rolled her beneath him. "That's what I'm thinking. There's not a damn thing that could be wrong right about now."

She shifted her legs, giving him room to settle his weight between them. His hands framed her face, his thumbs stroking her cheekbones. "But you were thinking. What were you thinking about?"

Hmmm…she might need ten more minutes. Maybe fifteen.

Emma pursed her lips and pretended to think on it. "Let's see. I was thinking about how you may need to show me one more time how much you like me. I'm still not convinced you do."

He sighed dramatically. "Well, I'll need to pull out some more tricks in my arsenal. Let me think."

He pressed a kiss to her forehead, then her eyelids, on each cheek, the corner of her mouth, but avoided her lips. The kisses continued down along the line of her jaw. When he reached the length of her throat, he alternated using his lips and his teeth. Emma began to writhe beneath him and small puffs of breath left her body.

He thumbed the silver anchor laying in the valley of her breasts. "I see you wear this often. I like it."

She reached up automatically to touch it, and her hand closed over his. "I like the symbolism."

"Which would be?"

"Hope. I wear it to remind myself of that."

"Hope," he murmured. He kissed the pendant before his mouth traveled down between her breasts. His hands caressed her skin, fingers lightly pinching her nipples until they were rock-hard beneath his fingertips. The quick bite of the pinch heightened the pleasure, and the heat in her lower belly intensified.

He continued mapping her body with his mouth, driving her nearly to the edge of insanity.

"Shane, please." She arched her back while his hot mouth skimmed over the plane of her stomach. Her hands gripped the sheets beneath her. Lifting her hips, she used them to try and guide him to where she wanted him most.

He reached up and fisted their hands together on either side of her hips. "Be still, Peaches. I'm going to do to you what I didn't get to last night."

She looked down her body at his face. "And what would that be?" she asked, breathless.

"Take my time. Make slow love to you." He moved lower, his breath blowing over the curls covering her sex. "I like the way you're made, Emmaline Reynolds. I'm going to enjoy every inch of you."

Shane moved to her right thigh, raining kisses over it. Her head dropped back on a sigh, closing her eyes and enjoying his perusal. A second later, her eyes popped back open, and she remembered the ugly, several-inch-long scar on the outside of her left thigh. Shane moved to that side and stopped. She lifted her head again and his eyes met hers. She opened her mouth to explain, but he simply shook his head once.

"Later" was all he said before he lowered his head and, with his eyes on hers, kissed the dark pink, puckered skin, treating it to the same sensual exploration he had provided to the rest of her unblemished body.

To her horror, tears pricked behind her eyes, and she dropped her head back to the pillow. Her chest filled with emotions she couldn't name, to the point that breathing was almost impossible. He held her spellbound with his words and the adoration of her body. The scar on her leg became a forgotten memory. For the last hour or so they'd been together, his hands had stayed busy in other places.

Not like now, when she laid exposed to his eyes, vulnerable. Even in her more serious relationships, she'd never allowed herself to be defenseless.

His journey ended at her toes, where he grinned at her toenails, painted fire-engine red. "The red is sexy."

He crawled his way back up her curves, settling his head between her legs. With his eyes on hers, he draped a hip over each shoulder, leaned in, and flicked her clit with his tongue. Closing her eyes, Emma threaded her fingers through his hair and arched her hips toward the hot mouth working her over. Shane plunged his tongue inside and tasted every part of her with an intimacy she'd never experienced before. She moaned and writhed, all rationale in her mind unraveling. "I'm close, Shane."

"That's right, Emma. Fall apart for me. I'm here for you."

With each lick and suck of his tongue, pressure built in her chest, down to her core until her orgasm tore through her body, causing her to cry out his name.

Emma closed her eyes and melted into the bed, floaty and boneless. Shane kissed the inside of her thighs then continued his lazy perusal up her body with that magical mouth before capturing hers in a scorching kiss.

She ghosted her hands up his strong, muscled back and pulled him closer. Need, desire, and feelings she didn't want to acknowledge coursed through her, ran under her skin, threatening to take her under. She needed him, needed to feel him on her, in her. She wanted a taste of all his power.

The lust building in her veins gave her strength and confidence. She pushed at his shoulders and rolled him over on his back. Straddling him, Emma gripped his wrists and pulled them up over his head. With her gaze holding his, she wrapped his fingers around the wooden slats of the headboard. Damn, his hot gaze made her want to sink down on him. But she wanted to return the favor. "Don't move your hands."

In response, his tongue flicked at a nipple that brushed across his mouth. Son of a bitch, he was sneaky.

Emma gasped and her core clenched against his cock. "Hmmm...you don't play fair."

"And yet I'm the one with no defense," he said through gritted teeth, bucking his hips against her. The head of his cock slid against her slick heat. One small shift and he'd be inside her. But before that...

She sent him her naughtiest smile and moved down his body, dropping kisses along the center of his chest. His hard pecs twitched under her touch. Her mouth joined in the fun when she licked his nipples before continuing further down his body. A groan rumbled from his chest and she smiled against the warm skin of his torso. With one hand, she trailed her fingertips along his ab muscles and along the well-defined sex lines above his hips. Emma licked her lips, mesmerized by the hot as hell V Shane sported. The man looked as though he were sculpted by Michelangelo himself.

Emma's gaze lifted to his. A grin curved his lips. "Like what you see?"

She hummed her appreciation. "How about you?" she countered.

"Fuck yeah," he replied without hesitation, lifting his hips slightly towards her. His cock twitched as though reaching for her.

"Patience," she whispered and kissed just below his navel.

Shane groaned and leaned his head back into the pillow. "You're killing me, Emma."

"At least you'll die happy."

His chuckle was strangled by a moan when she dragged her tongue down his happy trail and nuzzled his cock with her nose. She wrapped a hand around his long, thick length, stroking him several times before dropping her mouth to the purple head. He tasted salty and uniquely Shane.

"Fuck, Emma. Damn. Your mouth." More curses filled the air as she worked her mouth up and down his shaft and a hand cupped his balls. His knuckles were white where he continued to hold onto the headboard. He lifted his head from the pillow and his gaze met hers as she moved over him. Having Shane under her spell made Emma heady with power. Lust roared through her blood and made her clit weep for his touch.

"Emma, stop. I want to be inside you."

She released him from her mouth and, moving like a cheetah on the run, Shane shifted their positions. Braced on his elbows above her, he leaned down and captured her mouth once again. One hand moved down to her clit and he stroked the bundle of nerves until she teetered on the edge.

Tilting her hips, she moved against him, telling him what she needed without words. He broke off the kiss and leaned over to grab a condom from the nightstand. Once sheathed, he teased and rubbed against her slick entrance. She jerked from the overstimulation, but managed to hang on. The next time she came, she wanted the sensation of him inside her.

"Since I've been in Madison Ridge, you're the only woman I can think about. You've monopolized my thoughts ever since I walked into Maggie's Diner."

She swallowed the intense emotions rising in her throat and wrapped her legs around his waist. "Then what are you waiting for?"

The words barely left her lips before Shane slid his length inside her, filling her, leaving no space between them. Every touch, every movement was heightened by the desire that burned like an inferno between them. His eyes held hers as his hips moved against her in a rhythm designed to make her crazy. "Look at me, Emma. I want to see your eyes when you come apart this time."

She couldn't have looked away if her life depended on it. Every one of her nerve endings stirred and tingled as the pressure built low in her core. He lifted one of her legs to his shoulder, changing the angle to where he was deeper inside her. His hips picked up the pace and the storm building inside her left her panting every time he hit that magic spot inside her.

When she broke apart, her mouth opened on a silent cry, the edges of her vision dimmed, and shivers ran down to her toes. Shane grunted, and with one last thrust into her, he stilled, his cock twitching with his release inside her.

Under her hands, Shane's chest heaved from exertion. She wanted to cling to his strength, never letting go. With his face buried in her neck and his heart beating against hers.

Oh, her heart. Emma had a sinking feeling it didn't belong to her any longer.

FOURTEEN

Put Me Back Together

"IT LOOKS BLUE."

Emma stood next to Amelia, staring at the half-painted wall in front of them, frowning. "It's supposed to be gray."

"That, my friend, is blue," Amelia stated, an amused tone in her voice.

Emma sighed and swiped at her brow. She wasn't blind. She could see the damn wall wasn't gray. Crouching down, she read the color on the can. "Pewter sky. That's what I ordered." She glanced up at the wall. "What the hell happened? It doesn't look anything like the sample."

Amelia tilted her head to the side. "I like it. It's a soft and neutral color. Plus, it brightens the room, actually." She glanced around at the furniture covered by plastic in the middle of the room, her lips pursed. "And this is one room that could use some brightening."

Emma couldn't disagree. It had been her mother's bedroom and after she'd passed away, she hadn't been able to bring herself to do anything with it. She'd decided it was past time to get started on small renovation projects.

She stood up straight, twinges of pain running down her back—another daily reminder to help stay sober—and looked at the wall again. "You're right, I like it too. Besides, it's probably one of those colors that looks different with furniture and lighting." She picked up a paint brush and bumped Amelia's shoulder with her own. "Wanna help?"

Amelia shook her head. "I'd love to but I got that date." She lifted a hand that held a pair of sparkling gold stilettos. "I just came to raid your closet of awesome shoes for tonight."

Emma rolled her eyes, but smiled and dropped the paint brush. "Fine. I'll walk you out." As she started out of the room, she glanced back to her cousin. "And what do I get out of helping you with shoes?"

"I'll give you all the details about the great sex," Amelia said after a pause, following Emma down the hallway to the staircase. "No, I'd better not do that. I know it's been a while for you."

Emma nearly tripped down the stairs before catching her footing. Thank God, Amelia wasn't really a mind reader, although her astuteness sometimes made Emma wonder. "Yeah." She cleared her throat and tried to calm her racing heart. "It's been a while." That is, if Amelia's version of a while meant less than twenty-four hours.

If the situation between Emma and Shane were different—meaning, if he wasn't her boss—she would have told Amelia all about it. And about the slippery slope she found herself trying to solidify.

"Seriously though, Em," Amelia said when they reached the foyer. "I will help you paint next time."

Emma gave her cousin a one-armed hug in deference to Amelia's clean clothes versus her once-was-black-and-now-it's-pewter-sky T-shirt. "I know. Just giving you a hard time. It's a small thing, the painting, but every little bit helps."

Amelia's eyes widened, pulling away. "Did you get the mortgage thing straightened out?"

Emma held up crossed fingers. "I'm getting close. If that art piece sells in the next week, I'll have all I need. And having the job at KVN is helping me keep things afloat otherwise." She sighed, her heart dropping when she thought about how long she'd need to save for renovation costs. "Still, it's going to take some time before I can get to that point."

"Emma, I really wish I could help you financially." Amelia's face was as serious as Emma had ever seen. It made her heart melt to know that Amelia had that much faith in her.

She held up a hand. "No. It's fine, Ame. I wouldn't take it from you even if you had it. Your mom already offered to help me and I refused. I have to do this on my own." Emma smiled and breathed deep, the calm of working it out herself spreading through her limbs. "It's part of the steps."

"I'm so proud of you, Emma. We all are." Amelia gave Emma's hand a squeeze before releasing it. "I gotta go. I'll bring the shoes back tomorrow," she said, opening the door.

On the other side of the threshold stood none other than her boss. And newly minted lover. And damned if he didn't look yummy enough to climb like a tree in his well-worn jeans, navy-blue T-shirt that skimmed his muscles, and the sexy as fuck brown leather jacket.

Shit. Emma would've given anything to have the floor open and swallow her at that moment.

"Well, hello, Shane." Amelia gave Shane a megawatt smile.

"Good afternoon, Amelia. A pleasure to see you again." Shane returned Amelia's smile with one of his own. It sent Emma's hormones into overdrive, and shorted out her brain, making her forget about her state of disarray.

"Likewise. Please come in. I was just leaving." She turned to Emma, mischief dancing in her eyes. "Call me tomorrow, cousin."

Emma nodded and resisted the urge to shuffle her feet. "I will. Have fun tonight."

"Oh, I will." Amelia bobbed her eyebrows and waved her fingers. "Bye!" she called out, and shut the door behind her, leaving Emma and Shane in the foyer together.

Emma wrapped an arm around her middle. "I'm sorry about that. Her." She rubbed her bicep, wanting to curl up in a ball to hide her sloppy appearance from him. "And excuse how I look. I was painting."

Shane grinned and walked closer to her. His eyes skimmed from the ponytail piled on top of her head to her black sweatpants, which also bore gray-blue accents that matched the wall upstairs. Hell, even her bare feet had a sheen of spatter on them. She was a hot mess.

"I think you're adorable as hell." He stopped in front of her, and with his index finger, gently lifted her chin until she met his eyes. "Hello, Emmaline."

Damn it, she couldn't stop the warmth that spread through her when he said her name. She smiled. "Hello, Shane."

His lips brushed over hers in the lightest of kisses, but the zing ricocheted around her body and landed squarely in her lower belly, causing her thighs to clench.

Shane lifted his head. "There's more where that came from, later. First," he held up a cardboard tray she hadn't noticed when he arrived. "Hot chocolate. You like chocolate, right?"

She leaned back, the smell of cocoa and the sweetness of marshmallows hitting her. "Like it? I could eat it every day." Emma took the tray from him and lifted one of the cups out. She sipped the rich, hot chocolate. "Mmmm...so good." She licked her lips and Shane's gaze followed her tongue. A wicked glee filled her chest. "Oh, did you want one of these?"

Shane leaned in close to her, but kept his hands to himself. His eyes were dark with desire and her pulse quickened. "I promised myself I'd have some restraint and not haul you off to bed as soon as I saw you. Have some mercy on me, Emma." His voice was low and so sexy her breath caught in her throat.

She cleared her throat and held up the tray. "It's all yours." Her words came out breathy and weak. Damn, she needed some control.

Shane's groan was low when he stepped back. He took the drink and sipped, his eyes on hers. When he lowered the cup, a pensive smile curved his lips. She eyed him warily. "What?"

"When was the last time you took a walk around the property?"

"Uh, it's been a while," she said slowly, her head swimming a bit at the change in conversation.

"It's a beautiful day. Why don't we go out and get some air? I really..." He sighed as his eyes raked over her from head to toe, "really need some air."

Emma's skin flushed under his gaze. She swallowed hard before she could speak. "Sure. Just give me a minute."

Upstairs, her heart raced as she stripped down and put on jeans, a thick sweater, and boots. She let her hair down and fluffed it. With a shaky hand, she applied some lip gloss and called it done. Blowing out a breath, she tried to calm her nerves. Seriously, the guy has had his mouth all over her body. Why was she so nervous now? Adding a scarf around her neck, she headed downstairs.

"Okay, I'm ready," she said, stepping off the last step.

Shane took her hand and looked her over. "You're beautiful."

Emma ducked her head with a smile, a blush warming her cheeks. It wasn't just his words but the way he said them. He acted like she'd walked down in a dazzling ball gown instead of jeans and boots.

They struck out toward the flat expanse directly behind the house that led out to the pond and then gently rolled into hills. As they walked the land in comfortable silence, she realized in that moment, she needed someone to talk to, and that someone was Shane. "I don't mind telling you about it. About my scar."

He continued to walk, but glanced over at her. "Okay," he said simply.

Now that she'd brought it up and wanted to talk to him, how much would she tell him? The inside of her mouth was dry as sawdust. Was she ready for this? One hand rubbed on her leg where the scar lay underneath her clothing.

What the hell. She'd laid it out there without thinking. Time to follow through.

Emma cleared her throat and shoved her hands in her coat pockets. "Two years ago, I fell down a flight of stairs. I missed the top step and fell all the way to the bottom." She didn't have to tell him she'd been drunk as a sailor on leave. "I hit my head twice on the way down and they had to put me in a medically induced coma for a week to heal my injuries, especially my head. Among various cuts and bruises, I had a concussion, internal bleeding, a shattered femur, and broke my back in three places."

She rubbed absently against the scar under the denim. "I have pins in my leg to hold it together and wore a back brace for longer than I care to remember. They told me I was lucky they were able to put me back together and I'd be even luckier if I ever walked again." She smiled. "But I did, and I don't limp anymore." The smile faded. "Unfortunately, I don't run anymore, either." Even now, her heart ached at the loss of being able to do one of her favorite hobbies. Following on the heels of that ache was anger. Anger at herself and her fucking addiction that had tried its hardest to kill her mind, body, and spirit.

"Sounds like you're lucky to be alive. And even with the injuries you had, it could have been worse."

She nodded. "A lot worse. I know I'm blessed. Even if I can't do certain things like I used to do."

They stopped at the edge of a clearing. Shane faced her, his eyes studying her. She looked for any evidence of pity in his eyes but found none, for which she was grateful. "Like running," he said. It was a statement, not a question.

"Yeah, like running."

He stepped forward and wrapped his arms around her waist, pulling her close. Emma snuggled against his chest and closed her eyes, reveling in his warmth and heartbeat under her cheek. She inhaled the scent that was all Shane. This was the peace and contentment she wanted so desperately.

She knew it was fleeting and he wasn't hers. But she was going to enjoy it while it lasted.

FIFTEEN

Rock, Meet Hard Place

I COULD HOLD *her like this forever* was the thought that kept running through Shane's mind. She was soft and smelled so fucking good. He closed his eyes and bit back the nausea that hit him in the gut. Her body language and the fact that she told him about her accident made it clear she trusted him.

Jesus, he was stuck in his own private hell. He didn't have a clue as to what he was going to do now that he knew about the property.

She leaned back. "Ready to head back?"

He nodded and they started toward the house hand in hand. Shane gazed around while Emma pointed out different things about the trees and told little anecdotes. His business brain took over and he was in heaven thinking about all the possibilities, which only made the guilt dig its heels in.

"When did they close down the B&B?"

She continued to walk but looked down. "Not long after my dad died, so a few years ago. He handled the excursions, and after he died, my mother tried to keep them up because they were profitable add-ons, even after all the expenses that came with them."

Another moment passed before she continued. "After my dad sold all the horses to pay off his gambling debts, he went back out and gambled again. This time, he had to cash out his life insurance policy to pay off the debts because he'd mortgaged the house and the land. After a while, my mother couldn't afford to keep the help, couldn't afford to keep the place open at all." Emma sighed. "The rest of the family had no idea his gambling had gotten so out of hand. He'd had issues before. My uncle Paul bailed him out a couple of times. But after the last time, my father swore he would never do it again." Her mouth hardened into a straight line. "He did, he just kept it well hidden from everyone."

With the bits of info he had from the broker and what she'd told him, Shane was beginning to put the pieces together. It wasn't a pretty picture, and it made him hurt for her. Which made the situation shittier for him. "That's when you sold your business, isn't it?"

She looked away, her eyes unreadable. "It was the only thing I could do. I made a lot of money during my run in business. I was able to sell it for a pretty penny." She shrugged. "It wasn't what I wanted to do, but my mother needed it. Her health was failing and she faced losing the last thing she had—the house and the land. I told her we wouldn't lose them, and we didn't. But I'll admit it's hard to keep up with things now, day in and day out."

He looked around at the expanse of dormant, yellow grass covering her acreage, dotted with islands of trees here and there. "How many acres of land do you have here?"

"Um, just a little over forty." A smile lit up her face. "Come with me, I want to show you something."

Emma pulled him toward a large tree where a tire swing hung from a large branch. "Hey, look at that. I always wanted a tire swing," he said, smiling.

"It's really old," she said, looking up to the thick ropes wrapped around the tree. They were anchored to an old, thick branch of a massive oak tree. "It was here when my mom was a kid. Although my dad changed the ropes a couple of times, it's been a while. I hope it will still hold me."

Shane tugged hard on the ropes that were as thick as his bicep. They reminded him of ropes on a large boat and didn't budge an inch. "They seem secure to me."

Emma grinned. "Perfect." She climbed in and perched on the edge of the enormous tire, then began to rock back and forth, trying to gain momentum. She bit her lip, concentration etched all over her face. His Emma knew how to focus.

His Emma? When the hell did that happen? Pushing the thought aside, he turned his attention back to what she was doing.

"Want some help?" he asked, after a couple of moments.

She turned her face to him. "Please? It seems I've forgotten how to get this going."

Shane pushed the tire, sending it swinging in a pendulum, pushing it again when it came back his way. Emma laughed as she sailed through the air, her dark hair flying behind her.

She was a beautiful sight, one that took his breath away again and again. He wasn't sure he'd ever get used to it, wasn't sure he would be able to walk away from her when the time came. And the time would come, because he couldn't continue this...whatever it was with an employee. Not to mention he was only in Madison Ridge temporarily. Shane didn't do long-distance relationships. Hell, he didn't do any type of *relationship* anymore. Not since Marlene.

Shane also knew that once she found that he was trying to buy her house, Emma would never speak to him again. And he'd have one fewer employee. He had to figure out how to get out of this mess he found himself in. But, for the moment, all he wanted to do was spend more time with her. However long that time may be.

She dragged her feet along the ground, kicking up dust, trying to slow down the motion. When the swing finally came to a stop, her cheeks were flushed, turning that creamy skin into a rosy color that had his body tightening.

"Ah, that was fun. I haven't done that in ages," she said, laughter still in her voice. "Now let's see if I remember how to get out of here."

Now was his opportunity to touch her and still look like a gentle-man. Shane leaned down. "Put your arm around my neck." She followed his instruction, and he gathered her up, one arm under her knees, lifting her out of the tire.

"There. I've got you now." His voice was low and as tight as the hardness growing behind the fly of his jeans.

Her free arm came up to join the other, her eyes bright. "And now that you do, what do you plan to do with me?"

"Well, at the moment, you have the advantage, Peaches."

She cocked her head to the side. "Why do you call me Peaches?"

"Well, the first time I met you, you wore a peach-colored uniform, you were born in the Peach State, but most of all, it's because your skin is soft and you taste sweet." He brushed his lips against hers. "Just like a peach." The thought of tasting her again didn't do anything to help the discomfort below the belt.

She swallowed hard. "Okay," she croaked out. "Peaches it is." Her eyes narrowed and her arms tightened slightly before releasing. "It does appear I have the advantage here." Emma pressed her chest to his, moving against him sensually and taking little love bites out of his neck.

Son of a bitch. If she didn't stop doing that he was going to take her right on the ground, and he said a little prayer that he wouldn't drop her.

"Emma," he said tightly, "I know I said you had the advantage, but I really don't want to drop you."

Her chuckle was soft and seductive against his neck. "You won't drop me, Shane. I trust you."

A pang of guilt twisted in his gut. He should walk away, right now. He was a selfish prick. But in that moment, desire to be near her and touch her again won out. "We need to go back to the house. Now. Before I fuck you up against that tree."

She lifted her head up, her smile that of a woman who knew exactly what she was doing to her man. "Dirty boy. But as hot as that just made me, the idea of bark burn isn't really all that appealing." Emma dropped her eyes to his lips before raising her eyes back to his. "However, I'm not opposed to rug burn." Her lips curved into a wicked grin.

Damn, he wanted to eat her alive in all the best ways possible.

"Time to go home," he said shortly. He set her down on her feet, only to pick her up again in a fireman's hold.

"Shane!" Emma yelped. "Put me down!" Her hands slapped his back as she squirmed.

He smacked her ass lightly, making her squeak. "Be still so I don't drop you."

"Only if you promise to do that again when we get to bed."

"Your wish is my command," he replied and picked up the pace to the house.

By the time they made it to the back door, Shane's dick was hard as a steel rod and walking was painful. He set Emma on her feet and she turned to open the door. They'd barely cleared the doorway when Shane walked Emma backwards until her back connected with the wall.

Her amber-colored eyes darkened to that caramel color that was as sinful as it was sweet. He joined their hands and lifted them over her head, caging her with his body. The tip of her tongue peeked out and lined her top lip. "Well, Mr. Kavanaugh, now that you have me, what ever will you do with me?"

Shane gave her his best wicked smile. "Oh, I have plenty of things I'm going to do with you, Ms. Reynolds." He nuzzled her neck with his nose and nipped her soft earlobe. "Be patient, Peaches."

He covered her mouth with his and swallowed her moan, their tongues sliding together in a dance as old as time. Shane slid his hands over the curves of her breasts, hips, and ass, never breaking the kiss. She twined her arms around his neck and when he hitched her up, she wrapped those long legs around his waist.

"Shane," she murmured against his mouth, "I want you. I want to feel your skin on mine again."

He groaned. "Hold on. I don't want to drop you."

"This works for me." She nipped at his jaw.

He grit his teeth and recited baseball stats. "No way. As much as I want to take you right here, the bed's going to be more comfortable for the plans I have in mind. We can try this position later."

And they did. In fact, they christened the kitchen, the living room, and the dining room. Later that night, when the winter sun set below the horizon and the sky darkened to a deep indigo, Shane gathered Emma to his side. Something deep in his gut pulled at him when she snuggled against him and fell asleep. He lay on his back, stroking the velvety skin of her arm flung across his chest. He couldn't remember ever having a better, completely off-the-grid day. It was liberating.

But he should have left sooner. Hell, he should have never come over in the first place. By doing so, they'd officially moved past the ability to call whatever they were doing a one-night stand. Shane knew things about Emma now, personal things, including the plans she had for the house. Her plans didn't include selling it to any interested parties.

It was time to regain focus, and that focus was on business. Opening the winery, buying the perfect property, and saving the family company from destruction, before it was too late.

SIXTEEN

My Baby's Got a Secret

SHANE STAYED the rest of the weekend until he had to fly out to California. Emma was thankful her house sat far enough off the road no one could see Shane's truck in the driveway. She didn't need to give the town gossips anything more to yammer about.

But she missed him and that was a problem. It'd been three days since they said their goodbyes. Three days and already the gnawing in her gut distracted her from things she should be doing. Like typing a simple email to a vendor. How the hell was she going to handle it when he left for good?

She dropped her forehead to her hand and sighed. This was one reason why she never mixed business and pleasure. It was just too sticky.

Especially when the pleasure made her obliterate every rule she ever made. Shane made sex an art form. He was patient and a master at giving and taking. She didn't want to think about how many women he'd been with to hone the skills he possessed, but one thing was clear. He'd ruined her for all other men. Even now, her skin flushed and the tingling in her core had her clenching her thighs together.

Blowing out a breath, she turned to her computer to lose herself in something that didn't deal with her heart. Or her hormones.

A couple of hours later, her stomach growled, reminding her that she'd skipped breakfast. A glance at the clock said it was lunch time. Needing some fresh air, she decided to head to town for lunch.

On her way out of her office, she walked straight into a hard chest.

Strong hands gripped her biceps to keep her from toppling over. "Whoa, I'm sorry. Are you okay?"

Emma lifted her face to find a man smiling at her. His eyes twinkled with male appreciation. The face was familiar and yet different. "I'm fine. Can I help you?" she asked.

He released her arms and held out a hand. "Colin Kavanaugh. I'm looking for Shane." A slow smile curved his lips, his eyes taking her in. They were the color of green sea glass instead of blue like the sea itself. "You must be Emma. I've heard a lot about you."

She returned the handshake and smiled. "All good, I hope. It's nice to finally meet you." She hitched her purse higher on her shoulder. "Shane isn't here, though. Did he know you were coming?"

Colin shook his head. "No, this is a surprise visit. I was in Virginia and decided to take a detour here. I haven't seen this place since our first trip out here."

"I was just on my way out to lunch, but I could give you a quick tour before I go."

"Or...how about I take you to lunch and then you can show me around? Tell me how things are coming along here." Colin paused. "If you don't have other plans, of course."

Emma glanced at her watch and found she had some time. "I'm good. My next call isn't until later this afternoon."

He gave her a dazzling smile that reminded her so much of Shane, she ached. "Lead the way."

She chose The Magnolia House where they would be able to sit and talk, but which was also known for its quick service during the lunchtime hours.

The dining room of The Magnolia House was one of elegance and grace. With crisp, white linen tablecloths, crystal hurricane lamps lit with fat white candles, and gleaming silverware, it was simple, but spoke of money. Now that she'd met Shane's brother, she could see that the Kavanaugh family was much like the dining room—comfortable, yet the undertones of money and wealth couldn't be denied.

When they settled into their seats and their drink order had been placed, Colin leaned back and smiled at her. "I've heard a lot about how you've taken over the operations of the Madison Ridge location."

"Well, that is what I was hired to do." She sipped her water and reached for a slice of bread from the silver wire basket on the table.

"Shane tells me you are turning things around, getting things done while he goes back and forth between here and California." He shook his head and tapped a finger on the white tablecloth. "It's tough on him, all the traveling."

"I know your father being sick is taking a toll on him as well. He tries to hide it,"—she shrugged—"but I see it. I was in a similar position myself not long ago." The pang in her heart still appeared when she thought about losing her parents so quickly and how she was still reeling from her own issues.

Colin raised a brow. "I figured you knew. Shane speaks highly of you.

Emma sat up straighter. "He does?"

He sipped his water and nodded. "Absolutely. You're an integral part of the organization." Colin gave her a pointed stare. "I know he's left a lot on your shoulders for someone who has only been with us for a month. But Shane has trusted you with the winery from the beginning. And he doesn't trust easily."

Her chest expanded with pride, but it was quickly followed by a sickening feeling in her gut. Shane trusted her, and yet she hadn't been completely honest with him, had she? Even though her reasoning for it was sound in her mind, didn't Shane deserve to know the truth about her?

She leaned back and stared down at her hands gripped together in her lap. Raising her head, she sent Colin a smile. "I don't blame him for not trusting easily. Trust takes a while." Especially once it was broken. Just ask any of the family members she'd screwed over during her active addiction.

Shit, shit, shit. How was she still managing to find trouble?

"Once the rounds of treatment are over though, Shane will stop traveling so much. He's ironed out a good bit of the issues we've had at some other locations he's juggled as well. He'll be around more, at least for a while yet, until the renovation is over."

When their orders arrived, they talked tourism in the area, how they could bring more local flair into the winery, and marketing strategy. Colin was definitely savvier on the administrative side of things. Shane was sharp on all fronts, but it was clear he'd spent more time in the field and knew grapes inside out. Colin's strengths ran to dealing with things in the office.

When she mentioned it, Colin nodded and set down his fork, sipping his tea. "Shane always had a head for learning the agricultural part of the business. He's more like how our grandfather always was. It works out well, actually." He paused as a smile spread across his face. "But he is more like our father in other ways."

"Oh? How so?" Emma asked, forking up lettuce. She was enjoying the insights to Shane from someone in his family. It pleased her to see that she was coming to know him. Well, it pleased her and it distracted her.

"He was ready to settle in Napa like our father. Shane was never one for jetting all over the place, like me. I love it. Always going somewhere new. But Shane? He's more of a settle-in-for-the-long-haul type of guy."

She frowned. "That seems a bit at odds with what he does now."

Colin nodded. "It is. Now. But before his wife died, he was ready to lay roots around Napa and work at the family headquarters."

Emma's blood ran cold. His dead wife? He had been married? Her fingers tightened on the fork in her hand so hard it was a wonder it didn't bend in half.

When she didn't say anything, Colin continued, seemingly oblivious to her shock. "Marlene could be wonderful, but more often than not, she was just trouble. Out of the blue, she asked for a divorce, and then died before the divorce had been finalized." Colin shook his head. "Messed Shane up for a while. Changed him. Now he takes all the jobs that require him to be as far away from California as possible, for as long as possible. The only reason he comes back is to check in on Dad."

The waiter stopped by, asking if they needed anything else, and leaving the check. Emma, still reeling from all of the new information about the man she was sleeping with, managed to come up with what she thought was the appropriate response to Colin's word-vomit.

"That's sad to hear. Shane seems to have bounced back okay, though."

Colin stopped, staring into his glass before raising his eyes to hers. The sounds of muted conversations and clinking silverware against fine china drifted around them. "He does seem to be in better spirits the last couple of times I've seen him. Better than I've seen him in the last few years actually." He eyed her. "I have some guesses on why that could be."

In spite of herself, hope rose in Emma's chest. She stomped hard on that hope, though, knowing it had no place in her mind. "Well, whatever the reason, I'm glad for it." She grinned and winked at Colin, even though she wanted to crawl in a hole, forgetting Shane. "Makes for a better boss if he's happy."

He returned her grin. "You know what? I like you, Emma. You're smart and one of the most beautiful women I've ever seen. If you didn't work for my family's company, I'd ask you out."

She shrugged a shoulder, a weight heavy in her stomach. "Another time, another place."

He held up his hands as though surrendering, but sent her a grin that probably worked well on most women. It was identical to his brother's, and it had worked on her like a freaking charm. "If you ever decide to take a job elsewhere, let me know."

In spite of herself, she laughed. Colin had charisma in spades, something it appeared he had no trouble doling out.

Colin paid for lunch and she drove them back to the winery. After a quick tour through the place, he said his goodbyes, taking a rideshare to the local airport. Emma went back to her office and found herself staring at her computer screen again, thinking about the information she'd received during lunch. What she didn't know was why Colin had imparted all that information to her. But for whatever reason, Colin chose to tell her more about his brother than she thought was appropriate. Emma had no doubt Shane would be pissed. She'd shared seriously personal information with him, and in all of their conversa-tions, he hadn't said word one about a dead wife, or even mentioned being married.

The bigger question was, what did she do now that she had this information?

SEVENTEEN

Perfectly Fucked Up

"WE'LL BE LANDING in about ten minutes, Mr. Kavanaugh," the blonde flight attendant informed him, her voice low in the darkened cabin.

"Thanks." He adjusted the reclining seat and lifted the shade over the small oval window next to him. The North Georgia Mountains and the small towns that dotted them spread out under the descending plane like an inky-black blanket with golden sparkles shot through.

Equal parts joy and guilt ran through him. Joy because these mountains held the key to happiness for him. Emma. But it was followed up quickly by guilt. The conversation with his father in regards to her land didn't go as he'd planned.

Of course, Shane had left out the fact that the woman he'd just hired to run his winery was the same woman whose land they were trying to purchase. Oh, and that he had slept with her as well. Without that little juicy tidbit, it made it hard for Shane to explain to his father why he didn't want to move forward on that particular parcel of land, as perfect as it was. All that acreage, a house already set up for guests, and the fact that the back side of the land backed up to the road that ran in front of the winery. It was fucking perfect.

And perfectly fucked up.

Shane ran his hands down his face. The fact that leaving Madison

Ridge was getting harder to do each time was another kick in the ass. And he couldn't honestly say it was just because the grand opening loomed closer every day. April might seem like an eternity away, but those couple of months would pass in a flash.

No, it wasn't just work that had his gut in a knot when he'd boarded the private KVN plane. It was Emma. In a short period of time, she'd burrowed her way under his skin, whether he liked it or not. And he wasn't entirely sure he did. After Marlene had died, he'd sworn that he would never let another woman screw with his head and his life the way she had.

It wasn't something he looked for anymore, the love thing. Home and hearth. He wouldn't be able to handle another roller coaster ride like Marlene. So for now, traveling and working on projects all over the country had been his lot in life. Maybe someday he'd have that ridiculously traditional picture of family and home he wanted. But now wasn't the time.

Or was it?

The woman with the whiskey-colored eyes made him feel a fissure of hope that he could find love again. With her. He still had the whole house issue to figure out, but maybe if he approached her the right way, he could make her understand. Emma wanted the same thing he wanted for her childhood home, and that was to open it to guests again. Shane nodded to himself. Yeah, maybe it could work after all...

Wait. What the hell was he thinking? There was no way it was going to work. He didn't even live in Madison Ridge. Even though California was littered with bad memories for him, it was still home. His father was ill and needed him to step up for the business. Especially now that Colin was making a play to sell off the family company if he became CEO. Shane had already allowed love to derail him from his duty to the family dynasty once. It wasn't something he would let happen again.

His tired, jet-lagged brain was losing it. Best to let go of all that love mumbo-jumbo he'd almost let himself get caught up in again. He could continue to see Emma—they'd just keep it casual, easy.

The wheels of the plane touched the ground in a near-flawless landing and the airliner taxied down the runway to an open area near a large hangar. After gathering his bag and saying his goodbyes to the crew, Shane stepped off the plane and walked down the stairs, his pace slow, weary. Only two more weeks and the treatments for his father would be over. At least, for the time being. Then they would have to go through the testing to see if the treatments had worked. But for a little while, Shane would be in Madison Ridge for more than just a few days.

Being around Emma for any length of time besides the hours in the office sent a flash of heat straight to his groin and a smile to his face.

"Need a ride?"

As if she'd materialized out of his musings, Emma leaned against his Range Rover. His body tightened at the sight of her in jeans that hugged her curves in all the right places, a red ski jacket, and knee-high boots. A smile that gave the bright stars overhead a run for their money curved those perfect pink lips of hers. A knit hat was pulled low over her ears, her hair spilling over her shoulders.

She looked so fucking good, he literally ached.

His long legs ate up the ground between them. Just before he got to her, he dropped his bag to the ground and took her face in his hands. He needed to taste her, and taste her he did. Shane crushed his mouth to hers and she responded in kind, her arms coming up to wrap around his waist. He plundered, reveling in the taste that was uniquely Emma. She tasted like secrets and warmth and sunshine, all wrapped into one.

When he finally pulled away, they were both heaving as though they'd just wrapped up a fifty-yard dash. "Well, hello to you, too," she drawled with a smile, that lovely accent laced through her words.

He leaned his forehead against hers, still cradling her face in his palms. "I missed you."

Her breath hitched for just a second before she responded. "I missed you, too. Come on, I'll take you home."

Shane stepped back and leaned down to pick up his bag. He tossed it in the back seat and settled into the passenger seat, grateful she took charge and drove them home.

He'd think about the fact that he'd just called Madison Ridge home another time.

Situating back in the seat, he angled himself toward her, one arm stretched out and toying with the ends of her hair as she smoothly maneuvered the SUV along the curves of the road leading away from the airport. "Thanks for picking me up. You're much prettier than the guy I usually get when I send for a car."

She smiled, glancing at him quickly before sliding her eyes back to the road. "You're welcome. When Lindsey told me what time you'd be getting back here, I figured you might want to see a friendly face."

She had no idea just how much he'd needed that. Shane rubbed a few strands of her hair through his fingertips. "Always thinking, my Emma," he murmured before leaning his head back and letting his eyes close. He must have dozed off because within seconds, Emma was nudging him.

"Wake up. We're here."

He looked around, bleary-eyed, to find his cabin—he still had a hard time calling the large house a cabin—spread out in front of him. "Already?"

When they got inside, Shane collapsed in a free fall onto the plush sofa in the two-story living room. "God, I'm so tired. Tomorrow is Saturday, right?"

Emma looked down at him from the end of the couch, her eyes narrowed and her arms crossed over her chest. "Yes, it is. When was the last time you ate, Shane?"

Shane rubbed his eyes with the heel of his hands, trying to remember when he'd last eaten. These coast-to-coast trips really screwed with his routine all the way around. "What time is it?"

"Eleven-thirty."

He half moaned, half groaned. "Hell, I don't remember. But I'm starving, now that I think about it."

She patted his feet. "Why don't you go up and take a shower and I'll make you some food?"

"You don't have to do that. I'll just eat in the morning."

Emma came around and sat on the edge of the couch next to him, laying a hand on his knee. "I don't mind."

He looked over at her and found her gaze expectant on his, as though waiting for him to respond. It appeared she really didn't mind, even though she must have had a long day herself. Reaching out, he lifted one of her hands and brought her palm to his lips, where he placed an open-mouthed kiss in the center. Her pulse quickened against his cheek and her eyes darkened. "Thank you, Emma. I appreciate that."

She swallowed, the muscles of her throat working under her creamy skin. "You're welcome." She leaned forward until he could see the ring of dark brown around the iris of her eyes. "I need my hand back," she whispered, her voice like silk.

"Right." He kissed it again, a quick peck this time, before letting it go. She rose and skirted around the sofa. His eyes slid closed as her boot heels clicked across the wooden floors. A few minutes later, the feeling of being lulled into sleep spread through his limbs, while the sounds of Emma working in the kitchen faded away.

He wasn't sure how long he slept, but when he woke, he was still fully clothed, with a blanket tossed over his body. The living room was dark, with shafts of light from the kitchen giving it a shadowy appearance. Sitting up, he looked around, drawing up short when he found Emma sleeping in the recliner across the room, a magazine touting the latest gossip spread across her chest.

He stretched before looking at his watch. It was the middle of the night and he didn't want to wake her to send her home now. In sleep, she looked soft and he wanted to curl her up against him so he could feel that expanse of silky skin. Instead, Shane lifted the blanket and laid it over her. She stirred and opened her eyes. A sleepy smile spread her lips. "What time is it?"

"Just after two thirty."

Her eyes slid closed again and a millisecond later, they went wide and she sat straight up. "Oh God, I fell asleep. I need to get home. Wait, I never made your breakfast. You were out like a light, and I didn't have the heart to wake you. I'll do it now."

She rose and he put his hands on her shoulders. "Emma, it's the middle of the night. What you need to do is just go back to sleep."

The shadows of sleep were clearing from her eyes, and she shook her head, licked her lips. He couldn't help it. His gaze drew down to her beautiful, bow-shaped mouth. "It's okay, I can call Aidan. He's on call tonight."

Fuck it. At that moment, his mind was clear, and he realized he wanted her. All of her. And not just for a night. He wanted to be the one to take care of her, not her police officer cousin. After Marlene, Shane didn't think he'd find a woman he wanted to commit to again. He didn't want the aggravation or the heartbreak.

But Emma was different than Marlene. She didn't come with all the baggage his late wife had. She was perfect for him. All the logistical stuff—working together, the house, the fact that they lived three thousand miles apart—they would figure it out. Without a doubt in Shane's mind, the woman standing before him, the one who wanted to make him breakfast in the middle of the night, was worth any trouble.

"Emma. Stay with me." He held out a hand to her.

Her eyes roamed over his face for a moment before she slid her hand into his. With her other hand, she pointed a finger at him. "I see that look in your eye, Shane Kavanaugh. First, we sleep. Then we do," she waved her hand between them, "all that."

He arranged his features into a serious expression even though his voice held the underlying tone of "yeah, sure right". "Whatever you say, Peaches," he agreed before pulling her up the stairs and into his bedroom.

EIGHTEEN

When Trouble Finds You

A DISTANT RUMBLE of thunder stirred Emma from sleep. Her eyes blinked open to the dark room. Something was different. There was a warm body pressed up against her back.

Shane.

Her lips curled into a sleepy smile and she pressed herself against him, feeling his warm, naked chest against her skin. One arm tightened around her waist, while the other slid up between her breasts and cupped one. His magical fingers worked her nipple into a hard peak, causing her to gasp softly.

He nudged his hips forward. She bit her lip when his cock pressed against her ass.

"Good morning, Peaches." His breath was warm against her ear, causing stirrings deep in her core.

"Good morning," she whispered.

"Sleep well?" His mouth found the slope between her neck and shoulder. Shane planted hot, open-mouthed kisses on the sensitive skin, his tongue snaking out to tickle her skin. Shivers ran down her spine like lightning.

"Hmmmm…" Emma moved against him, wanting every part of her body touching his. Everywhere he kissed, it was agony and ecstasy to feel the heat of his talented mouth mingled with the cool air. Her heart thumped against her chest in anticipation of where those kisses would lead.

The thought of another round of mind-blowing sex wasn't the only reason her heart hammered against her ribs. She knew that in the short time they'd been together, she'd managed to fall in love with him.

He was all wrong for her. Hell, he made his living making a product that had nearly destroyed her. He lived on the other side of the country when he didn't travel the world for his job. Oh yeah, let's not forget, she worked for him, too. Emma had obliterated her cardinal rule: never sleep with someone you work with or work for. Because when it ended—and didn't it always?—it would taint the working relationship.

Yet, she found she couldn't bring herself to care about her rules. Emma just wanted to be happy, something she hadn't been in more years than she could count. For her, that meant giving up a little piece of herself to him and trusting him. Because if there was any man she wanted to give her heart away to, it was Shane. He was kind, smart, loved his family, and was sexy as hell.

A small nagging in the back of her mind reminded her that he'd been married once and hadn't told her about it. She pushed the thought away. They were still getting to know and trust each other on a personal level. She hadn't told him about her addiction yet, had she? Emma swallowed hard and blanked out the thoughts of having *that* particular conversation with him. It was one she needed to handle sooner than later, as it was crucial to her recovery steps. Not avoiding the hard stuff.

But it would take a little more time to gauge how he'd handle it.

She rolled onto her back. He lifted up on his elbow and gazed down into her eyes.

"What's going on in that beautiful mind of yours, Emmaline?" he murmured, nuzzling his nose against her neck.

She smiled softly. He was the only person, other than her mother, who used her full name regularly. "There's just so much I don't know about you."

"All you have to do is ask." His free hand started to roam underneath the sheet that covered her. He ran a hand flat across her belly, rubbing side to side. "Your skin is so soft," he whispered, his face in the crook of her neck.

Breathing became difficult the more he touched her. "What's your favorite color?"

His hand continued its caress, but he smiled against her skin. "Blue."

"Dog or cat?"

He chuckled. "Dog, of course."

"Good choice." Her breath hitched when he kissed the tender spot under her ear, the tips of his fingers drawing figure eights on her abdomen, though with each pass, those skillful hands lingered a tad bit lower.

"Were you born in California?"

"Born and raised in Napa."

"Did you go to college?"

"I did. UC Berkeley."

"Smarty pants," she said with a smile. "What's your favorite childhood memory? I mean, I know you were young when your mom died, but there must be something you think of fondly."

"Favorite childhood memory," he murmured, rolling onto his back, reversing their positions. Pillowing his hands behind his head, he stared at the ceiling. "Well, let's see." He was quiet for a moment, and then a smile spread across his face. "When Colin and I were kids, we used to wander over this one section of the vineyards. It was an area they didn't really use for wine production because the vines just wouldn't produce enough grapes."

Emma shifted, a small smile on her lips. Her fingers played idly with the smattering of hair covering his hard chest where she rested her chin. Shane's face was relaxed, a five o'clock shadow covering the lower part of his face, his eyes a sparkling brilliant blue. Something in her belly fluttered, and her heart was light seeing him like this.

"Anyway, the summer after our mother passed away, Colin and I were playing in that area, and to our surprise, we found a bunch of grapes on the vines, and many on the ground. We decided to gather them all together, like our dad. We were going to make wine."

Emma's grin matched his. "You boys were going to make wine?"

"Yep. We found a large tub and stomped on the grapes until we'd made a decent amount of juice, put it in a bottle. Without de-stemming. I knew enough to let it sit for a while. Since Father's Day was a few days later, we gave it to him then." Shane laughed. "It had to be the foulest stuff. But he sat there and drank a glass right in front of us. We never saw the bottle again, but he looked like the happiest man on earth that day." He paused, staring up at the ceiling, absently stroking her arm. "I'd forgotten about that until just now." His voice was soft, but strained, as though emotion clogged his throat. Shadows filled his eyes and the lightness in her heart was replaced by heartache.

Emma sighed. "Your father sounds like a great man. I'm so sorry he's sick. I wish I could meet him."

Shane shifted and rolled until she was on her back, settling himself between her thighs. His hard, warm body was a delicious pressure that she wanted to wrap herself up in forever.

Shane looked down at her. "I hope you can meet him as well," he said softly. He ran a finger along her cheek. "I don't know what you're doing to me. You trouble me," he murmured. A smile touched his lips. Those intense blue eyes were serious, yet confused. His thumbs swept soothing, gentle arcs along her temples.

Man, this guy shot straight for her heart. A different kind of warmth spread through her blood, a kind that warmed her soul, not just her parts south of the border. She pulled him by the hair to kiss his lips gently.

She touched him, brushing her fingertips down his face, her eyes focused on her movements. "You trouble me, too. In all my life, I've never known a man like you."

His eyes darkened to that sexy navy blue that was like throwing gas on a flame for her libido. His Adam's apple bobbed when he swallowed hard.

The emotions that ran through her body were intense and overwhelming to the point where she almost couldn't breathe. They held each other's stares for a few moments until he cleared his throat and broke the silence.

He lifted his head and looked around. "Did I really hear thunder?" he asked, his tone a mix of confusion and wonder.

Emma smiled, leaning into his hand that lay along her cheek. "Yeah. That's Georgia weather for you. We have all the seasons in a week. It's cooler tonight, but it was pretty mild today."

He shook his head. "That's crazy." His eyes met hers and a sexy grin curved his mouth. "You know what's fun to do on a rainy day?"

She pursed her lips and looked up at the ceiling as though contemplating her answer. "Binge-watching Netflix?"

"That's one thing," he conceded. "But I had some other things in mind." He rolled his hips against her core and dropped feather kisses along her jaw. She bit her lip to hold back a gasp.

"Oh? Like baking cookies?" she teased. "Chocolate chip is my favorite."

"Mine, too. And maybe you can bake me some later today."

"I don't know, I might be busy."

His eyes narrowed. "Do you need some incentive? Because I can oblige."

As he moved down her body, she arched against him, pressing her naked breasts into his roaming hands and giving him full access to her neck. "A little incentive never hurt any...one..." The last word came on a gasp when Shane cupped one of her breasts and sucked on the nipple. "Um, yes. Yes, I think..." God, she *couldn't* think when he moved his tongue on the beaded flesh.

He lifted his head, his mouth hovering over the aching peak. "What was that? You think...?"

Their eyes held. Emma ran her fingers into his dark hair and held fast to the soft locks. Being with Shane brought out feelings she'd never had for anyone. What they had burned hotter than the white-hot sun.

"Show me what's fun, Shane," she whispered.

The grin she was now addicted to spread across his face. "With pleasure, love."

"I'm going to need a shower soon, though."

He moved back up her body and settled himself between her hips. "Care for some company in the shower?"

She matched his grin with one of her own. "Of course."

Before she could take the next breath, Shane scooped her out of the bed and carried her into the bathroom, a smirk of his own across his handsome face.

After another round of mind-blowing sex that gave her new appreciation for built-in shower benches, Emma made them a hearty breakfast of eggs over medium, thick strips of bacon, and sourdough toast. All of his favorite breakfast things, he said.

Once the dishes were cleared, she sat across from him while he read the local newspaper. Through the steam wafting up from the coffee cup balanced on her knees, she studied him.

A lock of dark hair fell over his forehead, his strong jaw and broad shoulders relaxed, his gaze scanning the paper in front of him. God, he was a beautiful man. A blush bloomed over her skin before she could stop it. But before she lost herself in him again, she needed answers about what Colin told her.

Sipping her coffee, she decided to go for it. "So, I had a visitor at the winery yesterday."

Shane looked up and gave his attention to her. "Oh? Who was it?"

"Your brother, Colin."

The relaxed demeanor disappeared and the ocean blue of his eyes turned into blue-gray thunderclouds. His fingers tensed for a moment before releasing and folding the paper. "What did Colin want?"

Emma raised a brow. Whoa. She'd never heard Shane's voice so flat and cold before.

"Well, he was there to see you. He wanted to surprise you and see how the renovation was coming along. But since you weren't there, he took me to lunch, and I took him on a tour of the building."

Shane sat back, his arms crossing his chest. "Did Colin have any ideas about what he'd do better?" His tone was razor sharp.

"No, he was impressed with everything. Loved the vibe and area, he said." Emma paused and picked her words carefully. If Shane was annoyed about that, Emma feared he might lose his shit on the next topic. But it was one that she needed to get off her chest. She couldn't avoid it any longer.

Emma cleared her throat, unsure about broaching the next subject.

Averting her eyes, she trailed a finger around the rim of her cup. "Colin also mentioned something else. I'm not sure why he did. I mean, it's not clear to me just what we…are. Whatever this is."

Jeez, she was fumbling this big-time. When he didn't fill the silence, she went on. "He told me about Marlene."

She studied his face for any sort of reaction, but he stayed impassive. His shoulders stiffened, and Emma wanted to appreciate the play of his chest and ab muscles, but she was more concerned with the invisible wall he'd just put up between them.

"Colin should have kept that to himself."

She paused. "Want to talk about it?"

"There's nothing to talk about." He shot to his feet, picking up his coffee mug and stalking across the kitchen. Emma jumped when the cup hit the sink with a crash, followed by a string of dark cursing. She stayed still and silent while Shane paced the kitchen like an angry, caged tiger.

He turned to her, his eyes shooting blue flames, his hands jammed on his hips. "You want to know about Marlene? Fine, I'll tell you about her. It won't take long. She was an addict wrapped in a beautiful package, who didn't give a shit about anything except her next fix of heroin."

Emma's stomach did a long, slow roll, and for a moment, the coffee she'd just consumed burned at the back of her throat, threatening to come back up.

Shit. Shit. Shit. His late wife had been an addict?

She was royally screwed.

Unaware of her shocked state, Shane strode back over to the table where she sat and dropped back down in the chair, where he continued. He sighed heavily. "I'd known Marlene since we were kids. We'd been friends for a long time. Her mother was the manager of the restaurant in our flagship winery, and Marlene would come in and help her sometimes. She was a fireball who would burst into a room and scorch everything before leaving. But she changed after college."

His voice was a heartbreaking mix of sad, resigned, and weary. "Our relationship was something I never expected." His mouth twisted in a wry smile. "Of course, I might have, if the sum total of our time as a couple lasted longer than six months. In that short time, we dated, got married, started divorce proceedings, and had her funeral."

He looked away and ran a hand through his hair. An errant lock of dark hair fell over his forehead. Emma's gut twisted over the agony that showed in his body language. "It was such a whirlwind, I didn't have time to see she was addicted to heroin until after she'd persuaded me to 'put a ring on it', as she'd been fond of saying. When I found out, I tried to help her. She'd go out with friends and end up in the ER, on the verge of overdosing. Every time, I tried to send her to rehab. She just laughed and refused."

Emma closed her eyes briefly. Although heroin hadn't been her drug of choice, she could remember her family trying to help her. And how she'd laughed in their faces. She'd spend the rest of her life regretting it.

Shane continued, his eyes glazed over with a look that said his mind was in the past. "After a while, she said she grew tired of what she deemed my 'stick in the mud ways' since I would never join her shooting up. It would piss her off because I rarely even drank with her." His gaze sharpened and slid back to Emma, a frown marring his handsome mouth. "It became obvious she hooked up with me because of who I am."

Emma agreed, but stayed silent. As an addict herself, she figured Marlene would have used Shane's money and power to stay high.

He shrugged. "Anyway, she found a guy who would shoot up with her anytime she wanted. Before long, she asked for a divorce. Two days before we were set to make the divorce final, I stopped by her apartment to pick up a few of my things, and found her and her new boyfriend in bed. Both overdosed."

Her heart ached for the man across from her, a man she cared for far more than was prudent. A man who had a history of being screwed over by a woman who hadn't been too terribly different from her. Well, the old her, but it was a fight she fought daily. And always would.

"Oh, Shane. I'm so sorry." She laid a hand over his, her thumb rubbing back and forth. He turned his hand over and wound their fingers together. Staring down at their joined hands, he spoke, his voice low and gruff.

"It's been two years since she died, and I still feel like I failed by not saving her. I loved her, but not the way a man should love the woman he's married to. I mean, we'd been friends for years. But after the initial shine wore off, we were more like friends with benefits. Benefits that dropped off like a stone a week after we'd eloped." His broad shoulders slumped slightly and his eyes met hers. Pain mixed with regret swirled in those blue depths. "Honestly, I'm not surprised she asked for a divorce. It was inevitable, and not because she had issues, but because we wanted different things. But she was a human being, and a good one when she wasn't high." His other hand fisted on the table. "I just wished I could have helped her."

"Shane, people who are in the throes of active addiction don't believe they need help. There was nothing you could have done for Marlene." Emma desperately wanted Shane to understand that there was nothing he could have done for his late wife. For a drug addict, feeding that beast was always the number-one priority.

She leaned closer to him, her eyes intent. "Addicts think they've got it all under control. It isn't until they lose that control and their lives become so unmanageable and they hit bottom that they realize they have no control at all. It's the first of the twelve steps."

Shit on a shingle. Nothing like giving herself away. Tampering down the panic crawling at her throat, she kept her face impassive. His eyes held hers, and she prayed he didn't see too much. The man could read her like a book most of the time.

"You seem to know about the subject."

Avoidance. It still came easy. "Addiction isn't picky. My dad was in Gamblers Anonymous. The first step is the same."

When he nodded and looked back down at their hands, she exhaled quietly and guilt tore through her. Avoidance and deflection. Yeah, she still had those down cold.

The ironic thing was that she could give him truthful comfort, even if he wasn't convinced. But it was clear that if she wanted to work for KVN, even if she and Shane were just short-term lovers, she would have to make sure her past never made it to Shane's ears.

NINETEEN

Strip Poker for the Win

SHANE WAS PISSED. What the hell was Colin trying to do?

The question was rhetorical because he already knew what Colin's strategy was. He wasn't in Madison Ridge to check out the winery. He stopped by when he knew Shane wouldn't be there so he could assess what progress had been made.

After learning Colin wanted to leapfrog over him into the CEO position and use Shane's past against him, Shane no longer underestimated his little brother. He still didn't know why Colin wanted to sell off, but it didn't matter. Because it wasn't going to happen.

And he was going to pay dearly for sharing a story with Emma that wasn't Colin's to share.

After their talk, Emma suggested they take a walk while it wasn't raining. There was no playful tire swinging this time, just a quiet, pensive walk to clear his head. When the thunder rumbled and lightning cut through the sky, they decided to head back to shelter before the late winter thunderstorm broke free again.

Between the physical exercise and the emotional heaviness from earlier, they agreed to go back to bed. In spite of Emma's stern insistence that they sleep, they only managed a couple of hours before desire won out.

When they woke, the day was still gray and dreary, with the sun hiding deep behind the charcoal-gray clouds in the sky. The winds howled, with no signs of letting up anytime soon.

The one bright side to the dismal day was that Emma hadn't brought up anything more about Colin's visit or Marlene. While there'd been an occasional silence from her, there had been no awkwardness between them, which surprised and relaxed him. She was the same Emma as always. Hours later, after a day of dozing and watching movies, Emma paced in front of the fireplace, looking like she was going to jump out of her skin.

It appeared his little peach had a case of cabin fever.

Laid out on the sofa, Shane feigned sleep, his eyes narrow slits that followed her movements as she prowled the room. His gaze traveled from the messy bun on top of her head, along the tiny white tank top and snug black yoga pants, down to her bare feet, where her toes were painted that candy-apple red that made his blood run hot. The pants did fantastic things to the curve of her ass and legs. The fire crackled behind her and cast shadows across her face. Emma was quite the sight, and for a moment, Shane forgot to breathe.

When she whirled to face him, he slammed his eyes closed. The sofa dipped under his feet when she sat down. He bit back a smile when she sighed dramatically.

Shane was a patient man. He could wait out his opponent. When she sighed again, louder, he envisioned her chest heaving against the fabric of her top, nipples on display.

But his patience was tested by his naughty fantasy. Shane wanted to take her back to bed and have his way with her again. After all, it had been a few hours since the last time, and he was hungry for her.

Again.

Take it easy, Kavanaugh. The poor girl needs to walk tomorrow.

With an inward sigh, he pushed sex from his mind.

"Shane, I'm bored. Let's play a game."

Shane opened his eyes and raised a brow. "What kind of game do you have in mind, Ms. Reynolds?"

Emma tapped an index finger against her pink lips. "Hmmm…how good are you at card games?"

Shane mentally rubbed his hands together, but his face remained neutral. "I can hold my own."

No need to tell her that back in college, he ran a weekly poker game that helped pay for his living. And Shane hadn't eaten Ramen noodles a day in his life.

"How about you?" he asked. "Are you any good at card games?"

She raised her chin and looked down her nose at him. "I can hold my own."

"Well, then." Shane sat up and swung his legs to the side of the sofa. "Let's play."

A few minutes later, they sat at the dining room table, with Emma shuffling the deck. "Do we agree on strip poker, Five-card draw?" she asked, passing out cards to each of them.

A smile spread across his face. His favorite type of game. "Strip poker, Five-card draw it is." Her technique in dealing was smooth and tight, causing him to sit up a bit straighter. When she finished dealing, he studied the cards in his hand. It should be an interesting game.

Emma picked up her cards, tucking her legs underneath her. "You're up, Kavanaugh."

He had shit for cards. Two aces were all he had to use. But he hadn't lived on poker winnings because he'd been lucky.

Shane lay three cards facedown and slid them across the table, one side of his mouth quirked up in a smirk. "You know, you have to be the sexiest dealer I've ever seen."

Emma gave him a side-eyed look, but she wasn't fooling him. His words had the intended effect. Those amber-colored eyes darkened to a caramel color. He bit back a smile. He'd never be able to look at the sugary confection the same way again.

She wagged her finger at him. "Nice try, Kavanaugh. Your smooth words aren't going to work on me." She lay down three and then dealt each of them their respective number of cards.

"I seem to recall them working on you pretty well before," he said, bobbing his eyebrows.

Emma rolled her eyes but chuckled. "Shut up and place your bets."

He picked up his new cards and studied them. The two aces he kept from his first hand were joined by a queen, a nine, and a four. He glanced up at Emma, whose face was impassive, but her eyes weren't. She met his glance, but quickly looked away and rolled her lips inward, tapping her finger on the top of the end card.

"Your pants. I win, your pants come off."

Emma raised a brow and a small frown played on her lips. "You don't start small, do you?" she muttered.

Now, Shane did smile. "Go big or go home, babe."

Emma glanced up, then away before sighing. "Damn," she whispered. "I fold," she said aloud. "Let's see what you got."

Shane laid out his hand and Emma's jaw dropped. "No way!" She flipped her hand over. She'd had a pair of aces, and if she'd played her hand out, she would have beat him with a king to his queen. "Are you freaking kidding me?"

Shane laughed so hard at her incredulous expression, his eyes began to water. She slanted her gaze at him, but it held no real heat. She pointed at him. "Okay, Kavanaugh, this means war."

"This means your pants are mine."

She sighed heavily. "Fine."

With her jaw set but a gleam in her eye, she stood and moved away from the table. With her eyes on his, she lifted her tank top until it brushed the underside of her breasts. Splaying her hands across her flat, toned stomach, she moved them slowly down into the top of the waistband of her pants.

Shane's laughter died and his cock hardened to the point of aching as he watched her. Emma tossed her dark hair off her shoulders without breaking his stare. Her hands moved under the dark fabric, continuing their descent toward what Shane considered his own private heaven.

Just before her hands made it down that low, they moved to her hips, and she turned around, giving him her back.

Shane's body was taut as a bowstring with the need to launch himself over the table and grab her. Push her up against the wall and...

Shit, he needed to think about something else.

But the little minx was making it hard as hell to think about anything but her. She glanced over her shoulder and then pushed the pants down her legs to her ankles.

Fuck me.

She bent over at the waist and picked up the pants. All he could see was the black lace covering her ass and sex. She stood back up with another flip of her hair and turned back to face him. Tossing the pants at him, he caught them against his chest. They were warm from her body heat, and he held them to his nose, breathing deeply, inhaling the scent that was uniquely Emma.

Two could play at this game.

"Hmm…smells like heaven," he murmured, his eyes on hers.

She sat back down across from him, pulling her top down over her belly and panties. Gathering the cards from the table, she began dealing another hand. "I know," she said with a smirk.

"Well played, Peaches. Well played." He smiled at her from behind the pants before putting them over one shoulder. Emma was a fire-cracker and could give as good as she got. It was one of the things he loved about her.

He froze. Loved? He liked Emma a lot. Adored her actually. He wanted to be with her, in spite of some issues, but was it to the point of love?

"Shane? Are you okay?" Emma's voice brought him out of his internal babbling and he focused on her.

He cleared his throat. "Yep. I'm great. Just strategizing of how I can get you out of those panties now."

Yep, bring it back to sex for now. It was ground he understood and knew how to handle.

"Yeah, keep strategizing, Ace. It's game on, now," she said, her jaw set and a determined gleam in her eye.

"Bring your worst, baby."

Although Emma lost the next hand—and her shirt—Shane's willpower was taking a beating of its own. With every piece of clothing that came off, it took all the skills he had to play the game in order to win. If he lost one hand, he'd lose the whole battle since he was commando under his jeans.

The next hand, her bra came off and those luscious, beautiful breasts were begging for his touch. Shane did his best not to squirm in his chair, but his raging hard-on made sitting difficult.

He lifted a brow and gave Emma a pointed stare as she shuffled the deck. "I'd say this is the last hand."

Her eyes darkened with desire and gleamed with challenge. It was a potent combination that punched him straight in the gut, and one that he wouldn't mind seeing for the rest of his life.

Shane shoved that to the back of his mind when she dealt his hand. Leaning forward with his elbows on the table, he picked up his cards one at a time, studying what he'd been dealt. He bit back a smile when he picked the last one and found he'd been dealt a hand he'd had only a few times.

Straight flush.

He was going to love seeing those lacy panties come off.

"Your call," she asked, her voice was flat as she stared at her cards.

"Check."

She narrowed her eyes at him and put a card down, drawing a new one. Her expression didn't change as she studied her cards. A moment later, her eyes met his. "Show me what you've got."

Shane finally let loose the grin he'd been holding back as he laid out his hand. Four, five, six, seven, eight of spades.

She tapped a finger on her cheek, her eyes wide. "That's an impressive hand."

He leaned back with a satisfied smile and crossed his arms over his chest. "Yeah, you could say that."

Emma stared at his hand for a moment, that finger still tapping.

"Don't be shy now, Reynolds. Lay it on me."

Her eyes met his again, but they were unreadable this time. "Okay."

His grin grew wider. There was only one hand that could beat...

Son. Of. A. Bitch.

The shit-eating grin he'd been sporting slowly slid off his face with each card she put down.

All hearts.

Ace, King, Queen, Jack...

Her face broke into a heart-stopping smile as she turned over the last card.

Ten of hearts.

His jaw dropped as he stared at the cards placed on the table. "You've got to be fucking kidding me." He raised a brow. "Did you learn from the Poker Posse?"

Emma laughed as she leaned back in her chair and crossed her arms over her bare chest. "I think you owe me a pair of jeans, sir."

Shane blew out a breathy laugh. "I think I just got hustled."

Emma shrugged, the movement causing her breasts to taunt him. "Luck of the draw, my friend."

Shane couldn't believe her luck, but stood. "A bet is a bet."

"Yes, it is." Her eyes were trained and hungry on where his hands lay on the top button of his jeans. She licked her lips when he unbuttoned the top button.

Oh yeah, two could play at the game she'd put him through.

When he started to lower the zipper, she held up a hand and stood. "Wait. As the winner, let me do the honors."

She came around the table and laid her hands on his chest. His muscles tightened under her touch as she drew them down his torso, her eyes following the movement of her hands. She moved his out of the way and he let them drop to his sides. Emma flattened her palms against his abs and slid them down in a slow torturous motion. With a smile and a devilish look from under her lashes, she caressed his hard length through the denim before sliding the zipper down slowly. Shane brought up his hands to grab her hips, but she maneuvered out of his reach before he could touch her.

She wagged a finger at him. "No, no. You lost, this is my show."

The whole game had been her show, but Shane wasn't complaining. He growled, making her laugh, but pulled his hands back, fisting them at his sides. Emma was driving him bat-shit crazy, standing so close and touching him without letting him touch her. The whole poker game had been an exercise in prolonged foreplay, and he was at the end of his rope.

That tether of patience was fraying. This woman was the only person in the world who tempted him without fail on a daily basis. She tortured him in every possible way, with her body, mind, and spirit. He couldn't keep his hands off her when she was within arm's length of him, and right now he wanted nothing more than to gather her up and haul her back upstairs to bed. To spend the rest of the stormy, winter day having his way with her.

But fair was fair. He'd lost the last round—although he still wasn't sure how—and he had to pay the piper. Shane had to admit, though, with her hands running all over him, her body covered in nothing more than a scrap of lace, and the anticipation of getting her out of said panties, it was a win-win situation.

When the button was undone and the zipper unzipped, Emma walked around him, her fingertips teasing and taunting as they danced back up his abs, then over his chest and biceps.

His muscles flexed involuntarily underneath her touch. Otherwise, he stayed still and let her scent wrap itself around him as she continued her perusal. The heat of her eyes on him warmed his skin, and the soft caress of her fingers trailing down his spine gave him chills. Her other hand brushed over his ass, and even though the touch was feather-light through his jeans, he was burned by it.

He closed his eyes in surrender when she placed an open-mouthed kiss directly between his shoulder blades and, God help him, he shivered. She continued to walk around, dragging her fingertips across his hip. Shane sucked in a breath at the light touch across his skin. When Emma stood in front of him again, she looked up into his eyes and, with a wicked smile, slid to her knees.

"Emma, you don't need..." He trailed off when her lips wrapped around the head of his cock. With her eyes on his, she moved down his erection and he'd never seen anything more beautiful. Reminding himself to breathe, he fisted a handful of all that gorgeous hair he loved while she worked him over with her sultry mouth. "Son of a bitch, Emma. You will be my undoing."

The howling of the wind outside mimicked the howling desire that coursed through him. The world fell away when she looked at him, her eyes darkened to a deep brown with lust. As much as he enjoyed her mouth on his cock, when he came, he wanted to be inside her. With herculean effort, he gently tugged on her hair until she pulled away.

"Come here." He said, his voice low and husky.

She stood and her arms came up around his neck and her hands tangled in the hair at the nape of his neck. She stood up on her tiptoes and pressed her body up against him, her warmth setting him on fire. His hands gripped her hips, but he moved them no further. This was still her show after all, and she was in control. Her lips came within a breath from his and her eyes roamed his face before settling on his mouth. "Shane, there's something I want you to know."

"What's that?" he asked, his voice rough.

"I'm on the pill." It took a moment for his sex-hazed brain to kick in, but he caught her meaning, and he nearly finished before he began.

"You're the only woman I've been with since my last physical."

The smile that curved her lips stopped his heart. "Touch me. Please." Her voice was a whisper and a plea, both wrapped in seduction.

It was all he needed to hear.

He wanted to drag her down to the floor, tear off the last scrap of fabric covering her with his teeth, and finally slake the all-consuming lust he had for her. But for all the caveman proclivities that played out in his head, he couldn't bring himself to follow through. Instead, he slowly, achingly moved his hands down and palmed her ass.

Her skin was warm and her nipples were pebbled hard against his chest. Emma purred under his hands while his lips brushed over hers, driving them both crazy. Shane hooked a hand behind her thigh, lifting her leg up over his hip. When he lifted her off her feet, she wrapped her long legs around his waist, causing him to harden further and push up against her core, which was right in line with his erection.

Their eyes held as he walked them over to the sofa. He sat down with her in his lap, where she lifted up and kneeled over him, one finger hooked into the side of her panties. "Care to help me get rid of these?" Her voice was smooth, seductive, and designed to make him beg.

"Yes, please." Shane gathered a handful of lace and yanked. "I'll gladly buy you some new ones." The tearing sound mixed with her soft moan sent another wave of lust through him and he tossed the destroyed scrap of fabric to the floor. Emma shifted to straddle him, grinding her core against him. A thrill shot through Shane knowing that she wanted it as much as he did.

"Your turn." She tugged at his jeans and he lifted his hips just enough for the denim to get past his hips. Shane couldn't wait much longer to touch her silky skin again.

His hands slid up into her hair and his fingers tightened gently against her scalp. "I'm going to kiss you now."

"Yes, plea—" Before Emma could finish her sentence, Shane brought her head down, crashing their mouths together. Her mouth opened for him immediately and he wasted no time devouring her. Their tongues slid together in a dance made for lovers since the beginning of time.

Shane slanted his head, deepening the kiss. The word *mine* flashed in his brain over and over, and the animalistic need for her clawed at his throat. There was a roar in his ears and breathing became a concerted effort. But as much as he wanted to possess her, he wanted to take his time.

Her hands alternated between curling into fists on his chest, searching for purchase, and lying flat against his pecs. Emma moaned into his mouth, becoming more and more restless. When they finally came up for air, they panted as though they were drowning. And in a way, he was. He was drowning in a sea of Emma with no life preserver. She continued to hold his gaze, her eyes a storm of emotions. Lust swirled with need and other emotions that he couldn't read.

His chest tightened with all the emotions she brought out in him. He wanted to put them to words, but something stopped him. Before he could think, Emma shifted again and sank down on his cock, enveloping him in all her sweet heat.

They moaned in unison at the connection. He brought his hands up to her hips and anchored her to him. He was deeper inside of her than he ever had been, and the intensity of it was unlike anything he'd ever experienced with any other woman.

She lifted up again and sank back down, adding a little hip movement that made his head fall back on the sofa and his eyes cross. Every time she enveloped him, she brought him closer to the brink of insanity.

"Son of a bitch, Emma. You slay me."

So far, nothing with Emma had been like anything he'd ever experienced. The void in his soul was filled when he was with her. She made him complete.

Other than small moans and groans, Emma never said a word. She let her body and her eyes do all the talking. He followed suit and simply let her move over his body, her pace picking up speed. Shane caught one of her swaying breasts in his mouth, clasping it on her nipple and sucking hard. Emma cried out and increased her pace, her nails digging into his scalp as she held his head against her chest. He lifted his hips up to meet hers when she came down, the friction between them almost too much to bear. Before long, tingling started at the base of his spine at the same time her inner core muscles began to tighten around his cock.

"Shane," Emma panted out.

"Right there with you, baby," he ground out, an instant before he held her hips against his and exploded inside of her. An animalistic roar broke free from his chest and mingled with her shouts of his name.

She dropped her forehead to his shoulder, her breath still coming in pants. He ran a hand up and down her curved spine, trying to catch his own breath, even though he was still inside her.

"Are you okay?"

She nodded against his shoulder before raising her head and smiling at him. With her Cheshire-cat grin, sexy tousled hair, and flushed skin, Shane's gut took a hard hit and his heart rate increased.

"I'm perfect." Her voice was a husky whisper and her words slow. "You?"

"Never been happier to lose at a hand of poker."

She chuckled and laid her head back on his shoulder. "I'd say we both won that one."

Shane didn't answer, just continued to stroke the soft skin of her back. His gut twisted like a corkscrew. He may have won on the sex front, but after today, that was the only place he would come out a winner when it came to Emma.

Because the one thing he guarded like Fort Knox was already lost.

His heart.

TWENTY

I'm Not For Sale

WINTER CAME BACK with a vengeance and settled in deep as the days moved into February. The good news was there hadn't been any more snow or rain, so the ground stayed dry. The bad news was, Old Man Winter had Madison Ridge and the North Georgia Mountains firmly in his grasp.

In spite of the cold, renovations on the winery were moving right along, and Emma was excited to see it all come together. The largest of the tasting rooms would be complete by the end of the next week. The kitchen and restaurant area were awaiting the final touches once all the other construction was complete.

"Noah, it's beautiful." She stood next to her cousin, looking over the large area that would soon be filled with tables for diners to sit and enjoy a meal from the chef she was trying to lure from Atlanta.

Noah gave her a rare, genuine smile. "It did turn out better than even I anticipated."

She nudged him with an elbow. "Yeah, it's good even for you."

"Ha-ha. Everyone's a comedian. You should take that show on the road, Emma," Noah replied dryly. He glanced around. "I take it Shane isn't here. I haven't seen him for the last couple of weeks."

"He's in California right now." Emma hedged around the truth, even though Noah would never say anything to anyone if she asked him not to. But it wasn't her place to tell Noah anything. And this was business. Right now, she wasn't Emma Reynolds, cousin to Noah Reynolds. She was Emma Reynolds, customer to Reynolds Construction and Renovations.

Noah made a noncommittal sound. "I'm looking forward to meeting with him to review what we've done. Make sure he's happy with it. Do you know when he'll be back in town?"

"Lindsey will know when he'll be back for sure."

Noah raised a brow. "You don't know?"

Emma leveled him with a stare that had him holding up his hands in surrender. After the last time she and Shane had been together, where he told her all about Marlene and they'd played strip poker—and didn't the memories of *that* just put a flush on her skin—there had been a shift between them. Shane was not completely closed-off but he also didn't banter with her like before.

And alone time? They hadn't been alone together since their rainy weekend spent in his cabin, unless it was at work—a place they agreed was strictly off limits.

"Emma?" Noah's voice pulled her back to the present.

"What? I'm sorry, what were you saying?"

"I said, I'm headed out. Talk later?"

She nodded. "Sure."

Noah eyed her with a strange look. "Are you okay?" he asked.

She nodded—it was all she could seem to do—and gave him an over-bright smile. "Yeah, I'm fine." Her cell phone chimed in her pocket and she pulled it out, the now-familiar Atlanta number on the screen. She frowned. This broker guy was starting to piss her off. Emma figured if she never called him back, he'd get the picture. But enough was enough. "I need to take this. See ya later."

She answered as she walked up the staircase toward her office and away from the sounds of construction. "Emma Reynolds."

"Ms. Reynolds? It's Tim Ford. How are you today?"

Emma bit her lip to keep her professionalism in check. "I'm fine, Mr. Ford. But I'm still not selling."

"I have a buyer who's very interested in your property," he said as though he hadn't heard her response.

Emma made it to her office and shut the door behind her, leaning her back against it. "Wait a minute. I was around a lot of construction noise just now. But I could swear you just told me that there is someone who wants to buy my house."

"Yes, ma'am. That's exactly what I said. They're willing to make a very generous offer and want to close within thirty days." There were a couple of taps of a keyboard from his end. "Oh yes, and the best part is they want to buy it as-is. No repairs needed."

Emma crossed to her desk and dropped heavy into her chair. "Hold on." She rubbed her temple with her free hand. She'd either lost her ever-loving mind, someone was punking her, or she'd fallen into the Twilight Zone.

There was no other explanation.

"How does the buyer know what my place even looks like? It isn't for sale, so I know whoever this buyer is hasn't seen it."

"The information was passed along to me by a broker from one of our offices on the West Coast. Hold on, let me see what I can find."

This was getting stranger by the minute. An out-of-state buyer wanted her house, sight unseen?

"I don't need to know because I'm not selling."

"Don't you think you should know all of the information before you say no?" He rattled off the offer the buyer was making before she could tell him to shove his information up his ass. The number he threw out there made Emma's jaw drop, and she almost fell out of her chair.

"I'm sorry, can you repeat that?"

He did, and her heart raced again. It was enough to pay off the house, the land, and replenish the savings she'd drained to pay off the old debts her parents left behind. She wouldn't have to sell any more of her art.

But while all of that was the easy way to do it, it wasn't what she wanted. Emma wanted to keep the house that her parents had left in the trust they'd set up for her years ago. She wanted to resurrect the B&B that had once thrived, and people had enjoyed. The area was becoming more and more of a destination for tourists. It was a great time to get back into the game.

Emma couldn't go back to the lifestyle she had before. It would kill her. Literally. More to the point, she didn't *want* to go back to that life. She loved being back in Madison Ridge and in the home she had memories in. It was something she wanted to share with others. Maybe she could even talk with Shane about discount tours with the winery.

Tim cleared his throat and brought her back to the conversation at hand. "Look, Ms. Reynolds. I can tell you that it is a legitimate offer, if that's what you're worried about. I can tell you who the buyer is if you'd like. I also know that there are some issues concerning the mortgage. Correct?"

Anger surged in Emma, but she kept a tight rein on it. "The house is not for sale," she responded through gritted teeth.

The man sighed. "All I'm saying is that for the area and the property, the offer is above fair market value. Way above. And they aren't even asking for repairs."

"What part of 'no' did you not understand? The house is not for sale." She spoke slowly, as if talking to a dim-witted child. "Tell your buyer thanks, but no thanks. Now, lose my number." Emma stabbed the red button to end the phone call and tossed the phone on her desk, where it clattered loudly.

When there was a knock at the door, she bit back a frustrated scream. She needed a damn minute to think. "Yes?" she said, her tone a shade too sharp. She was going to feel really bad if it was Lindsey on the other side of that door.

Noah leaned his head in. "Hey, you okay?"

"Hey," she responded. "I thought you'd left." Emma rubbed at a spot over her breastbone, the burn behind it making her feel like someone had lit a torch inside her.

"I got tied up with the electrician. But I saw you hightail it up here on the phone, and you looked pissed."

Emma sighed. "I'm not really pissed. Just frustrated and confused."

Noah walked in and closed the door behind him before leaning against it, his arms folded across his chest. "What's going on?"

"Someone wants to buy my property." Emma stood and began

pacing the floor behind her desk, hands on her hips, her head bent. As she walked back and forth, she stared down at her open-toed heels without really seeing them. When Noah stayed silent, she rushed on. "They want to buy it, sight unseen. No repairs necessary. And the offer...well the offer is ridiculous. Who buys something for that kind of money, sight unseen?"

"Well, what is it?"

He whistled long and low when she told him. "Holy shit, Emma. That's..."

"I know." She stopped pacing and stood behind her desk, facing him. "Noah, that land has been in the Reynolds family for generations. And with all the times that my dad almost gambled it away, but my parents managed to hang on to it, I'm not going to just hand it over. I don't care how much they give me."

"On the other hand, if you sell it," Noah began calmly, "you will get out from under the maintenance it takes to keep the place up and having to pay the back mortgage payments." He crossed the room and hitched a hip on the edge of her desk. "And it does mean something, Emma. It means your parents were able to save it in the nick of time. But let's be honest. They didn't save it as a legacy to the Reynolds family. They saved it to keep it going as a B&B."

He looked away from her, a shadow of emotion crossing his face before he turned back to her. "I don't want to speak ill of the dead. Plus, they were your parents. But there were some deep-seated issues between your father and the rest of the Reynolds clan. I don't pretend to know what happened decades ago. And I'm sure some of the tension died with both of our fathers. It's probably fair to say Uncle Charles and Aunt Emily aren't going to talk about it. My mother won't talk about it either."

"I'm aware of all that. But I have plans for the place. Plans for my future there. It's more than just trying to save a past, Noah." They stared at each other for a moment. She pursed her lips. "You think I should sell, don't you?"

Noah pushed off the desk and moved his shoulders in a shrug. "If I were in your shoes, hell yes. But I'm not. I can only give you the facts of what I see. The fact is, you're struggling to maintain that house, and you've spent your life's savings and then some to keep it from being taken over by the bank again. You've already sacrificed a helluva lot to keep four walls and some earth."

She sat down heavily and leaned her head against the chair back. "I'll be honest with you. The way my life was going before my accident, I was bound to lose my business eventually. As strange as it sounds, falling down the stairs was the best thing that ever happened to me, even though it nearly killed me." She paused and glanced over at him. "I can't go back to the life I had before. Madison Ridge is my home. I also know I can't work for KVN forever." Especially given the fact that she'd gone and fallen in love with the heir of the company. But she'd keep that little tidbit to herself.

Noah's brows drew down. "What does keeping the house have to do with that?"

"I'm going to reopen the B&B. Eventually."

Noah's eyes widened for a moment. "I didn't realize that's what you wanted to do. Well, you've got some mountains to climb to get there." He stood and looked down at her. "But if anyone can do it, it's you. I'll help how I can when you're ready." His eyes studied her. "What are the odds you'll get the mortgage payments in on time?"

Emma blew out a breath and glanced down at the red X's lining the boxes on her calendar. "It's not a complete long shot. But I'm sweating it."

"You know I can always—"

Emma wagged a finger at him. "No. Absolutely not. I already told you I'm not taking money from you. Now get out of here. I have work to do."

He raised his hands in surrender. "Okay, okay. I gotta go anyway." He stopped after he pulled open the door. "Just out of curiosity, who's the broker?"

"Tim Ford. Hattersley Brokers."

Noah raised his brows. "I know Tim. Good guy." Emma scoffed. "A little ambitious, I'll give you that."

"He's a pushy pain in my ass," Emma muttered.

"Hattersley is a highbrow outfit. International firm. They only list and represent the elite. Whoever is looking to buy your place is not only legit, but has some deep pockets."

"Be that as it may, I'm not interested. I didn't take a job in a winery to save my house and future just to sell it so easily."

Noah nodded. "I know." He knocked twice on her desk. "Well, I'm outta here. Talk later."

She understood where Noah was coming from. He didn't want to see her hurt again, but his judgment was colored by the family issues, as well. If his comment was any indication, he had faith, but she would be a fool to think there wasn't a part of him that figured she'd fail. He'd seen her at her worst. Hell, he was on her list of people to make amends with on step eight.

There was someone she could talk to, though. A man who the old Emma hadn't wronged, whose business acumen and judgment were sound.

She picked up her phone and brought up Shane's contact name to send him a text.

Emma: Need some business advice. Not work related. Talk later?

Her phone stayed silent long enough that she put it down and shook the mouse to wake up her computer. A few minutes later, the gray bouncy balls popped up on the text screen.

Shane: I'll call you later this afternoon.

Emma: Thanks, talk to you later. Hope things are going well in California.

He didn't respond, and she clicked the button for the screen to go black. She blew out a breath and settled down to work. At the end of the day, she still had a job to do, and needed to focus on what was right in front of her.

Her past and future would have to wait.

TWENTY-ONE

No Good Choice

SHANE TAPPED the red button on his phone screen to disconnect the call. He dropped his chin to his chest and sighed. It was worse than he thought.

"What's the verdict, son?" Alan asked from his bed.

Shane turned from the window and crossed the room to sit on the end of the bed. "The owner was less than receptive."

Alan had a coughing fit before leaning back on his pillows, exhausted. Shane stood, adrenaline running high, prepared to do whatever he needed to do. But it wasn't the first coughing episode he'd had today, and Shane knew there was little he could do except offer him ice water to soothe his throat when it was over. His heart twisted watching his father deal with the chemo treatments. For some reason, the latest round had hit Alan hard.

"What can I do?" Shane asked.

Alan waved his hand. "Just part of the fun." He closed his eyes, and once he caught his breath, opened them and looked over at Shane. "We need to capitalize on Madison Ridge. It's an emerging area for tourism. They've had several write-ups in prominent magazines lately. That land is a huge part of our plan to keep Colin from selling off the company."

Shane's gut twisted. "I know."

Alan sighed. "I tried talking to him, to figure out why he wanted to tear the company apart." He paused and leaned his head back. "He's still never said why. Just gave me reasons why he should take over." He folded his hands in his lap. "Okay, so what do we know? Have you reached out to the owner personally?"

Shane rubbed the back of his neck. How did he tell his dad that he'd already met the owner personally? Extremely personally?

"I've already met the owner. Several times actually." Shane shifted in the chair, and the hair on the back of his neck stood up when Alan studied him. Chemo might be ravaging his body, but Alan's blue eyes were clear.

"Really? How? Did you already speak to him about the property?"

Shane cleared his throat. "Well, the owner is female. And no, I haven't talked to her about the property, though I have had a couple of up close and personal views of the house and land." And the owner, but he kept that to himself. "Anyway, the trustee of the property is Emma Reynolds."

Alan's eyes widened, and a hand fisted the sheet. "Emma, as in the Emma that works for us?"

"One and the same." For a moment, Shane wished the deal would fall through. Emma was everything he wished for in a woman and had never found, even with Marlene. She was strong, smart, independent. Perfect, as far as he was concerned. In the pit of his stomach, he knew the land deal could put everything he'd had with her in jeopardy.

Professionally, he would lose a fantastic employee. One he trusted, which was hard to come by these days.

As Shane looked at his father, seeing the weariness in his body, he knew that everything lay on the line for the company.

Shit, what a mess.

"Well, that does make it more complicated. But not impossible." Alan gave Shane a hard stare. "Present it to her as a business deal. We have some wiggle room to sweeten the pot a bit more."

Shane nodded and ran a hand through his hair. "I'll set up a meeting with her." He stood and glanced at his watch. "Are you hungry? Abe said lunch would be ready soon."

Alan shook his head. "Not right now. I would like some coffee though."

Shane called Abe, and when the older man brought in a serving cart with coffee, Shane's phone pinged with a text.

Emma: Need some advice. Not work related. Talk later?

He frowned. Could his situation get any worse? With a sigh, he tapped out a response.

Shane: I'll call you later this afternoon.

The gray balls bounced before her message appeared.

Emma: Thanks, talk to you later. Hope things are going well in California.

He slid the phone in his pocket and pushed all business aside while he had lunch with his father. Studying his father's movements, Shane had a gnawing fear in his gut. He wanted to stick around longer with Alan, but he also knew one of the best things he could do for his father was to keep business going. It would be one less thing for the elder Kavanaugh to worry over. Shane figured fighting for one's life was stress enough.

After lunch, Alan was exhausted, and Shane had a plane to catch back to Georgia. On the ride to the airport, his broker called.

"Shane, it's James. I've got some news for you on the property in Madison Ridge." Why did the man sound like he'd just landed the winning lottery numbers?

"I heard from Tim already. She turned him down flat."

"Well, she may not have a choice. My guess is that she hasn't received the notice from the bank yet today." James paused. "The bank is set to move forward with foreclosure proceedings."

Shane's stomach dropped. He should be ecstatic that KVN had virtually just been handed the property, and for a price much lower than they'd originally intended to pay. Instead, it just left him cold and feeling like a shit.

"Well, that's…unexpected," Shane said slowly.

"You don't sound as thrilled as I thought you would, Shane. Has there been a change in plans?" James sounded a bit perturbed at the thought of things changing without his knowledge. Shane normally liked James, but at this moment, he wanted to tell James to go fuck himself.

But that wouldn't go over very well, would it? Especially since no one knew about the fact that he was sleeping with the owner of the property.

He closed his eyes and pinched the bridge of his nose but schooled his voice with the appropriate enthusiasm. "The news just caught me off guard after the call I received from Tim a little while ago."

"Well," James's voice was laced with barely suppressed glee. "Are we moving forward?"

His chest ached and his stomach was slick with unease. Why was it so fucking hot in the car?

"Shane? Are you still there?"

"Just give me a minute," Shane snapped, wiping a sweaty palm on his pants leg. "I need to think."

James huffed. "What's to think about? This is what you wanted. What's the problem?"

Shane mentally counted to ten to keep the anger in his chest from unleashing. "James. I can't think with you talking in my ear." He glanced out the window to see them pull up to the hangar. "Look, I'm about to board the plane. Let me call you when I land."

"Shane, we need to move—"

"And we will, James. Just hang tight." It was all Shane could do to keep from telling James to fuck off. But he just couldn't do it.

James's disappointment and frustration came through loud and clear when he sighed. "Fine. Call me later."

For the next five hours on the plane ride back, Shane tried to sleep, but his mind was a tangled mess of worrying about his father and the situation with Emma, both professionally and personally. Although he was certain that once she found out about the bank and her own employer trying to buy her house against her wishes, there would be no more personal.

When he landed, he was relieved to find Emma hadn't surprised him again to drive him home. The woman was sharp and observant. She saw things that he didn't think anyone else did, even when he didn't want her to. He wanted to see her, he ached from missing her, but he needed to call James. And effectively put an end to whatever it was he and Emma had.

Shane sat in his truck, leather cold under his ass, and called James. As the line rang in his ear, his stomach churned and his chest tightened to aching. He blew out a breath to keep the nausea at bay.

"Shane, good to hear from you," James said when he answered. "Are we moving forward?"

Were they moving forward?

Shane already knew the answer, even if it made him feel like he'd found the ninth circle of Hell. "Yes. Get the paperwork started."

"Great, I'll have the agreement to you Monday morning. Congratulations, Shane."

"Yeah, thanks." Shane hung up and tossed the phone on the seat beside him.

He needed a drink. It had been a while since he'd thrown back some liquor. Going back to his big, empty cabin where the sheets smelled of Emma and all the sexy, naughty things they'd done there didn't appeal to him. Driving through the downtown square of Madison Ridge, he noticed several cars parked in front of a building with a sign touting the Silver Moon Café. He made a quick right-hand turn into an open space just down from the front door.

The chalkboard sign in front of the door announced they had the coldest beer and hottest nachos in town. It was a charming little place made of whitewashed clapboard, with an upstairs patio he was sure had plenty of activity in the spring and summer. The muted sound of country music filtered out to the sidewalk.

Once inside, the noise level increased several notches, and the smell of beer and fried foods wafted through the air. Groups of people gathered around various tables, laughing and talking, letting off steam from the week. Shane made his way to the bar through the throng, finding an unoccupied stool. One of the bartenders, dressed in a black button-down, jeans, and a smile that Shane bet earned the guy a shit ton of tips, placed a drink napkin in front of him. "Evening. What can I get ya?"

"Got any Glenfiddich?"

The bartender smiled. "We do, actually."

"Great. A double. Neat, please."

"You got it."

The man pulled out a whiskey glass before walking to the other end of the long bar that had seen better days.

As his server poured a whiskey neat and deftly fielded calls from less patient patrons and barmaids, Shane was impressed with his style. He was charismatic, good-looking, and moved like someone with years of experience. He also looked vaguely familiar.

Whether or not he knew the dark-haired man, the winery was still staffing the bar in the restaurant and needed a strong leader who knew what he was doing.

A few moments later, a tumbler with three fingers of amber colored whiskey, neat, slid in front of him. The color reminded him of a pair of eyes he knew would haunt him for the rest of his life.

"Can I get you anything else?"

Shane slid a business card across the bar. "I'm staffing my new winery nearby, and I like how you work. If you're interested in some-thing different, give me a call."

The guy looked down at the card, and a smile spread across his lips before his gaze met Shane's. "So, you're the Shane Kavanaugh I've heard so much about. Wyatt Davis. Nice to finally meet you." He stuck out his hand and Shane shook it. Strong and competent handshake. Good sign.

"How'd you hear about me?"

Wyatt chuckled and crossed his arms over his chest. A black line of ink peeked out from his shirt. "Well, first of all, this is a small town. We might get a lot of tourists, but we know when there's a new resident. And this isn't my only gig. I work with Reynolds Construction. Did some work over at the winery a couple of times."

Shane narrowed his eyes. "I thought you looked familiar. You handled the stonework, didn't you?"

Wyatt nodded. "Yep. Well, once Emma handled the stone debacle."

Shane's gut tightened thinking of Emma and the shitty situation he found himself in. He shoved the thought aside and raised a brow. "You did an amazing job."

"Thanks. It was a fun project. Intricate, but I enjoy a challenge."

Wyatt Davis seemed like just the kind of guy Shane would like on his team. Enjoyed a challenge, got the job done, and done well. Noah Reynolds trusted him, and from what Shane had learned, that was saying something.

Shane picked up his glass and gestured with it to Wyatt. "Well, maybe working as a bartender for me isn't what you'd want to do, but maybe we can work together on another project sometime."

"Absolutely." Wyatt pulled out his wallet. "Here's my card. I work with Noah a lot, but I'm independent. Just let me know."

Shane sipped the whiskey and studied Wyatt's card. Clean, professional, and straight to the point. He decided right there that he liked the guy.

"Wyatt! Come here!"

"Yeah, come see us! We miss you!"

The two of them glanced toward where the slurred, feminine voices came from to see young blonde twins, mirror images of each other leaning halfway over the bar, their boobs barely contained in their sweaters. They gestured wildly trying to get Wyatt's attention.

Shane chuckled. "Fan club?"

The other man rolled his eyes and sighed. "Part of the gig." He nodded his head at the centerfold-worthy twins and gave them a smile that made the girls visibly swoon. "Hey, sweethearts. I'll be right there, okay?"

Shane smirked. "Just part of the gig, huh?"

Wyatt turned his head and grinned. "I don't kiss and tell."

Shane laughed and sipped his drink.

"Need anything else right now?" Wyatt asked.

Shane shook his head. "I'm good."

Wyatt strolled down to the other end of the bar, the girls nearly vaulting over the bar to hug him. Shane chuckled while Wyatt untangled himself from tanned arms wrapping around him.

No doubt Wyatt was a ladies' man. Shane figured the guy rarely had a cold bed.

Thinking of bed made him think of Emma, and the image of his gorgeous woman invaded his brain, and he missed her so bad he ached. But they both needed some space, he was sure of it. He couldn't avoid her forever, so he'd have to figure out how to act the next time he saw her.

But for the moment, he just needed to breathe and take a minute. Even if it was in the middle of a crowded bar.

Shane focused on the television screen hanging over the bar, idly watching sports highlights, sipping more whiskey. It hit his belly, and a satisfying warmth spread through him.

"You must be Shane Kavanaugh." A feminine voice drifted to him from his left. He turned to find a red-haired woman perched on the stool next to him. She was a tiny sprite of a woman, overly made up and overdressed for the establishment. Without all the makeup, Shane figured she was about his age, midthirties, but with all the caked-on colors, she looked older. She might have been pretty once, but she looked like life hadn't thrown her too many bones, and bitterness seeped into the lines of her face.

"You'd be right. I don't think we've met."

Her lips pulled into a smile that revealed two rows of perfect, stark-white teeth, as fake as the breasts her tight sweater barely covered. She held out a hand and pushed the mounds of silicone out. "Tara Moore."

He shook her hand so that he wouldn't appear rude. "Nice to meet you, Tara. What are you drinking? I'll have Wyatt refill it for you."

She giggled and put a hand over her bosom. "So handsome and a gentleman to boot. Vodka tonic, please."

Shane signaled Wyatt, who'd managed to fend off the twins and move them along. "Add a vodka tonic to my bill for Ms. Moore, here."

Wyatt narrowed his eyes at Tara with a frown. She gave him the same look back. "Leave me alone, Wyatt. I'm fine."

"Oh, I'm sure you are, cousin." Wyatt turned away and started preparing her drink.

"Sorry about that. Wyatt's my cousin and likes to protect me."

Wyatt set her drink in front of her with a hard click. "More like trying to protect others." He turned his gaze to Shane. "Whatever she says, take it with a grain of salt."

As Wyatt turned away to take another order, she sent him a death stare before smoothing out her features and turning back to Shane.

Tara gave him a once-over and licked her slick, cotton candy-colored lips. "So," she started, "you're renovating that new winery in town, aren't you?"

Shane nodded. "Yes, ma'am." Her eyes narrowed, and her smile faltered for a moment but then reappeared, twice as bright.

"That's just fabulous. You know, I read about your company. It's an honor to have someone of your caliber here in our little mountain town."

"I like this little mountain town. It has a lot to offer in terms of wine and other things." His thoughts drifted to Emma and everything she'd shown him he'd been missing.

"Yes, I suppose." Tara laid a manicured hand on Shane's forearm. "I've heard you're working with some of the Reynolds clan. Noah's a good man, but that Amelia can be a bit...forward at times. And Emma?" She rolled her eyes and placed a hand over her heart again. "It's just terrible about her. Frankly, I can't believe she's working in your winery, with her problem and all." She clucked her tongue on the roof of her mouth. "Those Reynoldses have a rep to uphold."

He smiled slightly, trying to keep her talking, but a cold feeling of dread started in his belly. "I'm not sure I follow you."

Tara leaned forward, the tips of her fake boobs brushing his arm. He shifted his arm away from her under the guise of listening intently. "The whole town knows about it. She's a drunk. Well, not anymore. Not since that drunken fall down the stairs that landed her in a coma. She went to rehab. She's been sober since."

Bitterness set in the lines on her face and filled her dark brown eyes. "Or so those Reynoldses say, anyway. I think they're covering for her just like they did for her daddy's gambling addiction." She sighed and picked up the fresh drink Wyatt had placed in front of her. "I guess the apple doesn't fall too far from the tree."

Shane's brain stuttered to a stop. Emma was an alcoholic? That couldn't be right. He focused in on the woman in front of him, who was sipping on the straw in her drink in a way that Shane figured someone must have told her was sexy once, but just made her look desperate. He recalled her tone when talking about Emma and her family. Bad blood and gossipmongering colored her words.

Still, wasn't there always a kernel of truth in a rumor? Fear, dread, and the all-around "what the fuck?" feeling raced through his veins. His throat constricted, making it hard for him to draw a full breath. His clothes felt a size too small, and there was pain in every nerve of his body. So many thoughts swirled in his mind, he couldn't keep them straight. All he knew was that he needed to get out of there.

Sending Tara a smile, he rose and tossed a few bills on the battered bar to cover his tab. "Gotta run, but it was nice talking to you, Tara."

She sputtered, but he walked off before she could form a coherent sentence. He needed to talk to Emma. All he wanted to do was find out if everything the over-made, bitter, town gossip had said about the woman he had come to trust with his business and, more importantly, his heart, was true.

If it was, he wasn't sure he'd be able to handle the betrayal.

TWENTY-TWO

Tell Me Sweet Little Lies

EMMA STARED at the letter in her shaking hands, her head light.

The bank was going to start foreclosure proceedings. What the hell had happened to the forty-five days she had worked out? How were they able to just change their minds? And did they send these letters on Fridays on purpose?

She knew the answers. It came down to the almighty dollar. And now she would have to wait the whole weekend to find out if she had any recourse. Not that she had all the money yet, but she would. However, it required more time than she had.

To add insult to injury, her art broker informed her that the painting she needed to sell hadn't sold at the last auction. The next auction wouldn't be for another three months.

Emma stared out the windows of the living area and racked her brain, trying to figure out what to do. Her negotiating skills were going to get a workout come Monday.

Her mouth went dry and she swallowed hard, the familiar longing deep in her being to escape. Just one drink or one pill to make it all go away. She fisted her hands and then released them. The demons were out in full force tonight, and for the first time in the last year, Emma was scared to be alone, unsure of what she'd do to dull the pain.

She pulled her phone out of her pocket to call Amelia and then find a meeting on a Friday night. Her usual one met on Thursdays and Saturdays. Emma wasn't sure she could wait until the next day and that scared the shit out of her. Before she could hit send, the doorbell rang. The tension in the muscles of Emma's shoulders released as she walked into the foyer. At this point, she'd invite in a drifter just so she didn't have to be alone.

When Emma opened the door, her heart soared at the sight of Shane. In spite of herself, a slow burn started in her belly. "Hey. I wasn't expecting to see you." She grinned at him, absurdly happy to see him. He returned her smile, but it didn't quite reach his eyes, putting Emma on alert. "Is everything okay with your dad?"

"Yeah, he's fine. For now."

She furrowed a brow at his clipped tone. His hands were tucked into the pockets of his jeans and he made no moves to touch her. Something wasn't right.

Emma stepped aside to let him in. "Want to come in?"

He stared down at her before nodding. "Yeah, we need to talk," he said, his voice flat.

"Okay." Dread settled in the pit of her stomach as he stepped over the threshold.

"When did you get back to town?" she asked, shutting the door.

"Earlier tonight."

In the back of her mind, alarms were sounding. Something was off. "You never called me back." Shit, her voice sounded petulant even to her own ears.

Lifting his eyes to hers, those blue eyes were cold and emotionless when he looked at her. "Things were a little crazy."

No apology, no emotion. His mouth was set in a hard line, and his eyes lacked the desire she'd come to recognize.

This man was the Shane she'd first met. The cold, hard one who kept her at arm's length. He was a stranger.

"Can I get you some coffee?" Emma crossed to where the coffeemaker sat.

He crossed his arms and leaned a hip against the counter next to her. "Got anything stronger?"

She shook her head and glanced over at him. "No, I'm sorry I don't."

"Nothing at all? No beer, whiskey, scotch?"

She dumped the coffee into the filter and turned to him. "No. Nothing at all." She mimicked his stance. "What's this about, Shane?"

"It's about you lying to me."

Her mind raced and she swallowed. "When did I lie to you?" she asked, choosing her words with care.

"Do you know Tara Moore?" Shane countered.

Shit, this was not what she needed tonight. Emma blinked and shook her head slightly, trying to figure out why he would ask her about the town's biggest gossip queen whose family hated her family going back decades.

"Yeah, I know Tara. She doesn't like me very much." Tilting her head, she studied him with one brow raised. "How do *you* know Tara?"

The stare he leveled at her was icy. "Tara and I had a nice chat at the Silver Moon Café a little while ago." Emma would've been burning with jealousy if she didn't know Shane better.

"Really? So, what does Tara have to do with me lying to you?" *Oh my God.* As the realization hit, her lips parted and her stomach began to roll, leaving her nauseous.

Tara knew about her past. Those in town who knew about her and her family's troubles had enough class not to go around spreading her business. Except for anyone with the last name Moore. Some long-ago spat between the two families had grown into a long-simmering dislike between them. But hell if Emma knew the reason for it all. It didn't matter why. All she knew was that Tara knew the one piece of business about her that could detrimentally alter Emma's future.

This time, it was Shane who studied Emma. "I'd say by the look on your face you know exactly what I'm talking about. Our whole relationship was, and is, a lie." He advanced on her, and now his eyes burned bright with anger. "I confided in you about Marlene. Told you about how she was an addict and how that fucked me up for a while. And you never said a word. You never said you were just like Marlene. An addict."

Terror tightened her chest to the point of pain. She vainly tried to rub it away. She swallowed hard before she could speak. Tears threatened to fall but she blinked them back. "You're right. I should have told you." He growled and turned away, pushing a hand through his hair. "But I was scared. I was scared of what I felt for you when I knew what we had was short-term. And I was scared you'd never hire me. And I needed the job in the worst way. I still do."

He paced the width of the kitchen, one hand on his hip, the other rubbing the back of his neck. Stopping, he pinned her with a look. "Were you ever going to tell me? As your employer, were you going to tell me? Especially working for a company that produces alcohol. I mean, legally you don't have to tell me. But morally, Emma? Do you know how much of a liability that could be?"

She bit her lip and closed her eyes. "I thought of that. But Shane, I've been sober for two years." She blew out a breath and crossed the room to the table, her hands shaking with desperation. "Can you please sit and give me a chance to explain?" she asked, her voice strangled.

He let out a humorless laugh. "Oh, you've 'told' me plenty already. What I want is the truth."

"What I told you before was the truth. I just didn't mention everything."

"So, it was your version of the truth, huh?" His voice was laced with a venom she'd never heard from him before.

Desperation clawed at her throat and this time, she couldn't stop the tears from blurring her vision. "Shane, please. I'll tell you everything. Whatever you want to know."

He relented and jerked out a chair before sitting down. He crossed his arms again, effectively shutting her out. "Fine. Go ahead. Explain away, Emmaline."

She sat down next to him and clasped her hands on the table. A couple of breaths steadied her. "The night I signed away my professional life, I drank myself into oblivion. I went out with some friends under the guise of a celebration that I had made millions that day. It wasn't what I wanted, though, and I was distraught. But I saw no other way to help my mother out of debt." The tears she'd held back since she'd opened the bank letter finally rolled down her cheeks, but her voice stayed steady. "My friends drove me home and that's the last I remember. Noah found me the next morning at the bottom of the stairs in my house. I was barely breathing and busted up pretty good."

Shane cursed under his breath and shifted in his chair, but she continued. "When I woke from my coma three weeks later, they told me they had to pump my stomach. In addition to the alcohol, I had a high concentration of painkillers in my bloodstream from where I popped several Vicodin through the night." She looked down at her hands that were clenched into fists, her knuckles white. Emma forced them to open. "I didn't try to kill myself. I didn't want to die. I couldn't do that to my family. In my soul I knew I'd done enough damage to them, I couldn't add suicide to my list of sins. I just..." She paused to swallow the knot in her throat. "It wasn't the first time I'd been wasted and high on pills. But I was careless."

She wiped away the tears. "Anyway, once I came out of the coma and could be moved, my family sent me to rehab. It was the only choice I had to avoid losing my family. This was my last resort."

She looked up at him and his eyes were unreadable. His shoulders were tight and he was as still as a statue. But the coldness that had been in his eyes before gave way to something else she couldn't decipher.

"I was devastated to lose her before I could show her I was truly better." She blinked back the fresh tears in her eyes. "After she passed, I found out she had no life insurance because she had to cash it in to pay off my father's gambling debts. And she had debt from the B&B so the only money left was mine from the sale of my business. That went quick, dwindling away with the mountain of medical bills. All I had left was this house and the land. And my sobriety."

Emma looked him in the eye and moved closer to him. She needed to make him understand, even if her best intentions fell short. She reached for his hands, and when he didn't pull away, she held them in hers. They were strong and capable, kind and sensual. His wide palms and long fingers dwarfed her petite hands. She studied them and how they melded around hers.

As if made just for her.

Emma raised her head and looked Shane square in the eyes. "I'm an alcoholic, Shane. Two years ago, I found my way to true sobriety."

Shane raised a brow. "True sobriety?"

Emma nodded. "For me, that means being sober and actually *wanting* to be sober. Not the kind of sober where I don't drink, but wish I were, and being so miserable because I'm not drinking. I had long periods of that kind of sobriety. But it wasn't real." She looked away, out into the backyard, where the darkness was relieved by a full moon. "It was always for something else or someone else."

"As though you were living life on someone else's agenda?"

She turned her gaze back to his, nodding her head slowly. "Exactly. I had to find my own way, when I was ready." She rolled her lips inward to ward off more tears, and was only slightly successful. "I know I should have said something to you, especially after you told me about Marlene and all that you went through with her. I'm so very sorry that you had to deal with that, and that she lost her fight with her demons." Emma squeezed his hand. "I fight mine tooth and nail every day. And I win. And I plan to win every day for the rest of my life, even if I have to do it alone."

"What about the rest of your family?" he asked gruffly.

She brushed away more tears. "Yeah, I have them, too. Please understand. I didn't keep my situation from you to hurt you or create problems professionally." She gave him a soft smile, and his posture relaxed slightly. "You are a surprise to me, Shane Kavanaugh. An exception to all my rules. You trouble me because I didn't expect you to be so important. You mean more to me than just mind-blowing sex."

One side of his mouth quirked in a half smile, causing her heart to lift in hope that they could get past this.

"But I didn't know that at first. I just didn't see the need to tell you something like that unless it was serious. But then you told me about Marlene, and I panicked. I screwed up, and I'm sorry you had to find out the way you did."

Shane stared down at their joined hands, his thumb drawing light circles on the back of her hand. "You're a surprise to me too, Emma." He raised his eyes and her stomach plummeted when the look in them wasn't one of reconciliation. In fact, he looked downright miserable. The roiling in her gut heightened when he pulled his hands away.

Please, God, don't let this be the end.

He blew out a breath. "I have something I need to tell you."

She nodded, her mouth dry. "Okay."

Her gut twisted as her gaze lingered over his face. The longer he stayed silent, the more pained his expression became. Emma squeezed his hand again. "Whatever it is, you can tell me, Shane."

He held her stare and let out a breath. "I know about the offer on your house."

Her brows lowered. "How...how do you know about that?"

"Because I'm the one who made the offer."

She held up a hand in a motion to stop as her stomach pitched. "Wait, hold on." She leaned forward. "What do you mean, you made the offer?"

He released her hand and leaned back on the ladder-back chair. "The broker who called you yesterday was contacted by my broker, or rather KVN's broker. The company has been looking for a property in the area to expand the winery. More lodging, horseback riding, a full-fledged wine experience. Your property is perfect," Shane said, flatly. Even though he had the grace to look thoroughly conflicted about the situation, she grasped at what he was saying. The world spun around her and her lungs refused to take in air.

"I don't understand, Shane." Her mind refused to believe that the man in front of her, the one she'd come to love and trust, would betray her in such a personal way. Her heart hammered hard against her chest.

"We were made aware of the financial problems the owner was having and decided to move forward with an offer. But Emma, I didn't realize you were the trustee who owned the house until it was too late. Things progressed quickly between us. And so did the land deal. I had a choice to make."

It was all she could do not to be sick. "KVN is trying to buy my house? The house I live in?"

Shane opened his mouth to say something, but seemed to think better of it and just nodded his head instead. She pulled in a shuddering breath. "When did you know the house belonged to me?" When he didn't answer, the tears fell faster and anger built in her chest. "Shane, when did you know I was the owner? Please, tell me it was after we slept together."

"Emma." His voice was quiet and he wouldn't meet her gaze.

"When, Shane?" Emma asked but when he looked at her, the answer was clear.

"It was before we slept together." His voice was low and anguished.

Emma's head snapped back as if he'd slapped her. She rose slowly and wrapped her arms around her middle, unable to look at him. When she turned back to him, her back was against the counter. Much like her whole situation with him. "Shane, do you understand the only reason I went after the job at KVN was to keep this place? To make my amends?"

He rose and came to stand in front of her. "I know, Emma. But if the company buys it, you can downsize, and you wouldn't have to worry so much about the upkeep. It would be a really great thing."

She straightened her spine. "For you, it will be a really great thing. But what about me? I'm about to lose my childhood home, the only tangible thing I have left of my parents, and you want to stand there and tell me how great it will be that I don't have to worry about the upkeep? I won't have a fucking place to live!" The last word ended on a high note and her anger had built along with the pitch in her voice.

He rubbed the back of his neck and sighed. "No, that's not what I meant by that."

"You sat right there and questioned my judgment about being a liability to your precious company, when the only reason I took the job was to keep the one thing I have left of my life. Where the hell do you get off telling me what I should do with it or trying to buy me?"

Shane shook his head. "No, Emma. What we have is real. I didn't use you. I'm not trying to buy you. I—"

"It doesn't matter what you're trying to do. I'm not selling. Especially to you." Her voice was hard and cold, even though the blood roared in her ears.

"We both know you may have to sell it or lose it anyway, Emma."

Shane's tone was one of wary acceptance, but it only served to make her see red. The surge in her blood pressure made her head pound.

"Get out of my house." The words were said in a low tone, and Shane gave her a look as though he were confronted by a rattlesnake.

"Emma, let me explain." He moved slowly toward her, but she slapped a hand to his chest.

"No. There is no explanation here. You come into my home, pissed at me because I didn't come clean with you. And yet you're no better. I was trying to protect you. But you? You're just trying to make more money, and using me to do it." She shoved his chest hard. "Get the fuck out of my life, Shane."

Her insides quivered, but she kept her voice and the cold stare she gave him steady. His eyes narrowed on hers and his jaw bunched, helpless anger in his eyes. It didn't matter what he said now. The fact he could judge her for the addiction she worked on every day when he was using her to grow his company was a deal breaker.

After what seemed like an eternity, he walked out of the kitchen, the front door slamming a moment later. A sob escaped her chest and Emma slid to the floor. Rolling on her side, she curled up into a fetal position. She sobbed until the tears ran dry.

Dragging herself upstairs, she went to the door of her father's office. A room she hadn't set foot in since he passed away. Standing up on her toes, she reached for the key on the trim above the door. The key slid into the lock and turned easily. The room was old and dusty, drop cloths covering most of the furniture. She ignored it all and went straight to the bottom drawer of the large oak desk, pulling on the brass handle.

The drawer slid open and she lifted the brown leather photo album out of the bottom. At that moment, Emma missed her parents with a deep, gut-wrenching pain. She wanted to see their faces and go back to when things weren't so complicated. Flipping through the family album, the photos captured the times before she knew what alcohol was, before the losses, and before she ever knew a man named Shane Kavanaugh. Sliding the pictures through her hands, she cried and laughed.

After a while, she closed the thick, heavy album and turned to put it back in the drawer. Emma pulled at a picture stuck between the side and bottom of the drawer, causing the bottom to shift.

What the hell? She pushed on the wood and it lifted, revealing a false bottom. Her heart lodged in her throat when she found a glass bottle lying there. She lifted it from the drawer and set it on the desk. Eyeing the bottle of Jack Daniels, she sat down in the large leather desk chair her father had occupied so many times, curling her legs beneath her.

Jack comforted her as well as any lover. The burn as it slid down her throat, the warmth that would pool and spread in her belly when it hit the bottom. The numbness would keep the pain that permeated every cell in her body at bay.

After hitting rock bottom two years before, Emma never wanted to feel that way again.

Never say never.

TWENTY-THREE

The Surge

THE SLIDING glass doors of the Norcal Cancer Center whooshed open in time for Shane to barrel through them. He barely registered the warm air hitting his face, a stark contrast to the unusual early March cold snap that had set up camp in the Napa Valley. Dread and fear coursed through his veins as he moved across the hospital lobby.

At the bank of elevators, he pressed the button rapidly. "Damn it, what is taking so long?" He paced, waiting for the slowest elevator on planet Earth, glancing around the lobby. It looked more like the lobby of a high-end hotel than that of a hospital. Hardwoods gleamed and overstuffed chairs were arranged in sitting areas. It was beautiful, but cold and impersonal.

He spun around when the elevator dinged behind him. "Finafuck-inglly," he muttered.

On the ride up, Shane leaned against the wall of the elevator and pinched the bridge of his nose. Three days after Emma ended things, he was still angry and confused. Angry at himself for being such an ass, although he'd directed some of the anger at Emma for shutting him out after he'd given her the chance to explain why she lied to him about her addiction.

Somewhere over the cornfields of the Midwest, when the realization he may lose his father soon and the first person he wanted to talk to was Emma, Shane knew he was in love with her. Too little, too late. He'd tried to call a couple of times and she'd ignored him. Shane couldn't blame her. He'd fucked up nice and proper with her.

When the elevator dinged on the fifth floor, he pushed off the back wall and did his best to push Emma out of his mind. He stalked up to the nearest nurse's station. "Where's Alan Kavanaugh's room?"

"And you are?" The nurse in front of him peered over her glasses to give him a bland look.

Going to have your job if you mess with me. Instead he said, "His son, Shane."

"You can come with me, Mr. Kavanaugh."

He turned to find an older woman standing behind him. She wore a set of dark green scrubs and held a tablet in her hand. "I'm Ellie, the hospice nurse for your father." Her smile was kind and her lilting Jamaican accent was soothing. "I can take you to his room. I'm headed there myself."

Hospice nurse? What the hell? He nodded and followed Ellie down the hall.

Her shoes squeaked on the vinyl flooring as they passed several rooms, some empty, others occupied with patients in various stages of their cancer battle. His hands curled into fists as the smell of antiseptic assaulted his senses and brought back long-buried memories. Shane hadn't set foot in a hospital since Marlene's death, and before that, when his mother had died when he'd been twelve. The fact that Alan had been brought into a facility didn't bode well. A heavy feeling weighed on Shane's shoulders, and he inhaled a few deep breaths, trying to calm his nerves.

Ellie stopped in front of room 5148 and pushed open the door. "Mr. Alan, look who I found roaming the hall." The nurse crossed the room to the machines beside his father's bed.

Shane stepped into the room, expecting to find his father lying in the bed, still and pale like he'd seen in the movies. He stopped in his tracks when he found his father sitting up in bed flipping through the latest *Time* magazine.

He looked up when Shane entered the room. A big smile split his face. "Shane, you made it. I was wondering when you were coming to see me."

"Dad?" Stunned, Shane couldn't move.

"Who else would it be?" Alan motioned for Shane to sit in the chair next to his bed. "Come, sit and talk to me."

Shane's brain finally caught up with his feet and he moved toward the bed. He was trying to wrap his mind around the idea that the man in front of him seemed to be on the mend.

He took the vacant seat next to the bed and glanced at the machines. Most of the displays were foreign to him, but he did see that his father's blood pressure seemed to be good. Shane couldn't tell if the other numbers on the machines were a good or bad indicator of his father's health.

"Mr. Alan, let me get your vitals, hon." Ellie pressed a couple of buttons, and a whirring sound started.

"You look good today, Dad. Better than the last time I saw you."

The older man smiled. "I feel good today. I'm going home soon."

Shane rolled his lips inward and looked away, picking at imaginary lint on his jeans. "Did the doctors tell you that?"

"No, but I feel it. I'm going home soon."

Shane glanced up at Ellie, who continued her work without hesitation. She pursed her lips, the only indication she'd heard Alan's response.

Shane looked back at his father, studying his face. He indeed looked healthier than he had in a while, in spite of the aged hands, frail body, and tubes hooked up to him. Shane blinked rapidly, unable to reconcile what was going on.

"Where's Colin?" Shane asked. "I thought he'd be here."

"Oh, he said he had a phone call to make or something." He smiled at Shane. "I'm glad you're here, son. Fill me in. How are the renovations going? Still on schedule?"

Shane shook his head. At death's door and the man still wanted to talk business. So he indulged his father, because why the hell not?

Ellie finished Alan's vitals and left the room quietly while Shane brought him up to date on what was going on with the business in

Madison Ridge and at the other locations, carefully avoiding the topic of a certain employee and a land deal.

But leave it to his father to get down to the heart of the matter. "Heard anything more on the property?"

Shane bit back a sigh. He'd had nothing but radio silence from Emma since she kicked him out of her house. Only Lindsey had talked to her when she'd called in first thing in the morning, saying she had the flu and would be working from home all week. All of her correspondence had gone through Lindsey.

"Emma is adamant about not selling."

"Hey, Shane." Colin and a tall, lanky, gray-haired man in a white doctor's coat stood at the door.

"Both of my sons are here. It's a great day." Alan's smile lit up the room.

Colin's mouth curved into a smile that didn't reach his eyes. "Hey, Dad. I need to talk to Shane for a minute."

Alan nodded and picked up his magazine. "That's fine. But I do have more questions for you, Shane. So don't leave."

"I have no plans to leave any time soon, Dad." His eyes met his brother's, who nodded to follow him.

Shane battled with the internal monster that wanted to lash out at his brother right now. Seeing Colin was just another reminder of all that was at stake for Shane. And all that he was on the verge of losing or had already lost. The pain in his chest was nearly unbearable.

Out in the hall, Shane crossed his arms. "What's going on, Colin?"

The younger Kavanaugh shoved his hands into the front pockets of his jeans and sighed. "You remember Dr. Krist."

"I do." Shane nodded toward the doctor. "He's looking well. Seems to have bounced back."

Colin dropped his head and looked at the floor. Tension rolled off him in waves, putting Shane on alert. Next to him, Dr. Krist put his hands behind his back and sighed. "Over the last few hours it appears that your father has been experiencing what you might call a surge."

"A surge? What does that mean?"

"Some patients with terminal illnesses experience a burst of energy, a surge if you will, before they pass on. They appear to be on the mend. They sit up and engage in conversations. They become very introspective about life, that sort of thing."

It was as though someone had reached in and gutted him. If he thought the pain was unbearable before, what radiated through his body and landed in the center of his chest right now nearly brought him to his knees. He blew out a breath to combat the nausea that set up camp in his stomach. "Well, how do you know he's not just getting better?"

"We've been monitoring him closely and will continue to do so. But medically, nothing has changed."

Shane glanced over his shoulder. A smile played on Alan's lips as he flipped through the pages of the magazine. Shane turned back and narrowed his eyes at the doctor.

"No." Shane shook his head hard and his hands sliced the air. "No way. Look at him. That's not what this is. He could be improving. Right? Isn't there a chance of that?" His heart pounded against his chest in hard thumps and breathing became a colossal effort. There was no way the indomitable Alan Kavanaugh was going out on a surge.

"Shane." Dr. Krist's eyes were kind and full of apology. "Your father's treatment stopped working. His scans show the cancer has metastasized. He decided to forgo any and all other treatments. It took a tremendous toll on his body, and it didn't work. He chose not to continue. There's nothing more we can do."

Pain and desperation clawed at Shane's throat. This couldn't be happening. Not so fast. Shane narrowed his eyes at the man across from him. "Then explain to me how the hell that man can sit there, looking like he is getting better." Shane paced, his hands in his hair. "I mean, he looks like he can stand up and walk right out of here without a wheelchair."

Dr. Kris sighed. "In my forty years of medicine, I've seen what your father is experiencing once or twice. It's unusual. But each time it ends the same." He shook his head. "Unfortunately, Shane, he's not getting better."

"But—"

"Shane, stop it." Colin lifted his head. His tone was hard but heartbreak left shadows in his eyes. "Dad's doing exactly what Dr. Krist is saying. Laughing, talking about what's important in life. He's talked a lot about mom. Things I've never heard him talk about."

Shane set his jaw and looked down the hall. They were right, but he didn't like it.

"The thing about a surge," Dr. Krist said, "is that we don't know how long it will last. We aren't even really sure how it happens to begin with." He looked between the two of them. "So, if you have anything you want to say to him, now's the time to do it."

He glanced into the room before addressing them again. "I'll let you two go see him now. For what it's worth, Alan is a fighter. I'm sorry there isn't more we could do." He looked as though he wanted to say more, but instead, turned and walked away.

The two brothers' eyes met. In that moment, Shane let go of the resentment and Colin was simply his brother. They were family. As one, they reached for each other and held on. Shane squeezed his eyes closed, his stomach dropping to the floor, wishing things were different in just about every aspect of his life. But now wasn't the time for tears or wishes for what could never be.

If what the doctor said was true, there would be plenty of time for regrets later.

Shane clapped Colin on the back and pulled away. He cleared his throat before he could speak. "Let's go in and talk with him for a while."

Colin put his hands back in his pockets. "You go ahead. I'm going to go call some of the family. Update them on what's going on. I'll be in soon."

Shane studied his brother's eyes, so much like his own. He was giving him time to say his goodbyes alone.

Shane nodded and held out a fist. "Thanks, brother."

Colin bumped his fist. "No problem." With his hands in his pockets, Colin walked down the hall, his shoulders drooped, and his usual quick gait lacking energy.

Shane ran a hand through his hair and sighed. He turned back to the room and found Alan staring out the window.

"Hey, Dad. Still want to talk?"

Alan lifted his head off the pillow and turned toward Shane. He patted the bed next to him. "Come sit by me, Shane."

He crossed the room and gingerly sat next to his dad, memories of sitting with the old man on his knee when he was just a small boy flooding his mind.

"So, tell me about the woman."

Shane's eyes widened. How the hell did he *still* know everything on the other side of the country while fighting cancer? "The woman?"

Alan shook his head and made a *tsk*-ing noise. "Don't play coy with me, son. You know who I'm talking about."

Shane looked down, picking at the nubby comforter covering his father's legs. His smile was rueful. "I don't know how you always seem to know things."

"It's a gift. Now spill."

Shane shrugged and looked at Alan. "There's nothing to tell. Not anymore."

Alan gave his oldest son his trademark I'm-not-buying-it-try-again look that never failed to pull the truth from his boys. Shane sighed. "Okay, we were dating, I guess. Just casual. Having fun. We spent a lot of time together…"

"You got close." It wasn't a question, but a statement of fact.

Shane nodded. "Yeah," he replied, his voice rough. "I got too close. And it was a huge mistake, given that she's an employee. And the owner of the property we're trying to buy."

Alan's brows shot up to flirt with his hairline and he whistled low. "You were dating Emma. Damn, son."

Shane dropped his chin to his chest. "Well, add to the fact that the only reason she took the job at KVN is because she needed money to keep the house out of foreclosure." He rubbed the back of his neck. "She's a recovering alcoholic, Dad. And yet she still came to work for us. All to save the house we are trying to buy her out of."

"Son of a bitch." Alan swore softly. His eyes wandered over Shane's face. "Did you know about her recovery when you hired her?"

"No. She didn't tell me. I found out about it later. I probably wouldn't have hired her if I knew."

"Why? Because of Marlene?" When Shane didn't respond, Alan

shook his head. "Shane, Marlene was a twisted, troubled soul. The drug use made her worse, but it was always there. And she never had any desire to get any help. But that wasn't your fault. You tried. You can't keep carrying that around forever. Or shutting out people who aren't perfect. Emma had an addiction issue, but she handled it, right?"

"Yeah, she's two years sober."

Alan tilted his head. "Isn't that proof she isn't like Marlene?"

Shane moved his shoulders, trying to work the "oh shit" feeling that had settled there in the past few seconds. "It doesn't matter anyway. I was only there for a little while. I've already lined up visits to the vineyards in Virginia to get started there."

Alan frowned. "What about the rest of the renovations in Madison Ridge?"

"Noah, the contractor, will take care of everything. He's the best I've ever worked with as far as staying on time and budget."

"What about Emma?"

Thinking about Emma, Shane rubbed his chest, over his heart, which began to hurt. And how he had really and truly screwed up the best thing that happened to him. "What about her?"

"Are you going to talk to her?"

"About what, Dad? Between her not telling me about her addiction and me trying to use her circumstances as a way to buy her home? There's a lot of shit there between us that I don't think can be fixed. Besides," Shane shrugged, even though his stomach was in slick knots and his throat had tightened. The pain moving through his body was too much to bear, so he needed to push it away. "I have too much going on right now with KVN. I can't even think about being in a serious relationship."

"Sounds like you already are." Shane scoffed, making Alan's frown deepen. "Tell me something. When she told you she was an addict, how did you react?"

"Not well, Dad, not well. I was cold, judgmental. Made her sound like a common criminal. Even though I saw for myself she didn't drink, that she never acted weird around work even though the word 'wine' is used around her on the daily." He rubbed his hands down his face. "And yet I was a complete ass. Made her cry. Then she cursed me and kicked me out of her house." Even now, his heart twisted into a pretzel for causing her enough pain to bring on the tears. It hurt him to think about how he'd reacted and how Emma must have felt. He leaned forward, placing his elbows on his thighs and pulled on his hair until his eyes stung.

Alan sighed. "Shane. Look at me."

Shane lifted his head and looked at his dying father, emotions hitting him square in the chest. "Do you love Emma?"

Shane glanced away for a moment then nodded. "Yeah. God help me, but I love her." The thought of not seeing her shattered his heart. Emma Reynolds had brought him the rest of the way out of his dark hole. He needed her and he'd never needed anyone in his life. "She's strong, so strong. Smart, funny, and so beautiful it actually hurts to look at her sometimes." His eyes met his father's, a cold sadness weighing him down. "I really wish you could meet her."

Alan smiled softly. "I will one day."

"That's not—"

Alan held up a hand, his eyes imploring. "I want you to listen to me, Shane. Okay?"

"Okay."

"Are you listening? I want to tell you something."

Shane held his father's stare. "Yes, I'm listening."

"I was there the day you were born. You were the tiniest little human I'd ever seen. You scared the shit out of me, quite frankly. But your mother, she knew just how to handle you. She was never scared." Alan smiled, his eyes going soft as he fell into nostalgia. "She was so beautiful when she held you. I loved her, heart and soul. But there were times I was an ass and made her cry. More times than I care to think about, actually. Being the passionate woman she was, she cursed me many times, before and after we got married, something that almost didn't happen because of the high-handed Kavanaugh ego I managed to pass to my sons." He rolled his eyes. "My point is this: if you love her, you make it right. No matter how many times I showed my ass to your mother, I made it right. And she forgave me. Now, I'm not saying it's going to be easy for you. You have a few more complications than your mother and I had. But you'll figure it out. And whatever you decide to do to make it right, I stand behind you."

Shane stared at his father and read between the lines. If Alan stood behind him, that meant KVN did.

"Shane," Alan said softly, "don't deny yourself love just because you made a mistake before. Marlene was not the woman you were meant to fall in love with."

"I didn't even love her like a man should love his wife." Even now, it shamed Shane to admit that little tidbit.

Alan nodded. "I know. That's why I'm telling you. Don't let what happened before ruin what you have now. Get past that. And make the other situation right, however that may be." Alan patted Shane's hand. "Go get her, Shane Connor. If you want that ending you didn't get before, if you want her, you'll find a way to get through the challenges. Every man needs the love of a good woman. When you find it, grab it with both hands and don't let go." He leaned his head back and smiled at Shane. "I love you, son."

"I love you too, Dad." Shane's voice shook with emotion.

"I'm going home," Alan whispered, a smile on his face.

The feeling of loss clawed in his throat. Helpless, all he could do was sit there and hold his father's hand while he closed his eyes and sighed for the final time.

The surge was over.

TWENTY-FOUR

Time for New Memories

EMMA DIDN'T KNOW who the hell kept ringing her doorbell, but she was going to kill them when she found out. She kicked the covers off and stomped down the stairs, muttering under her breath about shovels and dead bodies.

"Stop ringing the damn—" Her ranting came to an abrupt halt when she yanked open the door to find her front porch crowded with all six Reynolds children plus her Aunt Stella. Standing front and center was Noah.

"Good morning to you, too."

She shoved the bed head hair out of her face and pulled the robe tighter around her, trying in vain to appear less of a train wreck. "Morning," she mumbled.

Delaney, the *Property Ace* himself, stepped next to Noah. He flashed that Hollywood smile that lit up the TV screen every week in a new episode and daily in reruns. "It's freaking cold out here, could you let us in?"

"Yeah, sorry." She stepped back to allow the clan of seven into the foyer, the cold air coming in with them. Shutting the door behind the crowd, Emma stood with her back against it. "What are you all doing here?"

They stood shoulder to shoulder, filling the large foyer area, facing her. Emma couldn't help but feel as though she stood in front of a firing squad. Noah stepped forward, the apparent ringleader of this early morning coup. "Call it an intervention of sorts."

The connotation straightened Emma's back against the hard door behind her. She narrowed her eyes on him. "I don't need an intervention. I'm just fine. I've had the flu." She pulled the tie of her robe tighter, crossing her arms over her chest.

"Bullshit." Aidan coughed into his hand. Emma shot him a withering look.

Charlotte, the baby of the clan, stepped forward, white bag in one hand. She held it out like a peace offering. "We heard so we brought you some cake."

Emma stared at the young woman with her chestnut-brown hair—the Reynolds women all had dark hair like their mother—pulled back into a ponytail, her heart-shaped face free of makeup. When had Charley gone and grown up on her? She was a beautiful girl, just like her sisters, Amelia and Grace. Emma reached for the bag and murmured, "Thank you," then turned her attention to Amelia. "Shouldn't you be at your shop? It's your busiest time of day."

Amelia shrugged. "I have more important things to deal with right here."

Emma glanced at Grace. "And you? Don't you have a class of kids to teach?"

"It's Saturday." Grace replied with a "nice try" smile on her face.

Stella came forward and placed her hands on Emma's shoulders. "Emmaline, we're calling a family meeting."

She stared into Stella's eyes. Determination, worry, and sadness filled the older woman's eyes. Seeing that in her aunt's eyes and knowing she put it there was like ripping open a wound that wasn't completely healed.

Emma stepped around Stella and walked into the open living area. "Well, come on in, then. Let's get comfortable in the living room."

"I'll make coffee." Charley took the bag of goodies from Emma and gently shoved her toward the living room.

They all shuffled into the spacious living area, sitting in various places around the room. Emma sat in the corner of the overstuffed sofa, curling her legs up under her. "So, what's the meeting about?"

"You."

Her head snapped up to where Noah stood, legs shoulder-width apart, his strong arms over his chest.

"Me?"

Del came up and stood beside him, mirroring his stance. The easygoing smile from earlier dropped away and now concern lined his face. "Yes, you. And why you won't sell to KVN."

Emma closed her eyes and let her head fall back on the couch. "I don't want to talk about it."

"Too fucking bad, Emma," Aidan said from his spot in front of the fireplace. He threw Stella a sheepish glance. "Sorry, Mom." She raised a hand in a "don't worry about it" gesture, and he continued. "Emma, enough with the evading and avoiding when the hard conversations come up."

Emma shot to her feet, anger built in her chest and every muscle in her body tensed. "You think I haven't had hard conversations, Aidan? My life has been nothing but hard conversations for the last two years. You have no idea what I've dealt with when it comes to hard conversations."

"Aidan isn't saying that you haven't had them, Em," Grace began in her calm way, as though dealing with one of her unruly students. "All he's saying is that we need to talk about why you want to hang on to something that is doing nothing for you."

"I can't sell the house. I made a promise to my mother, one that I plan to stick with. It's my future." Emma looked at each of them, including Charley, who'd come back in the room and leaned against the archway, her heart aching with the thought of losing the last tangible thread to her parents. "If I sell, it will just be one more failure on my part."

She crossed her arms over her middle, unable to meet the eyes of the people she loved—and hurt—the most in her life. "I know my family hasn't always made things easy. And I helped add to the misery by continuing the lovely addiction gene and almost killing myself. I put everyone I love through the wringer with my terrible decisions, and, for years, I didn't even care that I did it."

The shame running through her veins threatened to swallow her whole. Her body trembled from head to toe and she bit her lip to keep the sob swelling her chest from escaping.

"You have an illness. We know that," Stella said, her voice calm and caring.

Emma waved it away and dropped back down on the couch. "I know, but I still have to live with the fact that I acted like an ass to all of you. Keeping this house is my way of showing that I'm better. I'm more responsible. And like I said, it's my future."

Amelia rose from her spot on the other end of the sofa and perched on the coffee table in front of Emma. "Isn't that what the twelve steps are for? To help you work through that?"

Emma nodded looking down at her hands clasped in her lap. "Yeah, that's why they're there. And I'm working through them. I'm getting back to the basics. I have to." Her eyes welled up and a tear fell down her face. "I came this close"—she put her forefinger and thumb a hair's breadth apart—"to relapsing the other night. I found my father's prized bottle of Jack was still in the bottom drawer of his desk. I didn't even know it was there. I just sat there, staring at the bottle. Thinking of how just one drink, just one, would ease the pain."

Stella frowned. "What happened to push you so close?"

Emma met her aunt's gaze. "That's the thing, Stella. For an alcoholic, nothing has to happen. It just is, sometimes." She sighed and looked down at her hands fisted in her lap. She decided to keep the fight between her and Shane out of it. "But this time, something did happen. I received a letter that the bank is moving forward with foreclosure proceedings." She held up a hand to ward off what she knew was coming. "And no, none of you can loan me the money. That's one of my hard-and-fast rules. Don't mix finances with family."

She had to stick to that rule, because look what had happened the last time she'd broken one of her hard-and-fast rules. She'd ended up falling in love with a man who'd made her feel whole, and she'd forgotten about that dark part of her soul. She'd been normal with him.

And then he'd ripped her heart out and stomped on it.

"Oh, Em." Amelia's eyes were sad when she patted Emma's knee.

Emma stared off into space, thinking back to that night mere days ago that was like hitting rock bottom all over again. "But I called my sponsor and she reminded me of all the things I learned in rehab, and in those rooms. I need to live life on life's terms. And sometimes that means feeling the pain even when it would be easier to numb it all." She blew out a breath. "So, I poured my father's seven-hundred-dollar bottle of Jack Daniels special edition whiskey down the drain." Her smile was rueful. "I figure he'll be haunting me soon about that."

"The fact you dumped it says something," Graee said. "You can stand on your own, Emma."

Emma nodded, tears burning her throat, leaving her unable to speak.

Stella moved forward to sit on the edge of the recliner. She picked up Emma's hand and held it tight. "Emma, listen to me. I love you like you were my own daughter. I know what you dealt with. Your parents loved you, but there were issues no child should have to deal with. God rest their souls, they did try. Your father was a great man, when he could get away from the gambling and alcohol. I want you to hear me when I say that hanging on to this house is toxic. It won't bring back your parents or change anything about your childhood. Keep the memories. But if you keep the house, in the end, it will suck the life out of you, just like it did your mother. It won't change any bad decisions you made or any sins you think you committed. Nor will it atone for anything that was done to the family name." She squeezed Emma's hand. "This family is strong, stronger than any demon brought into it. If anything, you have shown everyone that our resolve is unbeatable. It's you, Emma. Not this house or the land it sits on."

Stella put a finger under Emma's chin and lifted her face. "It's you, baby girl."

Emma couldn't help it. All the things she'd tried so hard to do to keep things afloat, the fact that Shane was gone, and that she'd sent him away, crashed in on her. She crumbled into a ball of tears.

Within seconds, the entire family surrounded her in a group hug, murmuring to her and calming her down. After a while, her sobs subsided to sniffles. Her female cousins shed a few tears as well. Of course, Del, Noah, and Aidan looked uncomfortable, like men caught in an estrogen shit-storm. Emma snorted out a laugh when she looked at them.

"What's funny?" Noah demanded.

"I was just thinking that you three look like you're stuck in a gynecologist's office, having to talk about periods and cramps."

That made the three Reynolds men look at each other and grimace while the women laughed.

"First you cry, then you talk about stuff like that?" Aidan shuddered. "I don't want to know."

Emma let out a sigh. "Okay. I'm going to sell the property. To KVN. Let it all go. Make some new memories in a new place."

"You can come live with me for a while if you need to," Amelia offered.

"I may take you up on that." Emma wrinkled her nose. "Wait. Are you still a slob?"

"Yes," everyone in the room answered at the same time, causing Amelia to protest.

Emma shook her head. "For someone so clean in her kitchen, I don't get how you're so messy otherwise."

"Em, there's something else we came to tell you." Noah stepped forward, looking even more uncomfortable with his hands in the back pockets of his jeans.

She swallowed, wary of the solemn expression on his face. Fear clawed at her throat. "What is it?" Grace and Amelia sat next to Emma, holding her hands.

"It's Alan Kavanaugh. He passed away yesterday."

The fear turned to a hollow, sad feeling in the pit of her stomach. Tears came again, this time for the man she loved and the devastating loss he must be feeling. And for a man she'd never met, but had hoped to meet one day, so she could tell him what a fine man he'd raised, both in business and in life.

Now she'd never have the chance.

"Shane must be..." She lifted her head to look at Noah. "Have you talked to him?"

"Not since yesterday, when he called to tell me he wouldn't be back for a while, and that he'd need my help managing the rest of the renovation."

"I should call him." She stopped, tears clogging her throat again "No, he doesn't want to hear from me. We didn't end things well."

"He'd want to hear from you, Em. I know he would. He asked about you."

She stilled. In spite of the tears, her heart lifted and her belly fluttered. "What did he say?"

"Wanted to make sure you were okay. I told him I couldn't say. I hadn't seen or heard from you. It didn't seem to sit well with him."

Emma paused, mulling that over. "When's the funeral?"

"The day after tomorrow in Napa."

"You can fly back with me," Del said. "I'm headed out tomorrow morning for L.A. We can detour to Napa. I'll go with you to the funeral if you need a shoulder. I met Alan a few times. He was a great man. He'll be missed for sure."

"I think I can do more for Shane and KVN by staying here and taking care of their project. Tell Shane not to worry about anything here," Noah said.

Grace squeezed Emma's hand. "Are you going to go? You should, Emma." She pushed back a lock of hair behind Emma's ear. "I haven't met Shane yet, but from what I hear around town, he's a good guy. And I can see in your eyes how you feel about him."

Emma sighed, not responding to Grace's observation. She looked up into the face of her famous cousin who was willing to help her in the middle of his hectic Hollywood life. "When do we leave?"

TWENTY-FIVE

Happiness Denied Too Long

"ASHES TO ASHES, DUST TO DUST..." In the quiet of the cemetery, the minister's voice rang out clearly.

A mahogany casket perched over the rectangular hole in the ground. Large oaks shaded the mourners from the winter sun. Shane and Colin sat in white wooden chairs at the edge of the gravesite, with the rest of the extended family, while others surrounded them, all gathered to pay their respects to Alan Kavanaugh.

It was an impressive turnout, but one that didn't surprise Shane. Alan had been an innovative and key player in Napa Valley and the international winery community. The Kavanaugh name had been synonymous with fine wine for over a century. As a direct descendant of the founder, everyone knew Alan.

Now everyone mourned him.

The minister closed the Bible in his hands and tucked it under an arm, clasping his hands in front of him. "I've known the Kavanaugh family for years. Alan was a kind man and one that never backed down from any challenge handed to him." The minister cleared his throat and rubbed a hand over his mouth. "Including when his wife passed, leaving him with two young boys to raise on his own. He never remarried, focusing on his family and raising two young men that he was proud of and cherished every day."

As the minister continued to memorialize the man Shane wasn't sure how he was going to continue to live without, Shane closed his eyes, trying like hell to calm the storm of grief that ravaged his body. There was a hollowness in his chest that mirrored his life now. He didn't know any type of world without his father, business or personal. He thought back to the last few times he'd sat with his father. For all the jet lag Shane endured over the last few weeks, he didn't regret a single moment.

Shane could only be thankful that he'd gotten his shit together in time to help his father before cancer stole his last parent from him. Rage mixed with grief. Fucking cancer.

He glanced over at Colin, who sat stone-faced as he stared at the coffin. His brother had hardly uttered a dozen words the whole day.

An occasional sniffle or quiet sob carried on the breeze. He glanced around and found in addition to extended family, Abe, Jenn and her husband, and several of the other local winery owners in attendance. He caught the eye of one, who nodded in acknowledgement. Shane returned the nod.

He shifted his gaze, and sleep deprivation must have been messing with his head, because he swore he saw Emma standing next to Delaney Reynolds. They stood away from the crowd of people, just the two of them, their heads bowed. Emma's face was pale and drawn, a look that caught Shane off guard. With Del standing tall next to her, she appeared sad, fragile even. The ache in his chest grew and his gut twisted.

In the midst of the heartache over the death of his father, Shane's heart lightened. She'd flown all the way out here, and that had to mean something, right? He couldn't take his eyes off her. He wanted to push through the crowd and gather her in his arms. Get lost in her warmth and the scent that was all Emma. Feel her touch when she ran her fingers through his hair. Maybe he'd finally find some peace in the shit-show that had been his life since he'd left Madison Ridge.

He brought his attention back to the minister as the service concluded. Several people milled away, headed for their cars or gathering in small groups. Shane stood and walked over to the casket. Placing a trembling hand on the sun-warmed wood, he closed his eyes. He wouldn't allow the tears that threatened to fall. His lips trembled while his mind scrambled to find the right words.

"Hell, dad. I don't know what to say." The words were like razor blades in his throat and Shane swallowed back the clawing despair. When he continued, his voice was a mere whisper. "I hope you know how much I loved you. And how much it meant to know you loved me even when I wasn't easy to love. I'll work like hell every day to make you proud." His eyes slid closed again and he blew out a ragged breath. "Goodbye, Dad. Love you. Kiss Mom for me."

He leaned down and kissed the smooth, varnished wood. Grief tore at his chest, a gaping hole in his heart now that would never be filled. His throat tightened and he fisted a hand over the coffin. He ran a finger over the smooth wood one last time before he moved away, giving Colin room to say his own goodbyes.

Several people came by to offer condolences, hugs, handshakes, and short anecdotes of his father. Shane hugged an elderly woman who'd worked for his father and his grandfather before that. She patted his cheek and told him to stay in touch before walking away.

Shane scanned the cemetery, looking for Emma and Del, but they were gone. He shoved his fingers through his hair and pretended not to hear when someone called his name.

Several hours later, Shane sat in his office at KVN Incorporated overlooking acres of grapes as far as the eye could see. Colin had made himself scarce after the funeral, which twisted the knife deeper in Shane's gut. The relationship between him and the only person left in his immediate family was already feeling the strain. And Shane didn't know how the hell he was going to handle the situation with his brother. But if he had to guess, he would handle it as badly as he'd handled everything else lately.

The blinking light indicating he had a voicemail caught his eye, but he ignored it. The only person he cared to talk to wanted nothing to do with her. He couldn't blame her.

Instead, he replied to some emails, including the one from the chairman of the board stating they would follow Alan's wishes for the company leadership going forward. This meant he was the new CEO and Colin was Vice President. On one hand, he should be ecstatic. It was everything he'd worked for, with all the flying back and forth and putting deals together. But there was no joy at all. Having the position meant he no longer had his father, the relationship with his brother was rocky at best, and he no longer had the woman he loved. Selling his soul would hurt less.

There were two emails he couldn't bear to open at the moment. The subject of one read *Madison Ridge Property Agreement*. The other read *Emma Reynolds Resignation Letter*. He would have to open and address each of them eventually, but right now, he just pretended like they didn't exist.

He sat back, rocking back and forth in the large leather chair, watching another sunset explode a mixture of crimson, yellows, and oranges into the indigo sky. The rich green of the vineyards sat in the forefront, with mountains in the background. It was as if nature was trying to cheer him up and bring him out of the dark hole he was falling further into as each hour passed.

"Hey, big brother."

Shane spun his head around to find Colin leaning against the doorway to his office. The disheveled hair and wrinkled suit were out of place on his brother. "Hey."

"I assume you've seen the email?" Colin asked, strolling into the office.

Shane nodded, but eyed his brother warily. "I have."

The smile that spread across Colin's lips was more caustic than friendly. He held his arms out to his side. "You got what you wanted."

Shane narrowed his eyes. "What did you have planned for me? Because you knew I wouldn't stand by and let you sell it off."

Colin scoffed, pacing the office. "Come on now, brother. You would have been offered a more than generous package. You would be richer than you could imagine and not have to deal with this bullshit anymore."

Shane shook his head, baffled by the man he was once closer to than anyone. "So I was just going to be out. What the fuck, Colin? Why?" He rose from his chair and advanced on his brother, shoving at

Colin's shoulder. "You never told anyone why you wanted to sell KVN off. Dad wanted the two of us to run the company. To continue the legacy."

Colin shoved back. "I don't want the fucking legacy, Shane. It was always your thing, not mine. I never wanted to do this. I have other interests that don't include fermenting fruit."

Shane's head snapped back. "Why the hell didn't you say anything before? Dad would have—"

"Yeah, I know." Colin sighed and his shoulders slumped. "But you said yourself, he wanted *us* to run the company. I just couldn't bear to tell him."

Shane rubbed his chin, his mind still tangled as questions bounced around in the corners of his mind. "So why now? Why put us through all of this?"

Colin ran a hand through his hair. "A friend of mine has a tech start-up down in the Valley. He wants me in on it and I want to be in on it. Badly. It's not cheap though."

Shane walked back behind his desk. He had to move away for fear he'd punch Colin. They were both too old to start throwing punches again. "So you did it for money?"

Colin closed his eyes for a beat then shook his head. "Not completely. I have enough for the buy-in. But I didn't want the burden of KVN. I couldn't abandon you and the family by leaving it." He walked over and sat in a chair as though he were weary of the world.

When Colin looked up at him, his eyes were sad and full of regrets. "I'm sorry, man. I didn't handle this well. I was rash and selfish. I should have just resigned." He shrugged and looked past Shane out the window. "But once I hit a certain point, there was no going back. Better to look like a heartless bastard than a fool."

Shane sat down in his chair, studying Colin. In spite of his anger, Shane's resolve softened a bit because he could empathize. It was not a foreign concept to Shane to want something you thought you couldn't have. Except in Colin's case, he could. His brother's plan may have failed, but now that Shane knew why, he couldn't fault his brother's passion for what he wanted. As his father said just before he died, they were family after all. And family looked out for their own, regardless.

"Colin, I think you should step down."

Colin's gaze snapped back to Shane. "What the hell are you talking about?"

"As CEO, I'm asking you to step down." Shane tilted his head. "Don't you have another interest to pursue? I think your attention would be spread too thin. As such, I think you should focus on what's important to you."

Colin stared at Shane for several seconds, letting what Shane was telling him sink in. "You're giving me an out? Why?"

Shane picked up a pen and tapped it against the desk, but didn't meet Colin's gaze. "Because I understand where you're coming from, little brother. To want something so bad, you'll do whatever it takes to get it." He thought of Emma and how if he only knew a way to get her attention. Shaking the thought off, he focused back on the task at hand. "You should go, do what you want in life. KVN isn't what you want to do, and it doesn't have to be. Go find what is for you."

Colin's Adam's apple bobbed when he swallowed. "I don't deserve your understanding, Shane. I didn't do the same for you."

Shane smiled sadly. "No, you didn't. But we're family. The only family we have left. You lost your way for a minute, but now you're back." He stood and rounded the desk, hand held out to his brother. "I wish you all the best in your next endeavor."

Colin stood slowly and shook Shane's hand, shock still filling his eyes. "Thank you."

"Come here." Shane pulled Colin into a hug, slapping him on the back. "I love you, Colin. You'll always be a Kavanaugh, so I expect to hear great things come out of the Valley from you."

He nodded. "Absolutely."

Shane waved a hand. "Go on. I'll handle the press release of your resignation." He winked at Colin.

"Have I told you lately that you're fucking awesome?" Colin asked with a grin.

Ah yeah, there was the brother he knew and loved. Shane laughed. "No, but you can tell me again."

"I'm headed to the house for a while. You coming?"

Shane nodded. "I'll be there shortly."

196

"I'll let everyone know."

"Thanks, man."

They bumped fists and Colin crossed the room to leave but stopped when he got to the doorway. "Hey, Shane?"

Shane stopped behind his desk. "Yeah?"

"You remind me of dad running this company already. He'd be proud."

Speechless, Shane could only nod as he sat in his chair.

"Oh, and another thing. You should really go after what you want as well. Make it right." He knocked on the doorway once before walking away.

Make it right.

He'd made it right with Colin. If only he knew how the hell to do that with Emma and his own life. For that, he didn't have a clue.

He rose and crossed to the wine fridge that was built into the wall of his office, selecting a vintage sparkling wine the KVN vineyard had produced years before. Looking down at the bottle, he remembered when his father had given it to him, telling him to save it for something special. He figured drinking it now was as close as he was going to get. A solitary drink to the memory of his father.

Snagging a glass from the dark, oak-colored sideboard, Shane walked back to his desk, setting the glass and bottle on his desk with a thud. He shed his suit jacket, tossing it on the desk, and rolled up his sleeves before sitting down with a heavy sigh. The pop of the cork from the bottle filled the room and he poured the golden liquid to the rim of the glass. Kicking his legs out, he tipped his glass in salute toward the windows. "This one's for you, Dad. Bottoms up."

Shane drank more deeply than was considered appropriate according to wine connoisseurs, but at this moment he didn't give a flying fuck what anyone thought. The only thing he cared about was forgetting about the impending changes in his life and a bewitching brunette he couldn't get out of his head. He was pissed off at himself for thinking about her so damn much when he had a full plate to deal with concerning the company.

He should have known better, should have heeded the bells and sirens that had gone off in his head the first time they'd met. The woman had troubled him and tied him in knots ever since he'd walked into that dingy diner.

Shoving a hand through his hair, Shane stared into the bubbly liquid that glittered in his hand. There was no going back now. The hell of it was, he was going to have to move forward without her, leaving behind a vital piece of himself that she didn't want, but owned anyway.

Buried in all the heartache of losing his dad was also the heartache of knowing the one good thing he'd had in his life—ever—was gone. They'd both done their share of hurting each other, but even knowing that didn't ease the ache in his bones. He didn't have a guide or plan to get over her, but forgetting her was crucial.

Halfway through the second glass, his father's voice floated through his mind. One of the last things he'd said to Shane before quietly going into that good night.

"My point is this: if you love her, you make it right. No matter how many times I showed my ass to your mother, I made it right. And she forgave me. Now, I'm not saying it's going to be easy for you. You have a few more complications than your mother and I had. But you'll figure it out. And whatever you decide to do to make it right, I stand behind you."

All Shane had ever wanted to do was make his father proud. And all this time, Shane thought that meant what he could prove to his father professionally. He knew now that his father wanted Shane to be successful in love as well. His father gave him his blessing.

He pulled his cell phone out of his pocket and found the contact he needed. "I need the jet fueled up and ready to go to Madison Ridge tomorrow morning. Nine o'clock. Perfect. Thank you."

Shane ended the call and began to formulate a plan, which included opening the dreaded emails he avoided the last twenty-four hours. They were essential to his plan. He was about to fight for the happiness he denied himself for too long.

Shane Kavanaugh always played to win. That wasn't going to change now.

TWENTY-SIX

Trouble Me
———————

EMMA WIPED DOWN THE COUNTER, her back protesting and feet aching from being on them nonstop for the last couple of hours. Why the hell had she agreed to take this shift tonight at Maggie's? Oh yeah, the same reason she'd worked at Maggie's before. She needed money.

It was a reminder that Emma needed to get back to walking every day. She'd become accustomed to sitting behind a desk again, which with her injuries, wasn't such a good idea anymore. But it didn't matter now, did it? She'd resigned from KVN, had emailed Shane her resignation, along with a sales contract for KVN to buy her property.

He hadn't responded in any way, shape, or form. Emma imagined that he was buried in work now that he was the CEO of KVN Incorporated, but a part of her thought he'd at least respond to one of her emails, the sales contract especially. Now that she'd made up her mind, Emma was ready to get the property sold and move on with her life. Find a new dream for her future.

Still, her heart twisted with the knowledge that it was well and truly over between them. That beating organ inside her chest didn't really much care about land deals and secrets. It was in pain anyway.

The bell on the door rang. Shit! Why hadn't she locked the door?

Not smart since she was here by herself. She bit back a sigh before turning around. She just wanted to go home and—

Her stomach dropped to her knees.

"Hello, Emmaline."

Shane stood at the door. His deep voice shot tingles down her spine like it always did. His ocean-blue eyes were dark, almost navy as he stared at her, a small smile on his full lips.

It was déjà vu, but this time she knew what those lips, hands, and what the man himself was capable of doing to her. God, he was sexy as sin. His dark jeans rode low on his waist and hugged his slim hips. The white button-down shirt pulled across his broad chest when he slid his hands in the front pockets. Strong forearms bulged where he rolled back the sleeves. As it always seemed to be with this man, she had zero self-control. It was taking everything she had not to wrap herself around him.

She cleared the shock from her throat. "Hello, Shane. What are you doing here?"

The deadbolt on the front door clicked when he locked it, sounding like a shotgun in the quiet diner and caused her heart to pick up speed. With his stare on her, he strolled over and settled onto one of the swiveling seats along the counter. "I once heard you won't leave this diner hungry." He paused, his gaze hot on hers. "I hope that's still the case."

Emma twisted the dish towel in her hands. "I'm afraid you'll be disappointed tonight. Bud's already left for the night."

"I wasn't talking about food."

Emma exhaled quietly, trying to slow down her racing heart and her raging hormones. "Then why are you here? I emailed and you never responded." She shrugged, hoping the nonchalant, I-don't-give-a-shit attitude came through loud and clear in spite of her quivering insides. "I figured that meant we would speak through our agents on the purchase agreement."

Shane tapped his fingers on the counter, his eyes never leaving her face. "I came to talk to you, Emma. There are things to say."

She tossed the towel on the counter beside her and crossed her arms. "I think we've said all we need to say. What more could you possibly have to say to me?"

"A few things, actually. But first, let me respond to your emails." He shifted in the chair and pulled out two folded documents from his back pocket. "This one?" Shane opened the flaps, read it for a moment and then turned it to her. It was her resignation letter. He ripped it in half once, then twice, letting the ripped paper flutter to the counter.

Her eyes widened. "Shane—"

He held up a hand. "I don't accept it. And I have something to say before I answer the next one. Do I have your attention?"

She swallowed hard. "You have my attention." Her whole body went cold at the thought of what he would say next.

"I love you, Emmaline Rose Reynolds. I can't imagine my life without you in it."

Her lips parted and the blood rushed to her head, making her sway slightly. "Since when?"

"Since always."

Emma looked away, but kept her arms crossed. He'd stunned her with his admission and while she wanted to run the streets of Madison Ridge square screaming how much she loved him, she had to know for sure. "I don't—"

Shane slid off the stool and made his way around the counter toward her. His pace was slow, deliberate, and the thought of being the prey to his predator ran through her mind again. Just as it had the first time she met him.

"The first time I saw you, you were standing in nearly the same spot you're in right now." His eyes traveled down her body and back up again as he advanced on her. Her skin flushed under the uniform she wore and she automatically took a step back as he moved forward. "In the same peach uniform. My life hasn't been the same since. And I'm damn glad for it."

Her back hit the counter behind her and all at once he was in front of her, so close his body heat radiated to her. She had to lean her head back to look into his eyes that rooted her to the spot. "Emma, I'm crazy about you. I'm sorry for lying and hurting you. I never intended for any of that to happen. Please believe me." He ran a fingertip along her exposed collarbone, sending a shiver along her skin. "I would be lying if I said I could live without you. I'd be alive, but I wouldn't be living."

Emma was officially speechless. Love and desire filled his impossibly blue eyes. When she finally found her voice, she said, "I'm sorry that I wasn't more upfront with you about my past. I never wanted to hurt you either. Because I love you too, Shane. And it scares me just how much I do."

He smiled and pushed a wisp of hair behind her ear. His knuckles grazed the skin beneath her earlobe, causing her body to tingle. "You scare me, too. Now," he reached over and tapped a finger on the folded papers. "About this deal." Shane laid his hands on the counter on either side of her hips and leaned in close. The scent that was Shane and the piney aroma of his soap surrounded her and drowned out the diner smells that permeated the air. "If KVN buys your house, there is one condition."

"What's that?" She held her breath.

He pinned her with a look. "You have to move in with me into the cabin I'm buying. That's non-negotiable."

Her brows lifted in surprise. "You bought a cabin in Madison Ridge?"

He nodded, his eyes soft with love. "I bought our cabin. The one we made our own without knowing it." He grinned. "I made the owner an offer he couldn't refuse."

"So..." Emma stopped and swallowed, worried if she made any sudden moves, the dream would shatter and she'd be alone in the diner. "You're moving to Madison Ridge?"

"Yep." He glanced over his shoulder and out the windows with a slow nod. "I like it here. It reminds me of Napa in a lot of ways, but without all the baggage that's there for me now. The people have kinda grown on me too." He turned his head back and looked down at her, a slow, sexy smile spreading across his face. "Not to mention there's a woman here who has managed to take my heart. And I've recently learned she's not going to give it back to me so easily. I've also learned I have no desire to get it back from her." He lifted her hand and placed it on his shirt over his heart. "My heart is yours, Emmaline. Always and forever."

"And my heart is yours, Shane." Tears of joy coursed down her cheeks as Shane wrapped an arm around her waist, pulling her to him. One hand cupped her face, his thumb sweeping away the waterworks.

"No more tears, baby."

"No more tears." She nodded and smiled as his lips descended on hers. He kissed her with an intensity that was fueled by all the love and desire that existed between them.

Shane pulled back and looked into her eyes with a smile. The bright blue in his eyes reflected all the love that filled her own. "You showed me what it really means to love someone. I love you in ways I didn't know anyone could love. Will you trouble me for the rest of my life, Peaches?"

Her grin was so big, her face ached.

"Only if you promise to trouble me for the rest of mine."

Epilogue

Two Months Later

"SHANE, IT'S GORGEOUS."

Emma looked around the large, open room of the winery. The setting sun just beyond the wall of windows cast a golden hue on the room, the dark chocolate hardwood flooring warm against the glow. Retro looking string lights ran along the beams in the ceiling adding to the ambiance. Along one wall, the centerpiece stacked stone fireplace that had caused her so much grief ran up to the ceiling in all its majestic glory.

It was the cherry on top to the beauty of the room and worth all the headaches it had given her.

Wait staff bustled around the circular tables dotted around the room where friends and family would join them in celebrating the completion of the winery before it opened to the public. Tea lights glowed from the center of each table covered in crisp white linen cloth. Glasses and silverware gleamed.

It was a perfect setup. Cozy, warm, but elegant.

Quintessential Kavanaugh style.

Pride swelled in her chest at how well the winery had turned out once renovations were complete. There were still some things to be finalized in the guest rooms on the second floor and then there would be renovating her old home.

Yeah, that had been the best decision she'd ever made. Selling the old family land and house to KVN had kept her from losing the place, losing her mind, but keeping the promise to her mother.

Oh, and not to mention she'd ended up with a sinfully sexy, kind-hearted man who loved her with all her flaws.

"You like it?" Shane's strong arms went around her waist, and he kissed the side of her neck.

Just like that her breath quickened, and she wished that guests wouldn't be arriving in less than five minutes.

"Yes, I love it."

"Good." He turned her around and set her back at arm's length. His gorgeous blue eyes tracked her from head to toe. Desire and love lit them up when he met her gaze. "God, Emmaline. You're stunning."

"Thank you."

When he looked at her like that, she felt stunning, loved, and cherished.

But wearing the fire-engine-red wrap dress that hugged her curves, stopping just above the knee, didn't hurt either. Nor did the matching lingerie under said dress. She couldn't wait to see the look on his face later when he peeled the dress off her.

She moved into his arms, running a hand up his flawless dress shirt and curving around his neck. When she ran her nose along his collarbone, he groaned low in his throat. She inhaled his scent, the combination of cologne and man that was all Shane Kavanaugh. He'd make even more millions if he bottled that shit up.

"You make my knees weak in this suit," she whispered against his skin.

His hands gripped her hips and tightened her body against his. "You're too fucking hot in this dress. If you don't knock it off we're going to give some people quite the show." His voice was a low raspy grumble against her ear.

She chuckled and stepped back, but he caught her hands in his before she could get too far away.

Shane stared at her a little longer before blowing out a breath and shaking his head. He glanced over his shoulder. "Could you guys give us a moment, please? Thank you." He addressed the room with a professional but polite smile.

With murmurs of "yes sir," the staff shuffled out of the room, leaving them alone.

"Shane, we don't have time for that." But she couldn't help the trickle of excitement along her skin that maybe they could figure out a way to release some tension real quick.

Shane laughed and looked at the floor, his hands tightening against hers. After a moment, he lifted his head, and his stare locked onto hers. Panic flitted through her body at the serious look on his face. "Shane, is everything okay?"

When his lips curved into that panty-melting smile, she relaxed, especially when in his eyes, there was love and adoration for her. They were things she'd never thought she'd ever see in another's eyes. Not after all she'd done in her past.

"Everything is amazing. You are amazing. You're everything I've ever wanted and so, so much more. Not only do you make me want to be a better man, I *am* a better man because of you and the love you give me. You take my breath away, Peaches, with the way you move, the way you love, the generosity of your heart, your loyalty. You're everything I could have ever hoped for, all wrapped up in one exquisite package."

Her vision blurred from his words. Her heart banged against her ribs when he reached into his pocket and dropped to one knee. "I know I've already asked you to trouble me for the rest of my life. But I want to make it official."

Emma gasped, and her jaw dropped when the deep navy velvet box snapped open revealing the most dazzling ring she'd ever seen.

"Oh my God, Shane. It's spectacular." Her words came out in hushed tones. The center diamond solitaire sparkled like an emerald cut sun, and the intricate, diamond-studded vine motif wrapped around the center stone made the ring as one of a kind as the man kneeling in front of her.

"Emmaline Rose Reynolds, I would be honored if you would be my wife, my lover, my soul for the rest of my life. Will you marry me?"

"Yes, yes, yes!" Tears streamed down her cheeks as Shane stood and slipped the ring onto her finger. It was a perfect fit, both in the style and size.

She'd have to admire it later because her fiancé slanted his mouth on hers and kissed the breath out of her.

"Well, she must have said yes!"

Shane lifted his head, and she turned around to find her entire family and closest friends standing behind them, Amelia out in front.

Shane wrapped his arm around her shoulders, and with a huge grin and fist pump said, "She said yes!"

Clapping and whoops of glee rang out, and like a wave rushing toward shore, the crowd of her loved ones moved toward them. It was a flurry of hugs and tears for several minutes, and soon the champagne started to flow. Sparkling grape juice for her.

When Amelia finally caught up to her, she squeezed Emma tight and pulled back, lifting Emma's left hand. "Good Lord, this ring is...I have no words." She lifted her gaze to Emma's. "It suits you."

Emma nodded, fresh tears filling her eyes. "Yes, it does."

She sniffled and then cleared her throat, a thought dawning on her. "Hold on a minute, did you know Shane was doing this?"

Amelia shrugged a slim shoulder and dropped Emma's hand. "Maybe."

Emma tilted her head. "Did you help him with the ring?"

Amelia shook her head with raised brows. "Oh no. This was all Shane. The man has flawless taste. He doesn't need help as far as that's concerned."

Emma stared down at her hand, dazed by the gleaming diamonds. "He did good."

"I'm happy for you, Em. Truly happy for you." Amelia wrapped her arms around Emma again. "You deserve every bit of happiness, cousin. Remember that," she whispered in her ear.

Emma could only nod against the lump of emotions lodged in her throat.

As Amelia walked away, Emma stood there watching her cousin. Someday Amelia would find her happiness too, and she hoped it would be soon before the girl worked herself to death.

She sighed and turned only to find the man who held her happiness in the palm of his hand striding toward her. She couldn't help the smile that curved her lips.

"Hey, gorgeous."

"Hey, handsome." She wrapped her arms around his waist and leaned her head on his chest. Under her ear his heart beat, strong and sure. She leaned her head back. "So, this isn't really a friends and family soft launch, is it? It's our engagement party, isn't it?"

He grinned. "No and yes."

She shook her head but couldn't help matching his grin. "What would you have done if I said no?"

"Well," he said on a sigh, "we would have had a soft launch and then I would have done everything in my power to win you back."

She cupped his cheek in her hand. "You've had my heart since the beginning, Shane. And it will be forever yours."

"And my heart is yours."

When he kissed her, Emma knew that no matter what kind of trouble they came across, they would be able to handle it together.

Always.

THE END

Want more Shane and Emma? Subscribe to my newsletter for instant access for a bonus scene! Give me my bonus scene!!

In the mood for more steamy, small town goodness? Turn the page for a preview of Remind Me, book two in the Madison Ridge series!

Remind Me: Chapter One

WELCOME HOME, ACE

DELANEY REYNOLDS NEEDED a coffee the size of his head. Better yet, mainlining the rich brew his sister's cafe served up would suit him just fine, which is why he was beating feet to her place at the moment.

He'd had a rough night, a common occurrence for him over the last six months. But today he needed to get his shit together. He wasn't looking forward to the meeting that awaited him at the end of the next half hour. The summons from Lee Mitchum, his family's attorney, was cryptic and bad timing. He had enough on his plate with the end of his show and trying to fulfill a contract before he was in legal hot water.

Ten seasons was a long time in the home renovation television show world. At thirty-six years old, he was ready for a new adventure. But the fact he was forced to change course pissed him off. He liked making his own terms, but it appeared life had other plans for him.

Too bad life hadn't let him in on what those plans were, though.

Truth be told, he was glad to be back in Madison Ridge. He'd missed his family and the town his ancestors founded two hundred years ago. His gaze took in the sights around him. There were some new shops here and there like The Sweet Spot, his sister Amelia's cafe and bakery she'd opened a year or so ago. But the old mainstays like the general store, the pizza shop, and Maggie's diner—this time of morning the place was hopping—still stood strong.

The mountain air was clear—unlike the air he'd never quite gotten used to in Southern California—and all was quiet in the late spring weekday morning, but Del knew the weekends would be crowded with tourists. That's what happened when southern hospitality meets a glowing write-up in a mainstream magazine. Del's lips quirked thinking some of the stalwarts of the town were probably sitting in Maggie's grumbling about people and yet making money hand over fist.

Even though he'd missed it, Del had his reasons for staying away. Unfortunately, some of those reasons he couldn't outrun no matter how many corners of the globe he'd seen.

He pushed open the door to The Sweet Spot and a bell rung above his head causing the dark haired woman behind the counter to turn and look his way. "Well, if it isn't my big brother, Mr. Property Ace!" His sister Amelia rounded the corner of the counter and bounded over to him. Del barely caught her when she launched herself into his arms.

"Hey, Ames," he said on a laugh before lifting her off the floor in a bear hug.

"When did you get back?"

Del set her back down on her feet and smiled at the adorable picture his little sister made in her apron, jeans, and messy knot on top of her head. "Yesterday." He glanced around the blessedly empty dining area. "The place looks great. You added seating."

Amelia put her hands on her hips and looked around with a proud look on her face. "Yeah, I've done some upgrades since you were here last." She focused on him, her denim-blue eyes serious and scanning his face. "You look tired."

Del grinned. "Good to see you haven't changed a bit, brat." She folded her arms over her chest and leveled him with a stare. Damn, but she looked like their mother, scolding them without saying a word. "Okay, yeah. I'm tired. But right now, I'm late. I'm headed to Mitchum's office and I need the biggest coffee you got."

"You got it." Amelia swung back behind the counter and started to fill a tall cardboard cup with coffee from a carafe. "So what's your meeting with Mitchum about?"

Del shrugged. "Don't know. He didn't give me any details." He picked up the cup she slid across the counter and sipped. A whole lotta *hell yeah* screamed through his blood when the caffeinated magic hit his tongue. "Ahhh, damn, that's good."

Amelia smirked. "Yeah, I know." The smirk dropped to a frown as her gaze shifted behind him. "You still get mobbed when you go places?"

Dread set up camp in Del's gut. "Usually. Why?"

Amelia lifted her chin to the door. "If you're in a hurry, you better head out. There's a group of young women headed this way that have tourist written all over them." She hitched a thumb over her shoulder. "Go, quick. Out the back."

Del kicked his expensive but battered work boots into gear and headed toward the back of the store. The bell of the front door and Amelia's bright greeting reached his ears as he opened the back door. "Good morning, ladies. What can I get you?"

The door led out into a small alleyway between two historical buildings. It was open on either end, but he took a left that would dump him out onto the sidewalk that ran along the storefronts on Main Street. He jogged across the crosswalk, weaved around the back side of the historic courthouse in the center of the square, and made his way to a two-story red brick building on the corner.

There were four sets of double doors across the front of the building, with gold stenciling scrolled across the last set, announcing Mitchum and Associates was on the second floor. Comfort settled into Del's bones, noting some things never changed.

But when he opened the door to the attorney's office, the main reason he stayed away from his hometown sat on the loveseat in the waiting room, typing away on her phone.

Addison Davenport.

He'd know that strawberry-blonde hair anywhere. In all of his travels around the world, there was only one woman whose hair was that special mix of red and blonde.

Del's stomach met his feet, which decided they no longer knew how to move. This girl—scratch that, she was all woman now—had monopolized his thoughts since he had first learned how to shave. But they hadn't spoken in nearly ten years, even though he'd caught glimpses of her here and there when he'd been home.

Hell yeah, he'd avoided her. She had a temper as fiery as her hair when the mood struck and he had no desire to be on the receiving end again. Even though he deserved her temper in spades.

He'd fucked up royally.

Keep reading Remind Me

Also by Eliza Peake

The Madison Ridge Series

(Standalone Steamy, Emotional, Small Town Romances)

Trouble Me

Remind Me

Wreck Me

———

Tormented Bastard

A Cocky Hero Club Production

(A second chance, sports romance written in

Vi Keeland & Penelope Ward's Cocky Hero World)

———

Love's Kaleidoscope

A unique collection of love themed short stories.

———

NONFICTION

30 Days Until "The End": An Inspirational Guide to Finishing Your Novel in 30 Days

If you're looking for humor, positivity, and a swift kick to your flagging motivation, Eliza Peake's inspirational guide to completing a draft in thirty days is a must have.

Get a Sneak Peek in All Things Eliza!

If you'd like exclusive content, first look at cover reveals, bonus material and other announcements first, join my monthly newsletter, The Sneak Peake!

If you'd like to be a part of my street team where you receive access to ARC's first, join my Elite Street Team!

If you like to talk about books, hot guys, and general fun stuff in a drama free zone, join my reader group, Eliza Peake's Reader Group. We have a fun group going and growing all the time!

Author's Note

Dear Reader,

I want to thank you for reading *Trouble Me*. I couldn't be more thrilled to share it with you.

Emma is close to my heart as I can understand the demons she deals with on a daily basis. While my recovery journey isn't alcohol related, the steps to becoming whole again are very similar. She isn't an angel, but she wants to make herself and her family proud of her. One of my favorite things about romance is the elements of hope and redemption.

Which brings me to Shane. He's special to me, as are all my characters are, but there's an understanding with him that I just get. Addiction touched him in a way that can be just as hard a journey as the person in active addiction. Shane wants to show his father that he's capable of leading the family company into the future. He's looking for hope and redemption in his own way and he found it in Emma, regardless of her past.

If you liked *Trouble Me*, would you consider leaving me a review? I can be found on Goodreads, Amazon, and Bookbub. I also have a super fun newsletter, The Sneak Peake, where you can get exclusive news, find out about all the trouble I'm getting into, join my Elite Street Team, author events, and upcoming books. If you want to talk more about books and hot guys and general fun stuff, join my reader group, Eliza Peake's Reader Group. We have a fun group going and growing all the time!

If you fell in love with Shane and Emma, buckle up. The rest of the Reynolds clan is coming soon and like any big family, they come with a whole lotta drama, love, and laughter!

Happy Reading!

Love fearlessly, and live intentionally,

Acknowledgments

They say it take a village and that couldn't be more true when it comes to writing a novel.

    This book would not be possible without my writing community. This story has been through many iterations and I'm so pleased with the one I landed on with the help of so many wonderful writers.

My Magster girls: Christina, Diana, and Terra, who lovingly told me what I needed to hear, when I needed to hear it. You three have been my rocks over the last couple of years and I love you! My fabulous editor, Kimberly who made my story better than I could hope for; my talented cover artist, Julianne Burke at Heart to Cover who made a cover I fall in love with every time I see it; the crew at Georgia Romance Writers that refills my creative well at each meeting; my lovely podcast co-host Adrienne Bell who listened each week when I had a new episode of my crazy life; and Happily Editing Ann's, who kick ass at proofreading and were amazing to work with.

To my family, who always has my back. My daughter, who has been my faithful cheerleader every day. You're an angel and I can't wait to see what you do in life. I love you, infinity times infinity. To Mr. P, I love you more than you know. You're one of the hardest working men I know and you're so much stronger than you give yourself credit for. Thank you for loving me through it all.

Finally, to you, dear reader. If you've made it this far, I thank you from the bottom of my heart. It means the world to me that you chose

Emma and Shane's story to entertain you. Stay tuned for more Reynolds family stories!

About the Author

Eliza Peake is an international bestselling author of sexy, swoon-worthy, contemporary romance. She writes stories with smart, sassy heroines, charming yet broody heroes who love their women in all the right ways, and happily ever afters with all the feels. She also co-hosts The Misfits Guide to Writing Indie Romance podcast.

In her downtime, she reads all the panty-melting romances she can get her hands on, drinks gallons of coffee, and tries to wrangle her addiction to Mexican food.

She currently resides in North Georgia with her family and dreams of retiring to the beach someday where she will continue writing steamy romance stories to her heart's content.

Sign up for her newsletter, The Sneak Peake for exclusive content and to first look at her latest news.

Find her at www.elizapeake.com.